To my wife, Claribel and my   out
you as my inspirations, I never would have gotten this far

And once again to my friend William Moll, who as before was ready and
willing to support me publishing this book

To my Kickstarter pledgers, I thank you. With special thanks to Terran Empire
Publishing and Lord Avatar II

Cover art by **Ruxandra Tudorică**
Methyss-art
©2017
methyss.art@gmail.com

Other Works by Michael Timmins

The Lycan War Saga

"The Awakening: Part One"

"The Awakening: Part Two"

"The Gathering"
TBA

"The War"
TBA

Shards of the Coven
Series

Prelude to the Shards Anthology
"Intellect"
"Race of the Witchguard"
"A Town Called Ghost"
TBA

The Lycan War Saga
Book One

THE
AWAKENING

Part Two

MICHAEL TIMMINS

Prologue

Calin sat perched on his horse and watched Adonia inform the local Druid about the end of the war. An Elder, he was one from the early days of the Druid order. Stick-like in appearance, the Elder's arms were thin, the skin drooping like wax trailing down the side of a candle. Being too old to join in the fighting, he hadn't left the village. The Elder's grey hair cascaded to his lower back, a shear wall of hair, a gray waterfall frozen in time. His greying beard rushed to try and catch it, a contest to see which would reach the man's feet first. Calin's gaze left Adonia and the Elder to survey the village. This was the fifth village they visited in the past several weeks and Calin, frankly, cared little for it.

The village topped a short rise, and by the appearance, housed no more than forty or so families. The town's center, where they currently waited, with the soft wind blowing and the ringing of steel on steel from the blacksmith's forge were the only sounds to be heard.

The blacksmith shop with its open walls breathed out the billowing smoke of the smelting fires, escaping like the angry breath of some fabled dragon. The definitive smell of burning metal accosted Calin's nose causing him to sniff involuntarily. A single room was all that housed the smithy's workshop, yet beyond it was an expansive living area. As Calin scanned the area, the blacksmith's apprentice stepped out and wiped his soot covered hands across his leathered apron. He dragged the back of his slightly less blackened hand across his brow, wiping his stringy hair from his forehead. The movement left a black streak, a smeared trail like some snake made of ash.

1

The apprentice was a hearty appearing lad in his early teens. The constant exposure to the smoke and oils common of his craft left his bare arms the color of dusk. Muscles stood out, well defined and sizable, even at rest. A lot of strength was needed to work the bellows and pound the hammer, and blacksmiths acquired those muscles early. The apprentice eyed him and Adonia, and after a moment, the boy's eyes widened. Their presence and appearance must have registered with the stories he heard around the village about the Lycans who had led the army against Kestrel.

Calin nodded to the boy in acknowledgement and confirmation. The boy rushed inside after nodding back, presumably to inform his master there were two Lycans in their village. Calin's presumption was confirmed promptly enough as the master also stepped outside.

The resemblance was uncanny. The man was the apprentice's father, as the older man appeared to be a larger, and more muscular version of the younger one. Calin nodded once to the older man before continuing his scan of the village.

By now, other villagers made their way outside their places of work and living. Noticing the local innkeeper step out from his establishment, Calin examined the inn. A quaint affair, the large common room where the locals could come and share an ale, could be seen through the open windows. The leather flaps had been flipped up to allow the warm light of the sun, a rare occurrence this late in the year, to pour into the room. Regardless, smoke poured out of the stone chimney, billowy, white clouds escaping into the otherwise cloudless sky. The fires were lit and burning strong within, enough to ward off the chill, which would creep up later this afternoon as the sun raced for an early exit.

The innkeeper, stooped and balding, his back arched from age and the constant bending over to wipe tables clean,

2

belied his height. The towel he repeatedly used for such cleaning was tucked into his belt at his side. His apron, which could have easily been held up from the man's rotund belly, was discolored, like a child's first attempt at painting. Given its peculiar roundness, his belly was odd for a man so tall. If he had been a woman, Calin would have guessed he was almost ready to give birth. A couple of patrons crowded behind the man as they tried to listen to the conversation between Adonia and the Elder. The patrons whispered back and forth to each other. The inn keeper, with a frown and a rolling of his eyes, shooed them back inside. With one final glance over his shoulder, he disappeared back inside the inn.

A group of younglings watched from beneath the storage hut. A round building, it was built upon stilts to keep it high off the ground, a wooden tortoise, designed to prevent rodent infestation. It was barely elevated enough for the tallest of the kids, a boy, about ten, to stand up straight. The children peered at him with wide eyes and open mouths –the wild excitement of youth. When he acknowledged their presence, they scattered like minnows in a puddle– dozens of directions, which eventually took them nowhere. A short time ago he would have smiled ruefully at their behavior. These days, a smile was something he no longer felt capable of.

Calin found he cared about little these days, especially with the loss of Sylvanis. She wouldn't wish for him to drag himself through the dark miasma of despair, but he had little choice in the matter. Although Sylvanis and he had never been anything other than friends, if you could call it that, she had been their leader, and he, her Captain. Their relationship had never been romantic, and yet, he had loved her so fiercely, her loss created a hole he struggled to climb out of.

With the war ended, and Kestrel's army destroyed, there was little for him to do these days. Katherine, Adonia, and he had spent a large amount of time at the Calendar following the events which saw both Druidesses dead. At first, they tried everything in their power to negate the spell Kestrel had cast. All attempts to remove the etchings

3

in the rock were thwarted by the power of the spell. Nor could her body be moved, or damaged in any way.

In the end, nothing they did had any effect on the spell, or Kestrel. The decision was made to wall the room up and bury the stairs. They told no one about the spell, except a few of the Druid Elders. The army, of course, knew of Sylvanis' and Kestrel's demise, but they knew nothing of the circumstances surrounding their deaths. The three of them decided to keep it that way.

The other problem they had to deal with was the Weres. They were still active in Kestrel's army, although it was resolving itself on its own.

Upon the death of Por and Answi, their Weres instantly reverted to normal humans. Which left Syndor's and Renwick's Weres. Syndor's Weres reverted to human form shortly after the war was finished which indicated Syndor was dead. How his death had come about, no one knew. The only other possible explanation would be Syndor had performed the Sundering, but it defied all reason. Syndor willingly 'detaching' himself from his Weres was unlikely. No. The only logical explanation was he was dead.

The Sundering. They had forced Renwick to do so with his Weres. They still held him in custody in hopes he would be able to tell them where, if any, offspring he had, lived.

While he had been somewhat willing to go through the Sundering, he had yet to inform them of any children he had. Though he was unaware of the spells cast by Kestrel and Sylvanis, he was still wary enough to suspect their reasons for finding his kin.

They had located a few prominent children of Por and Answi. However, those two had been known to rape women whenever their desire arose, which was often, so there were others they would never know about. All they could do was to try and give Sylvanis a better chance of defeating Kestrel upon her return. One or two less Weres to battle could be all she needed. It was all they could do. Well, it wasn't ALL they could do. But, Calin wasn't ready for the other, though he knew it needed to be done.

Adonia was finishing up with the Elder and peered back in his direction. Her face softened as she watched him. She knew how much he was hurting, but she also knew enough not to ask. After a moment of searching his face, she turned back to the Elder and bade him farewell. Striding back to him, her steps brisk and firm, she mounted up.

"It's late, but I don't believe it's too late for us to make it to the next village by nightfall, if we hurry," she suggested.

She was not in her hybrid form today. During the war, she was almost always in that form, but now with it ended, her days were filled with the monotony of being human.

Adonia was a beautiful woman, striking features framed by flowing reddish-brown hair which always seemed more brown than red, but when caught by the sun, as it did on this day, it burned with the color of fire.

Bright green eyes questioned him. It was odd to see them that color. They were amber in her shifted form that he was used to seeing them that way. A strong nose dominated her face, but not so much as to detract from her beauty. If anything, it gave her a regal quality, to match her demeanor. Most people deferred to Adonia. Adonia deferred to him.

"Very well, let us continue," he replied, his voice hollow even to his own ears.

Again, she peered at him, searching. He knew she wanted him to tell her he was fine, but he chose not to give voice to the lie.

They had four more villages in this direction to visit then they were to meet back up with Katherine and Shain, Connor's eldest son. Although Shain was not a lycanthrope, he had tried to fill Connor's place and help to inform the populace of the end of the war. It was

5

tedious work; travelling from one village to another to inform them of what most knew.

Word of the end of the war had travelled fast. But, Calin felt it was important for them to get the word out, regardless of what people knew, or thought they knew. In some villages, misinformation had reached them; Kestrel's army had won, while in others, the lycanthropes had killed everyone.

Eventually, the true version would reach everyone, but Calin didn't feel it should wait. The people needed to hear Kestrel's reign of terror was no more, and Sylvanis died to keep them safe. If only he could tell them of the real sacrifice Sylvanis had made, but the agreement was to keep Kestrel's spell and Sylvanis' counter-spell a secret.

Their horses trotted along a dirt road, hard packed with occasional tufts of grass marring the path like sprouts of hair on an otherwise bald head. The road, like a dark brown eel, meandering through the soft flowing hills of greenish-gray grass and the occasional farmer's field. Calin's mind drifted to the question plaguing him since Sylvanis' death.

The Sundering. The separation from your Weres. It was a logical decision to make with the war ended. But, Adonia and Katherine disagreed with him, and honestly, he couldn't blame them. To give up your Weres was a difficult thing to do. Although they would never admit it aloud, there was a certain pleasure to being in control of other people; to never being alone, because you always had a sense someone else's presence. But, Calin believed it was the right thing to do.

The only reason any of them had Weres following them was because of the war, and now, the war was over. Those people deserved to return to their lives, without having someone who could command them to do anything they wished. None of them would abuse this power, but the temptation to use it was immense. No. The others needed to be convinced to undergo the Sundering. For now, though, he would leave off trying to convince them and he would go through the motions of living, though for him, his life ended the moment Sylvanis drove the knife into her own heart.

They had done their best to remove any descendants of Kestrel's Weres, but Calin felt sure they would never find them all. There were too many variables and possibilities of where they could be. When Sylvanis rose again, he was sure she would face the full spectrum of Weres and so, Calin believed, their duty was to ensure she had everyone she needed to meet the threat, which meant doing something Calin wasn't ready to do. He didn't think he would ever be ready.

Chapter 1

Watching from the hospital window, Taylor watched as the tiger and wolf circled, pacing in what appeared to be a stand-off. At long last, they ran off into the distant thicket of trees. After a minute, Taylor turned to survey the room they had burst into a short time ago. Blain and Joseph stood around a hospital bed which held an attractive woman. Auburn hair draped her somewhat long face, like twin curtains framing a beautiful window. Tears fell from her eyes freely as she stared at Blain. Her senses would tell her Blain was the one who infected her, and she watched him with sharp eyes that never left his form, her lips quivered, and she shook slightly. Taylor couldn't blame her for being scared. Blain scared the shit out of him. The man was brutal and sadistic. If he had a moral compass, it was broken beyond repair.

"They've left," Taylor mumbled from the window.

Grunting, Blain acknowledged Taylor's observation. It didn't surprise him in the least the tiger and the wolf would run away. Blain had almost killed the both alone, so with two others like him, they wouldn't have stood a chance.

"Shouldn't we go after them, Blain?" Joseph's guttural boar voice broke the near silence. "The Lady won't appreciate you losing them…again."

Taylor couldn't help but marvel at Joseph's audacity. He continued to push Blain, regardless of how many times the other beat the living crap out of him.

Blain chose to ignore Joseph's insolence and continued to stare at the woman, and she at him. After a moment, he smiled in the strange seeming way he did in his boar form.

"We don't need to go after him, do we, darlin'? He will come back for you, won't he?"

The woman glanced away, wiped tears from her eyes and refused to answer. It was answer enough.

"Stand up, darlin'," Blain commanded.

The woman glared as she fought every movement her body forced her to make as she got off the bed and faced him. A hospital gown, hung loosely from her shoulders. Blain, of course, could not resist.

"Turn around," he insisted with a leer.

The woman slowly rotated herself but grabbed her gown and brought it across her backside to protect it from view.

"Tsk, tsk, little lady, don't go hiding the goodies. Move your hand away. Now."

The woman let her hand and her head drop. The open back of the gown parted, revealing a shapely butt and thighs. She had a nicely formed body. Taylor couldn't help but admire her form, while feeling ashamed for gawking at something he had no permission to see.

"We should get out of here, Blain," Taylor told him as Blain continued to visually violate the woman. Sadly, Taylor knew this would be the least violated the woman would likely feel in the coming days.

Tearing his eyes away from the woman's body, Blain eyeballed Taylor, knowing there was more than the man's desire to leave this place prompting his statement.

Taylor was pathetic in Blain's eyes. Only wishing to leave so Blain would stop harassing the woman, and to prevent any more casualties when authorities showed up, which wouldn't be long, by Blain's estimation. They had eliminated those who had been unfortunate to be in the hallway when they entered this floor, shifting to their Were forms as they exited the elevator, followed by screams of terror. Despite Taylor's reasons, Blain couldn't argue with the logic of it. Not that he minded killing a few more people, but the Lady insisted they needed to remain as low profile as they were able. They couldn't afford a full-scale response from the authorities, especially here in the States.

After a moment, Blain nodded his agreement to Taylor.

"Yeah, let's get out of here. I don't think the Lady will mind if we don't pursue those two, yet. After all, they'll be searching for us, and while they search for us, they won't be able to join with the other Weres and stop the Lady from killing the other Druid."

Glancing at the woman who was still standing there, head down, crying softly, her body on display, Blain spoke. "Taylor…no, Joseph?" Motioning for Joseph to come forward. "Gather her up. Make sure you hold on to her tight, we wouldn't want her to fall down or anything."

Blain stared at Taylor when he spoke knowing full well the reason he was choosing Joseph. He knew Joseph would take advantage of having a hold of such a beautiful woman, and Taylor wouldn't. Blain smiled, looking even more vulgar in his boar form.

Taylor wished there was something he could do to help her but knew anything he tried would most likely end with a severe beating from Blain and likely, a worse treatment for her in the long run. It was the type of man Blain was. He would punish her more for Taylor trying to help. The man was a monster, in more ways than one. Taylor was stuck with him.

Kat and Clint fled the scene, shifting to their human forms as they made their way away from the hospital. Kat couldn't help but wonder why the boars were not following. They must know they had the advantage. The bigger one would have come for them, she was sure. She got the impression he was someone who did not like losing and would stop at nothing to make sure they didn't get away –again. But, he wasn't pursuing. Perhaps he was smarter than Kat gave him credit for. They didn't need to chase them, he knew. If he held Sarah, eventually, they would come to him. This would give him time to teach Sarah how to shift, and he could use her against them, to their disadvantage.

Their only hope was this pull they were both receiving, which would take them to a place where they could get help. Though, if the others like them had similar run-ins with bad Weres, it's possible there might not be anyone who will be able to help them. This begged the question — where were the others?

Chapter 2

Thunk. The log split and fell to the sides. Sweat dripped off Hank's chest as he pried the axe blade out of the trunk he used as a break for splitting wood. Placing another log vertically on the break, he brought the axe up in a flowing arc and down again, splitting the log in two. A shiver went through his body as wind blew from the north, carrying with it the promise of frost. It was still crisp out, despite being June, as summers come late to Nova Scotia. Muscles bunching, he yanked the axe back out.

At eight inches over six feet tall and easily close to three hundred pounds, he was a towering man. It had been years since he had actually weighed himself though, those things didn't concern him. Luckily, most of the weight was muscle, the type of muscle you get from hard labor, not from working out. His arms and shoulders corded with thick muscles, same with his thighs. He carried a little paunch in his belly, but all in all, he was in excellent shape for someone pushing forty-five.

Taking a moment to wipe his forehead clear of sweat, he brushed a hand through his brown locks. The hair slicked back easily, drenched in sweat. Ruggedly handsome, his face had chiseled lines and was tanned from prolonged exposure to sun. Light blue eyes peered out below bushy eyebrows and above a blunt, crooked nose, which had been broken at least once, but not crooked enough to detract from his face. Two-day-old growth created a dark shadow along his jaw-line and above his full lips. His wife, Jennifer always called them "kiss me" lips. His lips curled in a half smile as he thought of Jennifer. He missed her greatly. It was five years ago she had died, although it felt it was like yesterday they were laughing and teasing with each other in the house.

"Dad?" Sim called from the side of the house. Sim was his son, well, Jennifer's son, from her first marriage. His son, Patrick, had died during childbirth, along with Jennifer. Sim was how Jennifer always called him, short for Simon. Sim had been eleven when he and Jennifer got married. Before, Jennifer had been a single mother for eight years, so he was truthfully the only father Sim had ever known. It was only natural after Jennifer died Sim would stay with him. Besides, his real father didn't want anything to do with him, so it worked out. Hank loved the boy, he genuinely did, but sometimes he felt cheated to never have a son of his own.

Glancing towards the house, he gave a contented sigh. It wasn't much, a quaint two-story out in the middle of the woods. Built mostly from wood, it was the closest you could get to an actual wood cabin, without freezing your ass off in the winter months. Smoke curled from a cobblestone chimney, making soft, white, curly-Qs as it drifted through the branches reaching precariously over the roof. Despite it being moderately insulated, Canadian winter months could still feel quite cold. Hell, up here in Nova Scotia, even the summers can get a little chilly at nights.

The first floor was an open floor plan. Living room, kitchen, dining room and office were all open. A wooden staircase climbed to the second floor which consisted of three rooms: two bedrooms and a bathroom. It was enough for him. Well, it was enough for him and Sim. His nearest neighbor was several miles away, and the nearest town, twenty. It was what he liked about this place. It was peaceful. Peace is what Hank needed. People and he didn't do well together. Never had. There were only two people he could get along with, and one was dead. The other was Sim, and he didn't have much choice. Sim was only seventeen and Hank was responsible for him.

Sim didn't care much for being out here. Hank knew. What seventeen-year-old would want to live out in the middle of nowhere? Miles away from any friends, not to mention, miles away from any girls. Nothing was said directly, but Hank picked up on it in the subtle ways he talked about missing events at school, or wanting to be on the football team, but not being able to get to practice. He felt bad about having the boy out here with him, but he didn't see where he had much choice.

Hank was short to anger, and a long time burning down. If he spent too long with people, it was only a matter of time before someone was getting hit, and it was normally Hank who was doing the hitting. The only time he had been able to stop his anger was in the presence of Jennifer. She was gone now.

"Daaad?"

"Yeah, Sim. What do you need?"

"Dinner's ready. It's getting cold," Sim replied.

Smiling to himself, he thought that this was another thing that he could thank Jennifer for. Sim was a wonderful son, doing his chores without complaint, and helped additionally without being asked.

Hank had totally forgotten about dinner, as he commonly did when he got into the rhythm of chopping wood. Sim saw him out here and knew he would forget, so he started dinner. Though it was doubtless only Mac & cheese, least it was something.

Taking a moment, he surveyed the scenery. His house was on two hundred acres of wild lands. This part of Nova Scotia was still wild. Most of the surrounding area was hardwoods, old growth which had been here for centuries. All manner of wildlife lived in these woods: wolves, foxes, porcupines, minks, and bears. It was part of what he loved about living here. The mix of silence, and the sounds of life.

Through no fault of his own, he was wealthy. His parents left him a fortune, not to mention investments. His family could easily live off the interest. Though he didn't need to, he made money on his own. Webpage design was what he did, and it made him decent money, but was more of a hobby than a career. It also kept him away from people for the most part. Ironically, it was how he met Jennifer.

She worked for a Seattle company in charge of advertising, and he was living in Seattle at the time, starting his business of web page design. With only one site under his belt, he evidently had talent and the site got him several clients. One of them, Jennifer's firm.

Jennifer called and asked if she could meet to go over what she had in mind for their site. Figuring he didn't need to meet with his clients to get their website started, it would mean there was less chance he could screw it up by letting his anger get in the way. He told her to fax over her ideas, and he would get her a draft site by the end of the week. If he wanted the account, he would have to meet her, she told him.

Later, she informed him, his attitude infuriated her as she was the type of person who had to deal directly with someone when they pissed her off.

He considered walking away from the account. After all, he didn't *need* the money and nobody had forced the issue before. Most places were more than happy to fax something over, if he got results. It intrigued him she insisted on a meeting, so he agreed to meet her over dinner to discuss her proposals.

When he arrived at the restaurant, he was in a foul mood. Some idiot had double-parked and blocked his vehicle and he had spent the next half hour arguing with him. He sorely wanted to hit the guy, but he was running late, otherwise he would have. Waiters rushed about, and customers created a cacophony of sounds that overwhelmed his senses. For a Monday night, he was surprised to see so many people.

15

When he told the host his name, the man had him follow. The host moved in and around the tables like a snake sliding through weeds. Hank figured out where they were headed. A young woman sat alone in a booth at the back of the restaurant, sipping wine from a glass.

Though she was sitting, her long, shapely legs were stretched out to the side of her chair. Wavy brown hair cascaded over her shoulders. She wore a black dress, formal, yet casual enough to wear out to a club, which clung to her slim figure with the light touch of a suitor. She stood to greet him. High cheekbones were noticeable, but her face was fleshy enough to not make them appear stark. Though she had thin lips, the soft pink lipstick accentuated them without turning them garish.

The dress was squared off above her bosom so as to not reveal too much cleavage. Clearly, she didn't attempt to use her beauty to get what she wanted. She could have. She was beautiful. Stunning, truthfully. Realizing his mouth was stuck open, he shut it. As the host bowed out of the way, Jennifer extended her hand, which he unconsciously took and shook lightly.

"Hank Keller?" She asked, dark and throaty, as if seduction had a voice.

Nodding dumbly, he was unable to stop staring at her.

"I'm Jennifer Heins. Please, have a seat."

She sat, and after a moment, he sat opposite her.

"I don't normally meet with my clients. My business doesn't require a one on one meeting." Not really knowing what else to say, Hank sputtered his words.

She smiled at him.

"I realize, Mr. Keller. However, I like to see whom I'm doing business with. I guess it is a quirk of being in advertising. It's the best way to figure out how to sell their product."

"Yes, of course." For the first time in his life, he felt calm around someone. All his earlier anger at the parking incident, melted away. It was a bit of shock. All his life he had little to no desire to be around, well, anyone. Now he couldn't wait to spend more time with her.

The dinner lasted two hours, and they discussed many things. He learned she had a son named Simon who was ten. Her first marriage had been a sham, and she had no intention of marrying another "dumb loser" as she termed the father. Worried he might fit into that category, he tried to impress her, and she appeared interested in him, and what he did.

In the end, he got the account, and a second date. From there, their dating went on for about six months. When he proposed, it was during one of their fights. They enjoyed fighting, because they got each other's blood pumping and, sooner or later, one of them would kiss the other and go right into having make-up sex. This time, though, it was different.

"You are afraid of commitment, Hank. I stay over here four nights a week, and yet, you have never asked if I would like to move in with you!"

"That is because you are pretty much living here! Why should I have to ask you something you do?"

"I don't know, perhaps because it would make sense? You know, I could stop paying for MY apartment, and share the costs of YOUR apartment, so it would become OUR apartment. Or, we could get a house for Christ's sake! But you don't even suggest it, which makes me think you don't want to be with me!"

"Don't be ridiculous!" He yelled. "Of course, I want to be with you; otherwise I wouldn't be with you! Why don't I go ahead and marry you! What do you think about that?"

"Fine. Why don't you?!" Jennifer yelled in response.

For a moment, they stared at each other.

"Did you just propose?" Jennifer asked in a quiet voice.

"Yeah. I guess I did. What did you say?"

"I think I said yes. More or less."

"Well. Which one? More? Or less?" He pressed.

"More," Jennifer said after thinking on it a moment.

"Okay." Hank stared at her, and she at him.

They both broke out laughing. They were married six months later. Simon gave her away, since her father died many years ago. The closer she got to him down the aisle, the more beautiful she appeared, she was breathtaking. It was beyond doubt the happiest day of his life.

A little over a year later she was pregnant with their son, Patrick. Nine months, two weeks and three days later, Jennifer and Patrick were both dead. It was the worst day of his life.

It was then he decided to move to Canada, buy land, and build a house. Simon was an afterthought at the time. Taking some time to track down his real dad, when he found him, Simon's real dad told him to "go the fuck away," Simon called Hank and asked if he could stay with him. Hank loved Simon. They had grown accustomed to each other during the courtship and marriage, and eventual mourning of his mother.

He had lost his son, and Simon wasn't his. He wanted to be alone with his grief. But, when he thought about Jennifer, he knew she would want him to take care of her son. So, in the end, Simon came and lived with him. They had grown a lot closer since. After all, there wasn't much to do out here but father/son bonding. They hunted, fished and hiked all over his property. They were terrific friends, and what's more, he called him dad.

Reaching down, he grabbed his flannel shirt off the stump next to where he was working and put it on. Making his way down to the house, he opened the front door and entered. Sim was at the table eating. He appeared a lot like his mother, with his brown hair just short of being too long and a touch wavy. He lacked his mother's cheekbones, and instead, got her fleshy face only, which made his cheeks appear a little chubby. His lips were thin as well. Tall, like his mother, he was well proportioned. Not all arms and legs like some boys were at his height. The years here had put some muscle on his frame. Rather a plain looking boy, which was surprising, since his mother had been beautiful. Must have gotten it from his father, Hank guessed.

Sitting down at the table, he smiled over the plate of Mac & Cheese. *Good ol' Sim,* he thought. Shrugging, he dug in. If it was tasty, he wasn't picky about what he ate. He could have eaten Mac & Cheese for a month, and not cared. In fact, he thought, there might have been a month a while back when it was all they had.

Hank paused in eating, "How was school today?"

"You know."

Typical teenager answer, Hank thought.

"In fact, I don't know, which is why I am asking. Did you see me in your classrooms?"

Sim grunted. Hank waited.

Glancing up from scarfing down his food to see Hank was still waiting, he sighed audibly.

"It was fine. I got an A on my History test and only got a B in Chemistry. They say Aubrey Williams is pregnant, but she said it wasn't true. I believe her because I know her boyfriend, Ben, and he told me he wasn't getting any."

That was more than I needed to know, but I got my answer, Hank thought.

"Well I'm proud of you on your History test, and I wish you had studied a little longer on your chemistry. Whether Aubrey Williams is pregnant, or not, is none of your business, and you shouldn't be gossiping about it in school. Also, Ben should know

19

better than to tell people those things, it's not respectful to his girlfriend."

Sim frowned at him but nodded.

They ate the rest of their dinner in silence. After, Sim went outside and gathered some of the firewood Hank had cut to start the wood stove before turning on the TV. Hank worked on the computer in the corner. A typical evening. Sometimes they would break out some board games if either one was feeling up to it. Tonight, though, neither Sim nor he was interested.

Sitting at his computer, he didn't do any work. Instead, he watched Sim out of the corner of his eye. Thinking back, he realized Sim had saved him. When Sim called him to ask if he could stay with him, he had been in a bad way. The death of Jennifer and his son had sent him spiraling out of control — drinking incessantly, going to bars to fight and being moody.

He could admit he had been hoping for someone to draw a knife, or a gun, and to end it for him. In full honesty, he hadn't wanted to go on. The truth was, he was miserable, and had been all his life. The one thing which brought any happiness to his life was Jennifer. When she was gone, it was like someone let him experience Heaven after being in Hell then tossed him back to Hell. Simon's call changed everything. It gave him back a piece of Jennifer and he would be damned sure to take care of it for her.

Standing up, he walked over behind Sim, leaned down and kissed him on the head. Sim almost jumped and stared back up at him with huge eyes. Hank couldn't blame him. When it came to showing emotions, he was a reserved man. It was indeed something to get a hug out of him. So, a kiss on the head, it shocked Sim.

Smiling down at him. "You know I love you, Sim? You know, right?"

20

Sim stared at him for a moment, making sure he wasn't playing with him. After a moment, satisfied Hank wasn't, he answered. "Yeah, dad. I know. I love you, too."

Staring down at Sim for a moment, Hank felt wetness well in his eyes. He turned away.

"Okay, well I'm going to bed. Try not to stay up too late watching that crap."

"Sure, dad. Good night."

Climbing the stairs, he didn't glance back. If he had, he might have seen Sim wipe tears from his eyes.

Hank lay in bed, staring at the ceiling. "*It was time for them to move back to the states. He couldn't expect Simon to live out here like this. He needed friends nearby, needed a less "rural" education. This life might be for him, but it wasn't for Sim. Yes. It was time to move back.*" Hank smiled as his eyelids drooped and sleep overtook him "*I'll tell him in the morning. Sim will love the idea.*"

Agony!

His whole body felt as if bursting into flames. Pain seared him from head to toe. It felt like someone was taking a tire iron to his body. The pain was so intense, he screamed once, and blacked out.

Sim watched TV, some late-night court show, but he wasn't paying much attention to it. He mulled over what his dad said before heading up the stairs. He knew Hank loved him, but in all the years they were together, he never said it – really said it. Oh, he responded with it when offered to him. But, he never said it first. He wondered if Hank was okay. There were times when Hank missed Sim's mom, he knew, as there were still nights when Sim cried himself to sleep with the loss of his mother. Life goes on, though.

A lesson he had learned early. From losing his mother, to meeting his real dad, and having his dad reject him, you must pick yourself up after, which is exactly what he did. He called Hank, and Hank took him in. By not turning him away, Hank saved him. If he had rejected him as well, if he had lost his last chance at family, he would have died.

He hadn't been sure Hank would take him in. He had loved Sim's mother a great deal, and therefore may have felt the need to keep a piece of her close. Which was what it was, at first. Sim believed it was a way for Hank to hold on a bit longer to Jennifer.

Though in the end, Hank grew to love and care for him, at least, Sim thought so. Judging from a few moments ago, Sim was sure he was right. How he would ever begin to repay him, he didn't know. The least he could do was to complain as little as possible about living here. He didn't hate it. He liked the place. It was just so far from everything. It wasn't like he could hop onto his bike and ride it down the street to hang out with his friends. Instead, he, and his friends, needed to plan a day where they would all meet in town and do something from there. Of course, it all depended on whether their parents could get them there.

That would change when he got his car. He had been doing chores around the house for years, and Hank would pay him for it. His pay depended on whether he was asked to do the chore, or if he volunteered to do it without being asked. If he volunteered to do the chores, he always got paid more.

It was easy to give a kid an allowance, Hank had told him, but what does the kid learn from that? That his parents are going to give him money all the time? No. It was better if he learned how to earn money. It was a much better way, and though Sim didn't like doing chores, he had to agree. It made him appreciate his money.

At first, he went crazy with it and bought candy, video games, and whatever he felt like. When Hank asked him how he was going to buy a car when he turned sixteen since he kept spending all his money, Sim went on a spending freeze. Apart from an occasional personal reward, he saved every coin. Now, he had enough money to buy the car he wanted, though it took him a whole year beyond his sixteenth birthday to do so.

Closing his eyes, he pictured the car in his head. He was visualizing opening the car door when a scream from upstairs shattered the vision. Panicked, he rushed up the stairs. Never in his entire life had he heard someone scream like that. It held so much pain, he couldn't imagine what it must feel like. Mounting the top of the stairs, he peered down the hall towards Hank's room. It had to be Hank. There wasn't anyone else here, but the scream was so… inhuman. He wasn't sure it had been Hank.

Taking measured steps, he moved down the hall to the door of his dad's room. It was open a crack, as it always was, and Sim paused outside to listen. Someone breathed roughly — like each breath was being forced out of a tight chest, huffing and blowing. It was louder than it should have been and once again, heart pounding, he thought of his dad. Reaching for the handle so he could throw it open, the door was ripped from its hinges like it was made of cardboard and not the solid oak it was and tossed into the room to fly against the wall with a loud crash! Something he had never seen before came through, its bulk blocking the doorway like the moon blocks the sun in an eclipse.

It appeared bearish, like they do when they rear up on their hind legs, but something was different. Its shoulders were located differently, as if the front legs were more like arms. To further this

23

appearance, where the paws should be, there were elongated, beefy fingers, ending in wicked looking dagger-like claws. Its back legs appeared more capable of allowing the beast to use only its hind legs to walk. Examining its legs, he noticed something more shocking. Shredded strands of blue and white cloth dangled like streamers from a blue waistband stretched to its limits around the creature's waist. Sim recognized it because it belonged to his father. It was his favorite sweatpants he frequently wore to sleep in. Noticing all this in seconds, the creature's right claw smashed into him, slamming him into the wall. It was the last thing he remembered.

Sim awoke to the worst pain imaginable. His body ached like he had purposely targeted each muscle group and gave it a good beating. Even with his eyes closed, he could tell he was no longer at home. There was a soft murmur of voices coming from somewhere to his right, like he was in class, with the door closed, when all the students walked by in the hall. It smelled different as well. The house smelled of pine and soot, this smelled of well, nothing. His left side ached tremendously. Tentatively he opened one of his eyes. He could tell he was in a hospital straightaway, lying on a hospital bed, sheets covering his body. A tray table on a swing arm was pushed to the side, empty.

Blinds covered the window, doing a poor job of keeping out the light. So, it was daytime. No longer night. Ten hours, at least, he had been out. He saw Hank in the corner chair, his head lowered, and he was holding the sides of his head with his big hands. Sim tried to sit up and pain shot through his abdomen. He gasped. *Yep, that was the muscle group that got beaten the most*, he decided. Hank glanced up, he appeared on the verge of tears, and had trouble looking Sim in the eyes. Hastily, he moved to Sim's side and motioned him to keep still. Sim took another deep breath. *As if I was going to try and move again after that pain*, he thought.

"I am so sorry. I didn't mean to. I don't remember too well what happened. The police are here, Sim. I told them you were climbing, fell, and landed on a stump. They are going to ask you some questions." Pausing, he gazed away.

"If you want to tell them the truth about what I did, well I understand. Just know, I never meant to hurt you, son," Hank said, tears welling in his eyes.

"Whoa. Dad. What are you talking about? Some sort of beast attacked me. Like a bear, though it wasn't really a bear. It was like a man-bear. It stood on two legs, and it had on your sweatpants...." Sim stared at him. Hank glanced away, again.

"That was you? How is that possible?"

"I don't know, son. The only reason I'm not flipping out right now is because my father told me about something like this when I was younger. His grandfather told him as well and made him promise to tell his son. Dad made me promise, too, but... well, that doesn't matter, now." His voice trailed off.

"Dad? Told you what? What are you talking about?"

Hank shook his head to clear the reverie.

"They told me there was a curse, or a blessing, they weren't sure which one, passed down from father to son since the early days. This curse is supposed to transform you into a lycanthrope."

"A what? What the hell is a lie-can-rope?"

"No. A lycanthrope, a were-creature. Like a werewolf, though it appears not all lycanthropes are werewolves. Evidently, you can be a werebear." His lip curled in a smirk.

"Obviously," Sim replied, a little too harshly.

Hank flushed. Sim, reaching out his hand as far as he could, covered Hank's with his.

"It's okay. Well, I guess it's not okay. I have a monster as a dad. I don't know what to say, truthfully. It is all overwhelming."

"I could have killed you. It's a miracle I didn't. I think the only reason I didn't, was I attempted to maintain as much of myself as I could." Glancing towards the door, he moved his hand away.

"Well, the cops wanted to know when you woke up. I'm surprised they let me wait in here, given their suspicions." He rested his hand back on Sim's upper arm. "It's okay if you tell them. I'm prepared to face up to what I did."

Turning, he walked to the door, and opened it.

"He's awake." Hank stepped aside allowing two officers into the room.

They were both tall men. In fact, they could have been brothers with the same generous forehead which climbed from their eyebrows impossibly high until it reached slicked-back brown hair. They both shared the same sunken in eyes and rounded chin. The only thing setting them apart was the bushy mustache the one on the right wore beneath his bulbous nose. Checking the nametags, they both shared the same last name. Both were Detective Shirkland. *Ah. So, they are brothers,* Sim thought. One of the brothers, the one without the stache, turned to Hank.

"Umm. You can wait outside, sir. We will call you when we are ready."

Hank nodded. Gave one more glance at Sim which spoke volumes and turned to leave, closing the door behind him.

The one with the stache sat at the edge of the bed and smiled. Or at least he tried, it didn't seem like much of a smile since his mustache was too bushy and hid his upper lip.

"Hello, Simon. I'm Detective Mark Shirkland, and this is my partner, and yes, brother, Detective Allen Shirkland. We were contacted by the hospital because the injury you suffered was thought to resemble injuries sustained from abuse. Now I understand this may be a difficult thing for you to tell us. You live alone with your dad, and perhaps you're afraid telling on him would put you in foster care or something." He was trying to appear concerned but was failing miserably. It was obvious he had rehearsed this prior to coming in and wanted to get through it as swiftly as possible so he could arrest Hank.

The detective continued.

"I can understand your fear. I'm here to tell you it will be all right. You don't need to be afraid. We can protect you. You need to tell us the truth about what happened. We'll take care of the rest."

Sim gazed into the detective's eyes and didn't know what to say. He loved Hank. Hank was twice as much his dad as the one who fathered him. He would never cause him harm. But, how was he going to be safe if Hank changed into that…thing, again? Hank, himself, didn't seem to have any idea of how to control the thing. So, what happened next time? What would his mom want him to do?

"I fell," Sim told the detective, matter-of-factly.

The detective sighed, a slow exhalation of breath in resignation to a response he probably expected.

"Simon. Look. We can't help you if you won't help us. You almost died, son. What if next time you get hurt worse?"

"Next time I will tie myself to the tree like I'm supposed to, so I won't fall. Now, if you will excuse me, gentlemen, I need to get some rest."

Detective Shirkland frowned at him.

"Very well." Pulling something from his jacket, he handed it to Sim. It was a business card.

27

"If you change your mind, call the number on the card."

Sim watched as the detective tried to hand him the business card as his vision went narrow, and his breath caught in his throat. Pain burned through his chest. It was weird. Suddenly, all he could hear was a beeping noise droning on as he watched. It was like peeking through a door viewer. Watching, he could see the two detectives rush to the door and throw it open. They were shouting, but that damn beeping noise drowned them out. Hank, he saw, had rushed into the room and scanned his face. Sim could tell he was calling his name, but again, beeeeeeppppp. He wanted to tell him it was okay, not to worry, but he couldn't seem to move his mouth. The expression of guilt on his face tore Sim up inside. He wanted to tell him this wasn't his fault. But the truth was, it kinda was.

Sim watched as doctors rushed in with several nurses. His tunnel vision narrowed to a pinprick. Then it was gone. Only the beep continued. Eventually, it disappeared as well. He knew nothing more.

Hank sat alone on a bench outside Sim's room, his large form filled the waiting chair to its max. He was a rock, an unmoving mound, and yet, below the surface, a roiling sea; its waves thrashing about in chaos. It had been almost an hour since the doctors had kicked him out of the room as they worked feverishly to try to save Sim. He didn't understand it. The wounds Sim received were bad, but not bad enough to cause him heart failure. The two detectives spoke to him shortly after they left the room. Not so subtlety implying if Sim died, he would be going to jail. He had no idea what Sim had told them, so he kept his mouth shut. They left.

It had been a while since he heard frantic people in the next room. He couldn't understand why no one was coming out to tell him if his son was okay. What was going on? Standing to knock on the door, it opened abruptly. Several nurses filed out of the room, all giving him a quick glance from which he couldn't discern anything. Trying to peer over their shoulders, hoping to see Sim, they opened the door only enough to pass through. As the last nurse stepped out, a doctor followed her, an older gentleman with kind eyes. Black peppered his gray hair and full beard, his youth trying to put up a sporadic fight. The doctor was tall and thick. Not nearly as tall or as thick as Hank, but he was a close second. Glasses, which were too small for his large face, rested precariously on the tip of his nose, ready to fall at the slightest lean forward, as bifocals customarily did. Closing the door behind him, he stopped in front of Hank.

"Mr. Keller?" Hank nodded. "Your son is fine."

A sob broke out of Hank. The last time he cried was when Jennifer died, along with his son. He almost lost his last remaining piece of Jennifer in his life. Not only that, but he almost lost his son. That was what Sim was to him now, his son. The doctor waited a moment for Hank to collect himself.

"Can I see him?"

"I think we need to talk about some other things." The doctor motioned to the bench for him to sit. Hank regarded him quizzically, and the doctor motioned again to the seat. Hank sat.

"Have you ever known Simon to be a quick healer?"

Hank froze. He never knew Sim to be a quick healer. However, *HE* was a quick healer. He never was in the hospital, despite having broken his arm and collarbone after a bad fall out of a tree when he was young. His parents didn't bother to take him, which at the time, he found strange, but after a few hours, his bones mended and the bruises covering the right side of his body where he had impacted the ground, disappeared. His father told him it had something to do with what grandpa told him about the curse he inherited — about the ability to change into a lycanthrope.

At the time, of course, he thought the whole thing insane and dismissed it. Of course, through the years he came to accept the fact he healed miraculously quick. Broken bones knitted in hours, something simple as a paper cut disappeared in seconds, not leaving a scar. His father told him the same held true for him, he could heal rapidly and tried hard to stay away from hospitals and doctors since they always had uncomfortable questions. Not to mention a battery of tests. Hank stayed out of hospitals, and away from doctors. It was something he managed to keep to himself. Jennifer hadn't known about it.

The problem was, Sim wasn't his kid. There was no blood relation between them. So how had he gained his ability to heal rapidly?

"I've never noticed, doc. Why?"

The doctor stared intently at him before answering, realizing Hank was not being all together truthful.

"All of Simon's wounds have healed. They seem to have almost entirely disappeared as well. I can't locate any scarring tissue."

Hank feigned surprise. "What? How is that possible?"

The doctor watched Hank's reaction intently before answering. "It isn't. That is why I would like to keep your son here for some more tests."

Hank didn't like it one bit. He didn't want them to start running tests on Sim, because he didn't think he would like what they found.

"You said he is fine though, right?"

The doctor nodded.

"Well, if it is all the same to you, I would like to take Sim home."

"Please, Mr. Keller. I think it is important for your son to stay here so we can better determine what happened. He almost died."

"But he's fine now?"

"I can't lie to you, Mr. Keller." Hank could tell he wished he could. "As far as I can tell, your son is in excellent condition."

"Okay, we will be leaving,"

Frowning for a bit, the Doctor finally nodded. Hank watched as he got up and proceeded down the hall.

Hank stared at the door to his son's room, not knowing what to tell Sim. Somehow, he had transferred his ability to heal himself swiftly over to him. He didn't care for what it could possibly mean. Standing, he went to the door, opened it and entered. Sim was sitting up, watching TV. Sim gave him a wide smile when he saw him. Hank's heart lurched. He loved his son, and he knew now how much his son loved him. Yet, he couldn't ignore the fact he had almost killed his son, and perhaps worse, cursed him. He didn't know if he could forgive himself.

"Why didn't you tell the police the truth, Sim?"

Sim's smile disappeared. "How could I? You may not be my biological dad, Hank, but you are more my father than he ever was." Sim took a deep breath. "When I called you to tell you my real father didn't want anything to do with me, you didn't hesitate before telling me to come back and live with you, though I know how you like your solitude. You could have as easily told me to get lost, but no, you took me in, and raised me as your own." Tears welled in Sim's eyes. "When mom died, and my real father turned away from me, I lost everything. I had no family, except you. You have done so much for me; I couldn't possibly tell the police anything other than what you told them. I fell out of a tree." Sim wiped the tears from his eyes, and Hank had to do the same. Sim smiled again. "Plus, there is no way they would believe my father turned into a bear and attacked me."

Laughing, Hank smiled at his son.

"I love you, Sim."

"I love you, too... dad," Sim replied.

Crossing the room, Hank gave Sim a huge hug and kissed him on his forehead.

Sim eyes lit up as he remembered something.

"Oh, and can you believe it? My wounds are all healed. The doctor said it was some sort of miracle, or something." Pulling his gown up, he showed Hank where he had been injured, and it was, indeed, unharmed.

Hank's smile faded.

"Let's get you home," Hank told him.

Sim gazed at Hank for a moment, wondering why Hank wasn't happy or surprised he had healed fully. "Umm. Okay." Standing, he went to the closet. Hank brought him a change of clothes, which he hurriedly donned.

It was true. He was totally healed. In fact, he never felt better. It was almost if he was on caffeine pills and pain medication. Feeling no soreness or stiffness, he felt overly awake. Sim didn't understand what was going on, but he was sure Hank knew something he wasn't telling. If it was true, it meant something bothered him about the information, or otherwise he would have told Sim. Hank was like that. He didn't shield him from much, he pretty much gave him the facts, no matter what they were, even if they hurt Sim's feelings... or his ego. And, though Hank had a short temper with most people, he was somehow able to keep it in check with Sim and expected Sim to also tell him the straight truth, regardless if it hurt or angered him. It was something Sim always admired about him.

So many of his school friends went through life ignorantly unaware of life's truths . He didn't envy them when they entered the real world and had to fend for themselves. The first times in their lives when someone told them the hard truth, it would crush them.

They arrived home a few hours later. Again, he mentioned how it was amazing he healed so fully to watch Hank's response. Hank wouldn't meet his eyes but nodded. He told Sim since he was feeling so much better he should get outside and start collecting firewood. Realizing Hank knew something about his miraculous recovery and didn't want to tell him, made Sim a little pensive. Watching Hank, he walked to the door. Meanwhile, Hank crossed the room to the sink and began to put the flatware away. Still, he wouldn't glance at Sim. Sim frowned and stepped outside into the warm sun, but cold air of northern Canada.

Hank stopped putting the plates away as soon as Sim stepped outside. Standing there, leaning on his hands, he gripped the side of the sink, head bowed. Sim was suspicious he knew more than he was letting on. But, how could he tell him what his fast healing could mean? How could he tell him whatever happened from this point onward was Hank's fault? Sim would hate him, possibly decide to leave. Squeezing the sink hard, he forced himself to release his grip, shaking his head. He would tell Sim when the time was right, whenever that was. Turning, he went upstairs to his room. He didn't glance back to see the deep imprints in the steel sink his fingers had made.

Walking deep into the woods, Sim searched for good-sized fallen limbs to take back to the house to use as kindling. Contemplating the meaning of his quick healing, he wondered what Hank's knowledgeable silence meant.

A wide stump, and the remains of an oak tree, uprooted and laying on its side, rested in a swath of destruction where it had fallen. The stump had broken away and been pulled out of the dirt before it finally separated from the rest of the tree, left behind by the force of the falling giant. The inside of the bole was hollow as it had been for some time for it to snap off during a high wind. A smile broke his face as he approached the stump. Ever since he moved to Canada, one of his favorite past times was to find stumps such as this one and to flip them over, or to try to lift them. Sometimes, as he got older he could lift them and would attempt to toss them as far as he could.

It was absolute fun. It was something he needed now. Striding over to it, he kicked at the few remaining strands of tree and bark connecting the two. They broke with ease, like snapping toothpicks. Lowering himself, bending his knees, he wrapped his arms as far around the stump as he could manage. Taking two deep breaths, he held in the third, and lifted. The stump lifted off the ground with such ease; he staggered back a few steps. Sim was stunned for a moment and examined the stump.

The rot devastated the bole, but hadn't affected the stump, so there was no reason for it to weigh so little. Cautiously, he hefted the stump experimentally a few times. It was like tossing a balloon which was an exaggeration, but it was a lot lighter than it should be. Sim peered around and found a fairly open area with a few trees and saplings. Taking a few steps forward, he launched the stump with all his might, his muscles bunching and releasing as the stump left his grasp. It arced high into the air and went about twenty feet before slamming into a tree yards away from where he should normally have been able to reach. It hit the tree about ten feet up, which means he could have achieved a lot more distance with his throw.

Not believing his eyes, he stared in the direction the stump. His arm itched a little and he glanced down. The roots of the stump must have dragged across his skin and scratched it in several places.

Numb from the experience, he felt no pain; so instead, he went over to where he had thrown the stump. Upon examining the tree trunk, it was gouged and dented as if run into by a car– a flying car. The stump itself had split partially upon impact. Again, he lowered himself down and went to reach around the stump. Catching sight of his arm, he noticed the scratches were gone from picking up the stump the first time. Not a single trace left. He stared intently at his arm, as if expecting the scratches to reappear by magic. Staring from his arm to the stump and back again, it was as if something in his head clicked into place.

Standing, he gripped one of the stump's roots by hand and lifted it easily off the ground. Sim found a much longer opening through the trees and swung the root back, bringing it forward with remarkable speed. When he reached shoulder level, he let go, sending the stump deep within the forest, a lump of nature traveling impossibly through the air. He couldn't be sure, but he guessed it traveled almost thirty feet before hitting the ground, and rolled another ten, maybe more. He smiled. Realizing what happened to him, he understood why Hank was so hesitant to say anything. He must have thought Sim would be upset. Well, Hank was wrong, Sim wasn't upset, he was ecstatic.

Hank was prone to brooding. There were times he would be in a funk for weeks. Of course, that had been before he met Jennifer. And, like most of his unwanted traits, that, too, disappeared with her lovely smile. When she died, he brooded again for the first time since before her, and he only came out of it because Sim needed him.

He was brooding now. And this time, he didn't know who could bring him out of it. Laying on his bed for over an hour, he had only gotten up once to go to the bathroom.

As was often when he brooded, he generally ate a lot. It wasn't uncommon for him to put on ten pounds or more during his brooding sessions. A growling stomach forced him away from his bed, he trudged downstairs. His mind was so focused on getting something to eat out of the fridge, he never noticed Sim sitting at the dinner table, waiting for him.

"Have you been able to rapidly heal all your life?"

At the question, Hank's hand froze on the handle of the refrigerator.

"You passed it to me, didn't you? Somehow, when you attacked me, you passed whatever it is to me, right?"

Turning his head, he peered in Sim's direction. It was impossible to read his emotions at the moment, but Hank felt it was the time for the truth.

"I believe so. I don't know for certain." His voice quiet.

"I thought so. I was outside collecting wood and scratched myself. Within moments, those scratches disappeared, so I know what happened today at the hospital wasn't a fluke." Sim glanced at him. "I know you are strong, but are you stronger than you should be, dad?" Sim watched him questioningly.

For the first time, Hank noticed Sim slowly rolling an iron spike back and forth on the table, making a soft drumming noise like a woodpecker searching for insects in the trunk of a tree.

"I don't understand your question."

Sim stood and approached him with the iron spike.

"I mean, can you do this?" Holding the iron spike up, using two hands, he began to bend the spike. Hank's eyebrows climbed as it did, indeed, bend slowly. Muscles straining slightly, Sim exerted some effort, but didn't appear to be straining at all. Hank's eyes widened in surprise.

"How on earth did you do that?" Hank asked.

"You mean you can't?"

"No. I mean I might be able to bend it a little perhaps." He confessed, his brow furrowed.

Sim's face scrunched up. "I don't understand. I would have bet anything this was the same thing as the healing, something you passed to me in the attack. I'm sure I couldn't do it before yesterday." Tilting his head in thought. "Here, take it." Sim passed the spike to Hank. "You try it."

Taking the spike from Sim who raised an eyebrow at him and a quick nod. Hank grabbed both ends of the spike and proceeded to pry them apart, to straighten out the spike. It bent with ease. He dropped the spike in surprise, but Sim let out a laugh and clapped his hands together.

"I knew it!" he exclaimed. "But, you said you didn't have excessive strength, right?" Hank nodded dumbly. "It means it manifested itself after your transformation." Sim tapped his finger against his bottom lip in thought. "When I realized you transferred the ability to heal rapidly to me and I suddenly had super strength, it was like a light bulb went off in my head.

"Suddenly, I remembered what I learned in psychology. During the early 19th century, many doctors considered lycanthropy a mental disease brought upon by the moon. Because of the effect it had on

37

some people, it moved into the belief, because of the moon, some people changed into werewolves. It was also commonly believed at the time, lycanthropy was a disease transmitted when a werewolf attacked someone, and the person lived through the attack. It appears, somehow those people got it right —lycanthropy is passed through the blood of the victim if they manage to survive an attack of a Werewolf, or Werebear in your case." Sim wore a satisfied smile on his face at the conclusion of his history lesson. Hank was impressed.

"You know, I've heard of lycanthropy and werewolves. Though my father told me I carried the curse in me, I never bothered to find out anything about it. In fact, I think I was so embarrassed my father told me something like that, I actively avoided learning about it. Now it seems I shouldn't have," he concluded.

"Well," Sim began, "the question is now, what do we do with the information?"

It was a question neither one had the answer for, but the decision was going to be decided for them soon enough.

Several weeks passed since the night of the attack and both Sim and he were exhausted over learning all things Were. They spent an inordinate amount of their free time together to research as much as they could. The information they found was sparse, at best. Were-creatures were beings of legends. No one had reliably witnessed one, though there were many who claimed to have seen Werewolves which was the most common, of course, and the most popular. Books, movies, and games all covered the minutia of Werewolves.

Little was mentioned of any other Were-creatures, though they did see some mention of werebears, wererats, and weretigers. Most fabled information was centered on Celtic mythology. It was said the Druids were shape shifters and could take the forms of beasts of nature. This, for the most part, was one of the origins of the myth — of Druids taking the form of beasts and humans shifting into half human/half animal forms.

The problem was the Druids, for the most part, kept no written histories. Everything was passed down verbally. And, like all things to get passed down in this manner, they were subject to the teller's interpretation. After several weeks of in-depth study, both Sim and Hank believed they were well versed in all things involving lycanthropes, from myth to supposed scientific studies. In the end, there was nothing conclusive.

There was one sticking point they both could agree on. Almost all information surrounding lycanthropy tied it directly with the full moon. However, when he first transformed there was no full moon. Neither one could make a guess as to why it was. Either the mythology got it all wrong, or there was something else to trigger it. They were going to find out this evening, though. For tonight was a full moon, the first one since Hank's transformation and his subsequent attack on Sim. Tonight, they would find out if there was any truth to the myth. Sim joked they should call the "Myth Busters" and see if they wanted to prove or bust a huge myth.

Red and yellow flames danced about, creating a ring of glowing trees surrounding Hank and Sim, as Hank dropped a fresh log onto the fire. Sitting across from him, Sim wore a light coat against the night chill. They decided to wait outside for the possible metamorphosis. So, they sat, enjoying the campfire, both watching the full moon rise over the treetops. Something about it made it seem swollen and fat as it made its steady climb above the horizon. As it was nearing its apex; Sim and Hank were anxious.

"You know, if you are wrong, and I am the only one who changes, I might kill you this time?" He spoke to Sim across the fire.

"I know. But, I'm right," Sim said firmly.

"I hope so. If I start to change and you don't feel anything..." Hank stared at him to emphasize his point. "Run."

Sim snorted. "Obviously."

Hank couldn't help but smirk. Sitting back on his log, he resumed waiting. It didn't take long. A moment later he felt his body break apart as he grunted in pain. Sim watched from across the fire and had come partially off his log. The pain assaulted Hank so intensely he could hardly focus. The one thing he could tell, Sim was not changing. Sim had been wrong.

"Run!" Bellowing out to Sim, he doubled over. The bones within his body thickened and elongated; his muscles and skin adjusted to compensate. Sim stared at Hank for another moment, turned and ran.

Two steps and Sim cried out, crashing to the ground, sliding before coming to rest in a fetal position.

Somewhat aware of what was happening to Sim, pain wracked Hank's body. Consciousness slipped away, but he clawed his way out of the fog of pain to hold onto himself, barely managing to do so. Slowly, he rose to his full eleven-foot height. Flexing his arms to the sides, he spread his claws out wide. His paws were huge and the claws jutting from them were sharp and long. Glancing down, he saw his body was covered in fur and heavily muscular. He was most impressive.

Parting his maw, he let out a growl that rumbled out over the still night.

A growl answered him, and Hank gazed across the fire to see a bulky figure, almost his mirror, except in size, rear up from the ground. The Werebear across from him was roughly nine feet in height and not nearly as bulky as Hank. Hank's eyes grew big and he stepped back at seeing the feral aspect in the eyes of Sim. It was as if his son didn't recognize him. When he launched himself at Hank, leaping across the fire in a hard-headfirst slam, knocking him back, there wasn't much doubt. Hank twisted as he fell back, pushing Sim off him in one swift move.

"Sim! It's me!" Hank yelled, but was forced to dive to the side as Sim charged him. This time Sim reached out and dragged his claws across Hank's abdomen. Skin and muscle tore as one of the claws tore so deep it scored bone. Rolling, Hank sprang to his feet. He knew he could stop this, but he didn't want to hurt Sim. He tried to reach him one last time.

"Sim! It's your father." Hank watched as Sim turned and made to pounce once more.

"Stop!"

Sim stopped. Lowering the arm he had raised to ward off the blow, which would have followed had Sim pounced, he gazed at Sim. There was fire in Sim's eyes, but he didn't move. Hank didn't understand it. He hadn't been able to reach Sim, but somehow, he had gotten him to stop attacking. Slowly, Hank approached, but Sim made no more moves to attack. Reaching out with both arms, he settled his paws on Sim's shoulders and looked him in the eyes. Lips curled back in a snarl, Sim revealed sharp and nasty teeth. Hank searched his eyes for some sign of his son.

"Sim. It's Hank. Your father. Listen to me. You've got to hold on, son. Hold onto yourself. Don't let the beast take over."

Talking soothingly, Hank felt the muscles in Sim's arms release, and his vicious snarling ceased.

41

"Yeah, son. Don't give in. I know you are stronger than it. You've got to stay focused. Think of Jennifer. Think of your mom. Don't lose it, son."

In seconds, the fire that had burned in Sim's eyes dissipated.

"Dad? What happened?" For the first time Sim examined himself. "I was right. I knew it!" Sim peered at his father, and noticed the bloody cuts along his abdomen, closing even now.

"Whoa, dad. What happened to you?"

Hank barked out a laugh. "You happened to me, son."

Sim scrunched his forehead which came across as peculiar, given his current face structure.

"Never mind, it doesn't matter now. The important thing is we have both changed and have kept our sanity. So, hopefully, we can control ourselves easier when we change."

"You would think we would be able to change whenever we wanted. Or stop ourselves from changing if we wanted. Doesn't that make sense?" Sim questioned.

"Yeah, it does. But, I couldn't for the life of me think of how we could do that."

"Well, I guess that leaves trial and error, eh?"

He didn't like it, but Sim was right. In the end, it was Hank who figured it out. Examining his claws, he started visualizing what his hand normally appeared. Suddenly, pain shot through his hand, and he could sense his bones losing mass and the hair covering his paw recede slowly back into his skin to be reabsorbed for later use. It was at that moment he decided to visualize his entire self as he was when he was human and was 'rewarded' by the sudden onset of extreme pain as his body restructured itself back into human form. Seconds passed, and he was human again, his clothes lay shredded around him. His transformation left him so bulky his clothes couldn't possible hold his shape.

"How did you do it?" Sim stared at him eyes wide, slack-jawed.

"I visualized myself as I am normally, and I changed back," Hank told him. "Oh, and be prepared for..."

Sim doubled over, crying out in pain.

"... it to hurt like hell." Hank finished.

Sim righted himself after a moment, panting hard from the pain. "Thanks."

"No problem."

Sim glanced at his clothes, which were ripped at the seams in several places. This was a serious deal to take in all at once. "Do you think we can change back the same way? Or do we always have to wait for a full moon?" he asked.

"Dunno. Why don't you give it a try?" A sly smile made its way to Hank's lips.

Sim stared at Hank with hesitant eyes. "Okay." He started to concentrate, but a gasp from Hank's direction stopped him. Hank's body rippled and stretched impossibly without tearing. Sim heard the snaps of broken bones and could sometimes see them pop under Hank's skin. The most dramatic change came facially as Hank's face stretched forward from the top of the nose all around the jaw. Thousands of little breaks and rearrangements were made in seconds. Hank was no more. Instead, there was an enormous Werebear.

Hank's voice, deeper than usual, growled out, "It works, but it still hurts like hell, though I think it hurt less."

Following his lead, Sim formed a picture of himself as the Werebear in his mind and felt it lock into focus. The pain was instantaneous, but not long lasting. It was done, and they were standing together as Werebears.

Peering around for the first time, Hank realized he could see deep into the forest. Yes, the moon was at full illumination, but in the dense forest, he could see fine. This must be what bears see. Everything was a muted gray color of its original, though. Taking a moment to take a deep breath, he was assaulted by a barrage of smells. The smoke and pine from the fire. The freshly turned dirt from their earlier fight, and the smell of snow runoff from the creek some distance to the east. Another smell caught in his nose, he let out a soft growl.

Sim was too engrossed in his own discoveries to hear. "So, what do we do now?"

Hank let out a deep chuckle. "We do what bears do. We hunt!" Hank lowered to all fours and ran northwest towards the smell which caught his attention...deer.

Chapter 3

Sylvia watched the cursor blink on her monitor, and wondered for the hundredth time, what she did to deserve this? All she ever wanted to be in life was a journalist. When she was little she would interview family members and write newspaper stories about what she learned. When she got into junior high, she joined the school newspaper, and wrote several news breaking stories. In fact, one of her investigative reports was used on the evening news.

High school improved her skills. Devoting almost all her free time to the school newspaper, she was lead reporter, lead editor, and head writer all in one. In most cases, in high school there should have been some jealousy and bitterness, but Sylvia was so effective at her job nobody thought ill of her. She was also a nice, if a little self-absorbed, individual. She always came off as likable, she knew, but always distant, as if thinking of something else, which was generally accurate.

Running story ideas through her head, she had a unique ability to write an entire article in her head. It was a matter of sitting down and typing it, which is why most people didn't have any problem with the fact she almost single-handedly ran everything at the newspaper. It customarily took her about an hour to assemble and print, and it was always impeccable.

After high school, she went to Sydney University and studied Journalism as a major, and communications and biology as a double minor. The biology minor she took primarily as a personal curiosity was the cause of her most recent problem. Because of her animal knowledge, she was regulated to covering all stories to do with animals. This was not the position she had in mind when she applied to the Sydney Times.

Now, instead of covering critical stories about Australia's involvement in world events, or the current Prime Minister's new promise to make good with the Aborigines, she was covering dog shows and strange mutant animal attacks! Well, the latter was only once, but was the reason she was staring at her monitor now.

For several weeks, there were vicious attacks in the shadier parts of Sydney. It started with pets. Dogs and cats were found torn to shreds. Ultimately, it happened to humans. Initially it was thought perchance a rabid dingo made its way into Sydney, but an animal attack expert was called in and examined the bodies. He concluded the markings were almost identical to the way crocodile attacks appear.

Sylvia had dutifully reported what the expert said which caused a wave of panic to spread throughout Sydney. Outside animals suddenly were kept inside; kids weren't allowed to play far from the house at all. People went crazy. For a while, every day an Aussie would show up at the police station with a dead croc and claim it was the killer croc. Once again, the animal attack expert would come in and examine the bite width of the supposed killer croc, and it would always come up short. Supposedly, this attacking crocodile was one massive croc. Its bite radius was larger than an average croc.

Somehow this croc eluded all capture, even being seen, which was amazing, seeing how the complete police roster was combing the streets, Sydney harbor, and the sewer system for any sign of this quote, end quote, Killer croc. Once again, Sylvia placed her fingers upon the keyboard in hopes they might decide to write for themselves, but to no avail. She had nothing. No pic, no leads, no witnesses, only a case file of eight deaths attributed to this croc.

Flicking open the file, she fanned the pictures on her desk before her. The shots were gruesome and disturbing. Sizeable pieces of abdomens, upper thighs, even the side of one man's skull was missing. Perhaps the most disturbing of all the pics, and the reason why the police force and media were in a blitz, was of an eight-year-old girl.

Her name was Samantha Tosh, a petite, blonde-haired girl, like the ones seen in commercials, or calendars. Normally, you would expect to see a capricious smile and a twinkle in her eye, like a spark of laughter right before it came forth. Instead, all you saw was an expression of horror and agonizing pain on her face as the crocodile tore and shredded the lower half of her body. Entrails lay in a tangle heap, jutting from her severed torso. The lower floating ribs could be seen and the vertebrae down to her coccyx were visible. Her hands were each gripping part of her large intestine, trying to put it back inside her body as she died of shock and blood loss. Sylvia felt the bile rising in her stomach and turned the picture over. She had seen all types of deaths in her time studying journalism and being reporter, but this one hit her hard.

Sylvia thought of her niece. Tess was also eight years old, same as Samantha, and Sylvia could not imagine what those poor parents were going through. To have your young daughter taken from you, in such a violent way, was devastating. To have had to go into the morgue and gaze upon her face, a face revealing how much pain she endured before she died and identify her as your daughter. Sylvia wiped her eyes as tears welled in them. Thankfully, her niece was safe, at home.

Sylvia leaned back in her chair. It creaked faintly, a squeaky pulse, as it rocked back and forth. Pushing off with one foot, she rolled across the tile floor to the desk behind her and kicked on the police scanner. It was something she did now and again to see if she could

47

possibly scoop a story and get off the animal beat. As was obvious from the fact she still abided at this desk, she hadn't gotten lucky, yet.

The dispatch was finishing up telling an officer the location of a domestic violence call which had come in. The officer agreed to go check on it and would radio in when he arrived at the scene. Listening for a short while back at her desk, she stared at the monitor. The boss wanted the story for Friday's run, which gave her two more days to write it, and with luck, something might happen between now at then. *In the meantime*, Sylvia thought as she stood, shut down her computer and grabbed her purse, *she would go home and get some sleep*. The dispatch was coming back on as she switched off the scanner. Instantly, she turned it back on as she heard the address mentioned, recognizing it as right down the street.

"...Street next to the Jommy's liquor store. Witness said she thought she saw a large croc moving into the alley between the buildings. Probably, the witness is drunk, but better check it out. Please copy."

"This is car 82, we are less than two kilometers from locale. We will be there in two. Copy."

Staring at the scanner for a moment, she couldn't believe her luck. If this really was, in fact, the croc, now was her chance at a significant break in the story. There were no waterways nearby, which means it wouldn't be able to get anywhere to escape capture this time. Before she could think better of it, she grabbed a camera off the desk and ran for the stairs. She approached the alley location in less than a minute.

Lights blazed from Jommy's like flashlights pointing into the street, creating wells of light, but left everywhere else in oppressive darkness. The alley was a dark hole in which no light ventured. As Sylvia approached, she slowed. The streets were particularly empty this late on Monday night, with most

48

people having to work in the morning, the only ones venturing out were the drunks, whores and criminals. She had no desire to run into a thief or a rapist with a camera as her only defense. The camera, most likely, would be the reason for the robbery in the first place since it was an expensive piece of hardware.

Stepping over the curb, she hugged the side of the building as she moved closer to the alley entrance. Noises came from inside the alley, sounds she couldn't attribute to anything she recognized. This was it, she thought. It had to be the croc and it was within her reach. The police would be here in moments, she should wait for them, but it was possible they would interfere with her getting some useful pictures. She didn't want to risk it. The noises still came from the alley.

Standing at the corner of the alley, Sylvia listened. Down a side street, the flashes of red and white heralded the approach of the police. They had decided to run silent, not wishing to scare the croc away with the loud sirens, she guessed, but still, they had their lights going. Sylvia took a deep breath, rounded the corner of the alley, and pressed the button on the camera. Flashes illuminated the alley in quick succession like some strobe-lighted dance floor. Firing off a dozen shots as her eyes adjusted to the sudden light, Sylvia's mind registered what she saw. In all her life, she had never witnessed anything as horrific as she was seeing, or as impossible.

Standing deep within the alley was some sort of humanoid — it stood at least twice her height, somewhere over three meters tall, and was broad of frame. Its body seemed to shift from green to black but was made of large scales from head to toe. Its legs were lighter color on the inside, as was the abdomen, chest and under its neck. Its neck swept out into a long snout filled with teeth, gleaming as the flash's light struck them. Red colored eyes sat on either side of its head.

She had no problem realizing this was the creature everyone thought was the killer croc, because that was what it was like; a crocodile, standing on two legs. Another reason she figured this was the killer which had Sydney in a panic was the fact it was in the process of eating its latest victim. Its powerful arms held two halves of a body whose midsection was all but missing. Realizing now what those sounds she had heard were, she resisted the urge to puke. Blood, gore and ichor dripped from the gaping mouth of the creature as it froze from chewing. The flashes of light momentarily blinding it.

Sylvia realized her predicament and stopped shooting pictures. The alley went dark. Light circles swam across her vision as the sudden darkness left her temporarily blinded. Sylvia froze for a moment, not sure if what she had seen was real. She took several steps back from the alley's mouth.

It emerged from the darkness in front of her. As if from nothingness, the snout appeared first, followed by its massive body, like a demon stepping from a portal out of hell. Its eyes locked on her, and she could only watch in fascination as its inner eyelids closed over the eyes, retreating under the outer eyelids. It was then Sylvia knew she was going to die. Hopefully, the pictures in her camera would show the world what was hiding in the city. This monster was like nothing she had ever seen before or heard of.

Like a slow-motion action scene from a movie, she watched as the creature's right hand reached backwards, before slowly coming forward in a terrible arc towards her head. As the arm slashed in front of her she heard, detachedly, four hollow booms, and she caught flashes from her peripheral. The creature about to end her life rocked back as bullets ripped into its flesh. Sylvia saw two bullets bury themselves into its chest, one in the arm and the other in the abdomen.

Blood sprayed her, warm droplets of red rain, as the creature whipped around. Sylvia felt terrible pain. Flipping over, her head struck the pavement as its tail whipped around, catching her legs and knocking them out from underneath her. Head throbbing in pain, she watched from the pavement. The thing escaped with lightning speed down the alleyway. More shots were fired as one cop ran to the entrance of the alley, firing into the dark alley in hopes of striking the beast. The other cop knelt in front of her. Holding on to consciousness long enough, she heard the cop call for an ambulance.

Gordon knew he was fucked. His appetite, finally, got him in trouble. He ducked into his hideout, a block from where he got shot, though you couldn't tell anymore, as the wounds were now healed. Shutting the door behind him, he conjured a picture of himself as a human into his mind. With slight discomfort, he reverted to his original form. The man most people would recognize as Gordon Sands was of middling height and build, though he recently dropped about twenty pounds in which everyone at work desperately wanted to know what his diet was. This always made him smile, knowing they certainly wouldn't want to know he was eating other humans.

Short-cropped, sandy blonde hair topped his rather squarish head. Pencil thin eyebrows, which he worked tirelessly to keep, arched over olive green eyes. High cheekbones and a strong face made Gordon a man who got most ladies to give him a second glance. Not to mention the fact he was a doctor, a neurosurgeon, and a damn fine one. Gordon Sands was hardly thirty and a very successful doctor.

This was his life. An excellent job, wonderful pay, and all the toys he could buy and all the women he could want. At least, it had been his life, until a few months ago. It was the same day Stonehenge fell. He would never forget, and wondered again if it was a coincidence or if it had something to do with his initial change? The timing was too suspect. Researching it, as far as he could tell, right when the last stone fell is exactly the moment he first changed.

51

Well, his life, as he had known it, was over. Oh sure, he still pretended to be Dr. Gordon Sands, going through the motions, but it didn't bring him the joy it once had. The only thing to bring him joy now was the killing. He began to understand a little how some serial killers must feel. How thrilling it was to choose a target, then kill them, except, he was better than any serial killer. Something beyond them. Some serial killers pretended to be nice citizens, pillars of the community. Later they would turn out to be monsters. Monsters, yet still human. And as such, eventually they would leave some sort of physical evidence.

He, on the other hand, *was* a monster. When he killed, he wasn't human, and therefore, would never leave any physical evidence linking himself to the murders. Hell, the police didn't think of them as murders. They were animal attacks.

Gordon dressed slowly, not wanting to rush out of his hiding spot and appear suspicious. The perfect killer, he thought. No one suspected the crocodile killing people was a man. But, now. Now he had fucked up. Not only did he leave witnesses, but he was photographed. The cops would be on the lookout for some sort of person behind all of this. They couldn't ignore the evidence they had. Before, they were searching for a wayward croc. Now, they were on the lookout for, well, he wasn't sure what they would be searching for. They definitely would be widening their search parameters.

He would have to lay low for a while and not go hunting. He frowned. The truth was, he was beginning to enjoy the taste of human flesh. At first, it disgusted him. Now, he began to crave it, like some junkie questing for his next fix.

Stepping out of his hideout, he locked the door behind him.

He bought this cellar studio after he understood his abilities and his needs. Every few nights he came here, stripped down, and became the beast. Then, he would go and find a victim, eat, and return.

There was a club around the corner he went to afterwards. He always felt aroused after he fed. It wouldn't take him long to find a willing partner to take home to satisfy his lust. Climbing the stairs, he made his way to the front of the building when a cop came around the corner, shining a flashlight at Gordon's face, the intense light momentarily blinding him.

"Excuse me, sir. Can I ask what you are doing here?" The cop lowered the light a touch so Gordon could make out the features of his face.

"I own the studio down the stairs there." Gordon pointed off behind him at the unlit stairwell.

"Okay. Still does not answer my question, sir." The cop danced the flashlight down the stairwell.

Gordon flashed a smile. He was becoming irritated by this police officer's attitude. He shouldn't have to explain himself to this pathetic human, but he was trying to not draw attention to himself, so he tried to calm his frustration.

"Well, it's just I was going to hit the club across the street and I hadn't been by this property in some time. I decided to check on it and make sure everything was in order." He flashed another smile. His smile was disarming, or so he was told, so he tried to use it as often as he could to ease people's minds so they wouldn't see too close at the darkness inside him. "I checked, and everything is fine. So, if you don't mind, I'm off to the club."

The officer examined him for a moment more before smiling back.

"All right. I wouldn't want to keep you from the ladies. Just be careful out here, okay? The crocodile killed not too far from here this evening and is still on the loose."

Gordon feigned fear. "Really? It escaped again? For a crocodile, it certainly seems quick." Gordon finished smiling crookedly at the cop.

"Yeah, well the report just came in. Not sure I believe it, but, this crocodile walks on two legs."

Gordon's smile wavered, but he recovered and barked a laugh.

"That is the most ridiculous thing I have ever heard. It sounds like some cop trying to make an excuse as to how it got away from him."

The cop shook his head. "That's what I thought at first, too, but there were two cops and a female reporter who took some pictures of it. Also, the cops took several shots at it. They believe at least two confirmed hits and possibly a third. The thing turned and ran away." The cop shook his head again. "Even if it was Halloween, I would have trouble believing all of that. We will have to wait for the pictures. I'm sure you will see something about it in the papers tomorrow." The cop lowered his flashlight and clicked it off. "Well, have a good night."

As the cop turned and walked away, Gordon struggled to keep a straight face. Watching the cop drive off, he seethed inside. As soon as the cop was out of sight, Gordon spun and slammed his fist in the brick wall next to him. Several chunks of brick flew away as he shattered the first couple of inches. Bringing his fist back, he examined the sliced-up skin on his fist. It throbbed for a moment, healed, and the pain went away.

Gordon smiled. Seeing how much better a specimen he was than everyone else around him always made him smile. He was unstoppable. Four times he was shot this evening and now he was fine. He should stop worrying about what the cops and the stupid reporter saw. If they decide they have some sort of walking crocodile, they still aren't going to know it is him. If they were to find out, he would kill them all!

Gordon relaxed, straightened his clothes, crossed the street, and entered the club. After a quick visit to the bathroom to wash the blood off his fist he made his way to the bar. The club was full of hot, sweaty people dancing to the throbbing music. Bodies undulated in a chaotic, yet rhythmic dance matching the song being played.

There were women everywhere in various stages of undress. Most had small halter-tops, leaving their bellies bare and some had tube tops, hardly more than a strip of cloth scarcely covering their breasts. Almost all of them had on short skirts or shorts, allowing a little bit of cheek to show at the bottom. It was a pleasing sight to Gordon. His appetite for women was insatiable. The only thing he had an appetite for more, was tearing the flesh from bone and tasting the sweet nectar of someone's blood draining down the back of his throat.

Watching the crowd, he sipped his rum and coke. Someone brushed against his arm. He turned. An attractive brunette leaned on the bar next to him. Soft curls framed her attractive face. Brown eyes, like a baby deer, peered out over a small but flat nose, complimenting her large, petulant mouth. She had darker skin, not the bronze skin most women in Sydney had from their time on the beach or in a tanning bed. Her darker skin implied aboriginal heritage, a grandparent or great grandparent most likely. She was tall, almost as tall as Gordon.

Leaning against the bar next to him, her long legs stretched out behind her, one calf raised as her foot bobbed rhythmically to the music. She appeared unaware of his presence as she glanced around for a bartender. Conservatively dressed for the bar, she wore a long silky black skirt, cut below her knees but was split up the side to mid-thigh. Her top was a red buttoned down collared blouse, unbuttoned enough to see some cleavage and the edge of her black bra. Her Mojito was nearly finished.

Gordon turned and caught a bartender's eye and nodded once. Most of the wait staff knew him, and knew he was a terrific tipper, so he moved hurriedly to see what Gordon wanted.

As the bartender approached, the woman tried to get his attention, but Gordon brushed her arm. Turning to gaze at him, he smiled to her. She smiled back.

"Don't worry, I got it," he told her.

"What do you need, mate?" the bartender asked.

"A Mojito for the lady, and another rum and coke for me." Nodding in the direction of the woman.

"Gotcha, coming right up." The bartender turned and went over to the cooler to get out the Mojito.

Gordon stared at the woman for some time, giving a soft smile. She peered at him as intently, and then glanced down.

"I'm Gordon," he said while offering his hand.

"Sheila," she responded, taking his hand.

He almost lost it.

"Seriously?" Staring at her, eyes wide as a smile played across his face. Sheila was the word most Australians used to call a woman.

She quirked a smile and rolled her eyes.

"I know, I know. My parents thought they had a sense of humor. It gets kinda confusing out there in crowded areas when people are yelling out; 'Hey, sheila and I always glance around."

"I can imagine. I suppose you hate your parents for the travesty of a name they gave you?"

"You get used to it. And no, I still love my parents. I always give them shit for it, though."

Gordon smiled, and she smiled back. This was going well, and he was sure he knew how this would end up.

56

◈

It was four in the morning when Gordon snuck out of Sheila's house. So no one would spot him, he always left early. The last thing he wanted was to be seen leaving a house where a half-eaten mangled up body of a woman lay on blood-soaked sheets with bones and viscera strewn haphazardly around the room.

He walked about ten blocks away before hailing a cab.

Sheila had taken him to her home after he explained he planned on drinking and didn't want the temptation of driving home, so he had taken a cab to the bar. Initially she had offered to take him home, but when they got to the car and started making out heavily, she mentioned her home was closer if he wanted to stay the night, which was his intent the entire time. They drove to her house, went inside, had sex on her stairwell, and finished in her room. After, he went to the bathroom and transformed into the croc. Leaving the lights off, so she couldn't see him, he entered the bedroom. He didn't want her to scream, or someone would call the cops.

Crossing the room to where she lay in the bed, he could hear her breathing which came in a soft, steady rhythm, signifying she was sleeping. Lowering his towering form, his jaws lined up with her throat, he parted them, saliva dripped slowly from his gapping jaws like clear strings.

SNAP!

He tore into her throat, ripping free her esophagus and larynx in one quick bite, purposely missing the arteries in her neck. It wouldn't do to have her bleed out to quickly. Pulling back so he could see, her eyes flew open. Opening her mouth to scream– no sound came forth. Her hands reached up to the gaping hole below her chin.

Gordon managed to turn the light on next to the bed, so Sheila could see her attacker. When her eyes met his, they widened and her whole body began to shake. He felt himself become aroused, again. Grabbing her arms, he yanked them swiftly out of their sockets, so they flopped uselessly beside her.

She tried frantically to yell at him but could only gurgle. Maneuvering himself between her legs, she kicked at him. She wasn't hurting him but was succeeding in preventing him from getting between her legs. Grabbing one thigh, he slammed his hand, palm out against her calf, right below the knee. There was a sickening pop as the lower part of her leg snapped free of the knee socket, he repeated the process with the other leg.

Sheila stared at him and cried, the tears fell without feeling, now knowing she was going to be raped as the blood quickly seeped out from her neck. Gordon was furious. He wanted fear! He could feel the arousal passing. Anger surged through him, and he brought both his claws down, piercing her abdomen. Thrusting his arms out, he tore open her midsection. Blood and organs flew out to either side, spraying the walls to slowly slide down and pool upon the floor. Bringing what remained stuck to his claws up to his mouth, he dropped strips of flesh and muscle down his throat. When he glanced back down, Sheila's sightless eyes stared up at him. He went to work on the rest of her body.

After he finished eating, he changed back to his human form and took a shower. There was no way for him to utterly get rid of the evidence he had been there, he hoped he could tie his presence back to another day. Going to her purse, he put his phone number into her address book. He would call her later and leave a voice mail about how much fun he had with her the other night, and how he wanted to see her again. Hopefully, it would be enough to throw off any suspicion. They met, went back to her place, and he left. Whatever had happened to her, happened later.

Gordon's mind wandered as the cab drove him home with the driver going on about things which didn't matter much to Gordon. He hardly listened. Sydney was beginning to wake up as the cab turned down his street. The driver either ran out of things to say or realized he was talking to himself, for he had fallen silent. Gordon paid the man without saying a word and walked up the short flight of stairs to his condo. Seeing what was lying on his doorstep made him freeze. It was a picture of him, well, a picture of his other form to be exact. Right there on the front page of the Sydney Times with the headline *Monster Terrorizing Sydney, REVEALED!*

The picture was clear, and they had cropped it to hide the ripped torso gripped in his claws, but it was unmistakable. It was him. Maybe, just maybe, he had thought, the picture wouldn't have come out so high-quality, but it appears the woman had gotten a perfect shot. Picking up the paper, he flipped it open. There were several more shots of him in different poses.

Immediately, he opened his door and went inside. Gordon sank down onto the kitchen table chair and read the article.

As many of you know, Sydney has been gripped with terror over the recent attacks these past few months, made by what was believed to be a crocodile who had wandered into the city's sewer system. It has happened before, and so it seemed likely, this was the case. But, unlike before, the police and animal experts had so far been unlucky in catching the beast. As it turns out, the police and everyone else was searching for the wrong thing. By luck, though I question the use of the word; I happened upon this creature you see in the photos above feasting on, as of yet, unidentified victim. I managed to keep my wits, and my dinner, long enough to get off a few photos before I was attacked by the creature. If it wasn't for the swift action of Officer James Downy and Officer Pete Glitch, I would have been its next victim. The officers fired several shots at it. I am positive the creature was hit at least four times, though I was more worried for my life than paying attention to see if any shots had hit, so I can't be certain, though both officers believe it was how many hit it. The creature, after taking several shots, turned and ran away, as if it hadn't been hit at all.

I have spoken to several government officials and they have assured me all resources available are being brought to bear on finding this thing, whatever it is.

As always, Sydney Times will bring you the most up to date information regarding the creature.

Sylvia Tyrine, reporter.

He should have killed her and taken the camera away or destroyed it. Witnesses could be dismissed as seeing crazy things at night, but photographic evidence is hard to dispute. At least coming from the Sydney Times, it would be. Some tabloid paper you could discredit, but the Sydney Times was a reputable newspaper and wouldn't print stories which could be construed as fluff or bogus stories. What should he do about this? If anything? There was no way to connect him with the monster, at least, none he knew of. So why worry?

The problem was, he would have to curb his appetite for quite a while. He couldn't afford to get caught. Of course, he was damn near invincible, but, still, he could be caught. Once that happened, it would only be a matter of time before they would figure out who he was.

It was time to return to the normal life of the 9 to 5 doctor, as much as it grated on Gordon, it couldn't be helped. Let the city forget about the monster, let them assume it disappeared or went back to where it had come from. Tossing the paper in the trash, he went upstairs to sleep off the night's exploits.

The Sydney library was much like most longstanding libraries throughout the world; dark and dreary except for small pockets of light mounted above some work stations like fireflies in a field. Volumes of books lined hundreds of book cases ranging from the occult all the way to torrid romance novels. Sylvia would prefer to have been leafing through the latter, but instead, was flipping through one of the many books on the occult she had arranged before her on the work desk. With bags under her eyes, she could admit without any shame, she had appeared better.

The last few weeks had been chaotic, to say the least. As being one of the few who witnessed the monster, and took photos of it, she ran the gambit of talk shows, news interviews and everyday people on the street wondering what she saw, and how did she make it out alive?

Pinching the bridge of her nose, she closed her eyes as the migraines she still got, attacking her head like some strong man squeezing her brain. She knew she was lucky — very lucky. If those officers hadn't been there, she would have been ripped apart, and devoured.

Along with the migraines, also came the nightmares. Most nights she awoke, screaming as she saw the monster barreling down upon her, mouth agape, ready to tear into her flesh.

At last, the interviews had slowed to a trickle and she was only accosted by people on the street occasionally. It had been several weeks since the last attack and people began to forget. It was enough to make her scream. The attention span of most Australians was like a two-year-old. If the toy was in front of them, it was the most important thing in the world. Take the toy away for a bit, and it's like it never existed.

Evidently, the general populous didn't realize what she realized after the last attack. A second attack had occurred the same night of her altercation with the beast. A poor woman was ripped apart in her bedroom, which had been different than the previous attacks, since all of those occurred outside somewhere. This one occurred inside. There was no sign of forced entry, no damage to the home at all, which amazed her, considering the size of the thing.

For some reason, that didn't bother anyone, didn't set off alarms in anyone's head. Except for hers, she guessed. The creature had taken four bullets; she was sure of it. The thing had staggered from the impact of the bullets. It had taken four bullets, and yet, was perfectly capable of going somewhere, quite a distance away, without being seen, and commit another attack.

It bothered her. But, the thing making her suspicious was the sudden cessation of attacks the moment her story ran in the paper. With actual evidence of what they were hunting now, it was only a matter of time before they would capture the thing. Yet, if the creature didn't make any attacks, how would they?

It was smart, she realized. It wasn't some dumb monster. It was intelligent. It was smart enough to know it needed to lie low and keep off the radar for a while and let the situation cool. Unfortunately, after only a couple of weeks, the situation was indeed cooling.

Wondering again about what she was searching for, she sighed. Why was she knee-deep in occult books? What did she hope to find? Resting her head on the table, she was too tired to go through all these books. The whirlwind schedule she had maintained these last weeks, and the lack of sleep due to the reoccurring nightmares gave her little rest. The grains of the wood pressed into her forehead, a cold comfort, as she rested it on the top of the desk. Closing her eyes for a moment, she tried to let the stress flow out of her body. Once again, though, the image of the monster manifested itself in her mind's eyes and it attacked!

BAM!

Sylvia's head shot up at the sound of something slamming onto the table next to her head. Heart pounding, she peeked to see a large book, bound in a brown cover resting next to her. Standing behind the book was a wild haired gentleman, presumably the one who had slammed the book down on the table next to her. She took a moment to examine the bloke before ripping him a new one for waking her so rudely.

A stunted fellow, he had a blocky build. Gray hair, wild, yet not uncombed, reminding her of the pictures she had seen of Albert Einstein. A short, gray trimmed beard, framed a set of thin lips, scarcely visible because of it. Gold wired rimmed glasses rested comfortably at the end of a sharp, beak like nose. He wore brown slacks and vest, and a gray button-down shirt. A gold chain peeked out of his right breast pocket, most likely attached to one of those old pocket watches. Gazing down upon her through those glasses, he watched her. Instantly, she felt intimidated by him, as if he was her college professor, and she was his student who got caught asleep in his class.

Opening her mouth to talk, he stopped her.

"You are searching in the wrong place, Miss Tyrine."

"What?"

"What you are searching for, won't be found in those books you have there."

"What?" Asking again, stupidly. She was a little off kilter by his apparent knowledge of her and what she might be searching for. Plus, she couldn't come up with a better response.

He frowned down at her.

"You must have taken a more significant blow to the head than had been reported."

Gathering her wits about her, she responded. "No. Sorry." Sylvia frowned at the man. "It's just… you startled me. You threw me off by implying you knew who I was and what I was searching for. I find it remarkable, because I don't really know what I'm searching for."

"You are looking for a creature who thinks like a man."

Sylvia stared at him, eyebrows climbing slowly. He described it so plainly, it took her a moment to realize it was exactly what she was looking for.

"Why do you say I'm searching in the wrong place, mister...?

"Elliot, Jackson Elliot. Miss Tyrine, I can tell you are searching in the wrong place because I know where you should be searching." Tapping the large book he had set beside her.

Sylvia glared up at the man before her then back down at the book. Sliding the volume closer, she picked it up to examine the cover. The book's cover depicted a priestly seeming man in a brown robe carrying an odd-looking walking stick and wearing a crown made of antlers. The robed man faced an extremely huge bear, rearing up on its hind legs menacingly, though the priest seemed unafraid. In gold script was the title "Celtic Historical Mythology. A study at where truth ends, and myth begins by Jackson Elliot." Glancing back up at Jackson, she raised an eyebrow. Jackson nodded.

"What you need to find is in here, miss."

"Why don't you just tell me, since you wrote this, and you know what it is I'm looking for?"

"Because, I thought you, as a reporter, would understand."

"Understand what?" Sylvia questioningly stared at him, honestly curious.

"Knowledge is only appreciated if it's discovered, not given." Jackson gave a curt nod and walked away.

Sylvia watched him go. He walked robustly for a man of obvious advancing years. Posture erect, not bent like many elderly, so perhaps he wasn't as old as she first thought. He disappeared around a shelf of books. She waited a short bit to see if he would reappear, since he seemed like the type to show up again when you thought he was long gone.

Glancing back down, she examined the book. Did it hold the secret of the creature as Mr. Elliot claimed? Opening it, she began reading. It was a thick book but held many illustrations — it wouldn't take too long to get through it.

The cab came to a halt in front of a brick two-story on a sizable plot of land. The road wound its way through corralled horses grazing on the newly grown grass. Sylvia admired the horses and the rolling land Mr. Elliot's home stood upon. It took her three days to locate Mr. Elliot's home and she had to use much of her reporting skills to find it. Plainly, Mr. Elliot enjoyed his solitude. He didn't even own a phone. Not for the first time did she wonder how he had located her. She had read his book. Twice. It didn't take her long to find the answer she was searching for, but she was enchanted by the history and mythology of the Celts, so she read through the whole thing.

Like many, she had heard of Druids and their connection with Stonehenge. Werewolves, she had heard of as well, but not the other creatures some people could change into: wolves, bears, boars, snakes, rats, foxes and others. Lycanthropy, as it was referred to now, was believed, by some, to be a gift from the Druids to help protect them as they carried out their work to protect nature. It was believed to be passed down through generations.

Most of it was supposition, since the Druids did not keep a written history. However, there were those who dealt with the Druids who left clues to put together and put together Mr. Elliot had. If what he had been able to put together was true, the creature terrorizing Sydney was a Werecroc. Shuddering, she thought about what would have happened if it had bit her or scratched her, as lycanthropy was believed to be transmitted through bites and cuts.

It intrigued her there was a connection between this creature and the Druids, considering the fact Stonehenge collapsed shortly before the first attack. Going back, she checked, to make sure, and it had been about a week before the first attack. The two events were connected, she was convinced, and the only person who would have a reasonably clear idea if this was true was Jackson Elliot.

She was surprised how easy it was to believe the monster was some sort of Were-creature. It was outlandish, and insane, but it was the only thing which made sense. The creature was humanoid yet resembled a crocodile. It also explained how it could disappear so easily — it changed back to its human form. Further evidence was the last attack. It was inside a woman's home with no signs of forced entry by some sort of animal, or monster. It signified it wasn't a monster when it entered. She was a logical woman, and the Werecroc, no matter how crazy, was the only logical answer.

Stepping out of the cab, she asked if he could stick around for a moment, since she wasn't sure if the man was home. The driver nodded, and she made her way to the front door. As of yet, it seemed as if no one was home, for no one had stirred in the home when she arrived. Ignoring the hefty brass knockers, she knocked on the thick wooden double doors first. Using her fist, the sound it emitted was too light for anyone to hear. Lifting the knocker, she brought it down hard, three times. The door promptly opened on the third rap as Mr. Elliot swung it open.

"I heard you the first time! No need to... oh, Miss Tyrine. I expected you a few days ago. I didn't think it would take you this long to figure things out."

He appeared as she remembered him from last time, white hair, erect, like crazy wisps of solid smoke. Wearing the same brown slacks and vest, the same grey shirt, she was sure it was the same clothes. It was either an incredible coincidence, or he didn't have much variety in his wardrobe. She decided on the latter.

"Good day to you, too, Mr. Elliot."

"Jackson, please."

"Jackson. I'm sorry it took me longer to get here than you thought it would, but I assure you, I figured everything out quite a long time ago. It was finding you which proved more troublesome. However, since I am here now, why don't you invite me in?"

Jackson peered down at her through his gold rimmed glasses as if she was some bug under a magnifying glass he was trying to determine what to do with it. She hoped he wouldn't angle the glass towards the sun.

With a nod, he stepped aside and motioned her in. With a wave to the taxi driver, she entered. The foyer of the house was grand in scale. Its vaulted ceiling was illuminated by a pair of sky lights which did little to light the floor. A light-colored hardwood floor burst outward concentrically from the center of the rounded foyer like age rings on an immense oak. A broad stairwell emptied out at the far end of the room leading up to a balconied hallway. A dark red runner carpet crawled its way up the center of the stair like a river of blood.

To the right was another room, a large oak table ran the length of the room. A golden and silver chandelier dangled above with ten candles mounted on wax guards. It was an antique, for most people used electric and had done away with candle chandeliers ages ago, but she always liked them.

Her parents had kept one in the dining room until a few years ago, when one of the candles fell out and caught the table cloth on fire.

Afterwards, they got rid of it. It was amazing how you can have something for years, decades, and though it always had potential to be dangerous, nothing ever happens. Then, suddenly it blows up on you.

The table was flanked by four wooden chairs, each intricately carved. The chairs themselves seemed as if they were cut from one piece of wood. From where she stood she couldn't see a single join. She was probably too far away to see them. Either way, the chairs were expertly put together.

To her left was a traditional sitting room as you imagine most vintage British homes would have. A sizeable fireplace centered the wall surrounded by two cushioned chairs; their red upholstered cushions in stark contrast to the dark stained wooden legs, arms, and back, plus the fireplace mantle. An equally adorned ottoman sat with its back toward her, facing the fireplace. The deep colors and the warmth from the coals; red eyes buried under a gray blanket, created in her a desire to curl up and read a book, or to share drinks with a couple of friends over deep conversational points.

Spreading out from the fireplace was floor to ceiling bookcases, filled with row upon row of books. The whole place exuded manliness. The only thing to throw off the whole clichéd macho crib was the plants. They were everywhere. In the foyer, two giant ferns rested to either side of the entry doors, verdant sentries standing at attention. Several potted plants hung from hooks, descending from the vaulted ceiling to dangle above one's head.

Some plants spilled out from the pot to reach longingly for the floor, a waterfall of vines, though they were still a meter or two from it. White flowers spotted the vines intermittingly, white petals pealed back to reveal yellow coated stamen.

Bright flowers created a palette of colors emerging from pots running the length of the balcony on the second floor. The pleasant smell of a flower garden permeated the house and she breathed deeply, her muscles relaxed, and tension fled from her body. Feeling a sense of renewal and awakening, it must have been mirrored in her eyes because she caught Jackson watching her, nodding his head.

Smiling, he said, "It's like waking up after a decent night's sleep and stepping outside on the first couple days of spring, isn't it?"

All she could do was nod, as she was a little overwhelmed by the ease she felt inside. Peering again at Jackson, she felt as if she was seeing him for the first time. His demeanor had changed. Before, he had always seen gruff and grumpy. Even a moment ago, when answering the door. Judging by the light in his eyes and the smile on his face, she believed it had all been a show. Perhaps, one he had to use all too often and so became almost too natural for him to put on.

"You have questions?" Pointing to the sitting room.

"I do." Sylvia moved across the foyer and into the sitting room. Choosing the ottoman instead of one of the chairs, she sat. Now, more than ever, she felt like curling up on it and reading a book or writing one.

Following her in, Jackson took one of the chairs, turning it to face her a little more squarely.

"Ask." He placed his hands together on his lap.

Sylvia wasn't sure where to begin. She had many questions, but those took a back seat now to a more pressing question which had now worked itself to the surface of her brain after entering this house.

"Who are you?"

Jackson's eyes widened a little at the question.

"Not the question I expected, but I am pleased by it. I had a feeling you were a smart girl." He smiled widely at her.

For some reason, she felt a swelling of pride at his approval.

"Definitely, not the question I was expecting." He inhaled deeply. "And not an easy one to answer, I'm afraid. If I was to tell you, it would require a great deal of faith on your part to believe in the tale I would tell." Leaning forward, his eyes captured hers. "Do you have faith in me? Would you believe a story the likes of some fairy tale told by the Brothers Grimm?"

Staring into his eyes, she noticed for the first time how startling green they were. There wasn't much she wouldn't believe from this man, she realized, nodding.

Jackson leaned back into the chair.

"Very well. I will tell you my tale and it will answer some of your other questions I would imagine. Get comfortable, this will take a while, for the story spans many years, several thousand years in fact."

Chapter 4

"I was born at the sunset of the time of the Druids. At the age of thirteen, I was apprenticed to a Druid named Marloq. He was ancient by anyone's standards. He had been there since the beginning, or so it was said. One of the first to be called Druid." Jackson paused, expecting Sylvia to interrupt with a guffaw at what he was suggesting, but she remained silent and attentive. He continued.

"I knew little about Druids, but I always had an affinity for animals and nature. My parents felt it best to guide me along the Path, knowing full well what danger I would be in. They decided it was for my best to learn the ways of Druids.

"You see, this was the time of the Roman Empire, and they were like locusts, sweeping across the lands. When they came to the Isles, some of the Celts fought them. The Druids, the religious guiding force among the Celts, were swept up in the combat. Despite the mystical power of the Druids, there were too few who remained to give the Romans much trouble."

Again, Jackson paused for a reaction, but Sylvia appeared enthralled with his story.

"Tea?" he asked.

Staring at him a moment longer, she realized he was asking her a question.

"I'm sorry, what?"

"Tea? Would you like some tea?"

She smiled. "I would, yes, thank you."

Standing, Jackson left through a doorway towards the rear of the house. It was a long time since he had relived these memories. Stuffed away like a squirrel stows away a nut, forgetting it till needed, or perhaps, to never uncover it again. This time though, the nut appears to have grown on its own and was uprooting all he believed.

Absently he boiled the water and grabbed a pair of tea cups and bags. He headed back to the sitting room. Sylvia was there, standing, reading the bookends on his book cases. When he entered, she suddenly turned from them, as if embarrassed to be caught, and returned to the ottoman.

"It's okay. I don't mind if you explore my books. In fact, you can have them when I'm gone."

Scrunching her eyebrows at that statement. "Gone? Gone where?" she demanded.

"Ahh... Forgive me. I get ahead of myself." He handed the cup to Sylvia.

Taking the cup from him, she placed the bag inside. Pouring till the cup was about three-quarters full, he stopped, checking her to see if it was enough. She nodded, so he brought the kettle over to his chair and placed the bag in the cup and pour three-quarters full again. It was always the right amount for the tea to taste the best. It was a pleasure to see the girl thought the same way as him. Easing himself into the chair, he allowed a moment to settle his body.

Sylvia removed the tea bag from her cup, setting it on the small saucer Jackson had provided. "Why were there so few Druids left?"

Again, it was an excellent question, Jackson thought.

"There were so few Druids because of the civil war between them. As with most groups of people, there are always differing thoughts, and Druids were no different. There were those who believed nature and humans could work together to make a better world. Those people were, near the end, led by one called Sylvanis. A formidable Druidess, but she found her equal in the ruler of the opposing view, Kestrel, who believed civilization was a harbinger of death to nature. It must be scourged from the Earth, so nature could reign, she believed. To accomplish this, she used an ancient spell, seizing the totem animal of an individual and drew it out, merging it with the person. This spell was called Lycanthros. It created the first Trues."

"Trues?" Sylvia cut in. He could tell she was having a tough time understanding what he was telling her but was trying.

"Yes, Trues. The spell is complex and only works on certain individuals. Those whose totems were close to the forefront. The spell only worked on four individuals she was able to locate. Por, a Celt whose alternate form was of a boar. Renwick, another Celt whom took the shape of a rat. Two foreigners from Egypt became the other two. Syndor, the snake and the other Egyptian, Answi, became what you saw the other night." Jackson stood and began to pace. "They were called Trues because they were the first shapeshifters, their spawn were only copies — less than the Trues, and beholden to them as well."

Sylvia raised an eyebrow. "What do you mean beholden?"

Jackson gave a quiet smirk and sat. "When a True infects another, and they live, which isn't assured. The transmission of lycanthropy is traumatic to the body and often causes rejection, system shock, resulting in cardiac arrest. However, if the person lives, they are now a lycanthrope and can mimic the ability of the True who infected them. Oh, they will never be as strong, but they are formidable in their own right. The problem is simple, they are under the control of the True. Whatever the True wants, the victim will do."

"Sounds dangerous," Sylvia muttered. "I mean, if they can control the person, why wouldn't they infect as many as they could, and create their own army!"

73

"Again, I am pleased I was right about you, Sylvia." Jackson stood and began to pace. "Which is precisely what Kestrel proceeded to do. She had her Trues wreak havoc all over the land, infecting as many as possible. Thousands died from the attacks and more died by not living through the infection." Jackson stopped pacing and sat back down. Leaning forward with his elbows on his knees, he clasped his hands before him.

"Sylvanis was left with little choice. Searching everywhere for those who might undergo the spell and live, she only found four people as well." Pausing, he considered something.

"You see; nature always seeks a balance. I believe it's why Sylvanis was only able to find four, though she searched everywhere. Four became her champions. Her Trues. Calin, a Celt, believed to be the lover of Sylvanis, though it was never confirmed. His totem was the wolf. Adonia, whose form was of a fox. Catherine, was from far to the east, though no one knows where, but I believe it was Macedonia. The animal she transformed into was a tiger. And, of course there was Conner, another Celt who was as massive as a bear, and became one, too," Jackson said with a flourish and a smile.

Sylvia pondered this. It was incredible what he was telling her, but it was also impossible. According to him, Jackson was supposedly over two thousand years old. He was also claiming there were monsters walking the land, in the service of magic wielding Druids. The funny thing was, after seeing what she saw, she believed him. This story was too fantastical. Yet, she was trapped in the story with no hope or desire to escape.

"Tell me more. I'm not sure I believe any of what you are telling me, but it's an amazing story."

Jackson smiled.

74

"Well, I have been many things in my life, but a liar isn't one of them." Jackson smiled. "Where was I?"

"Sylvanis' Trues," Sylvia informed him.

"Ah, yes. Kestrel allowed her Trues to raise an army by force, so she could try to destroy civilization, but Sylvanis only took people who volunteered to become Weres. Her army was smaller, but because they were volunteers they fought with heart. The others were dominated and did not fight with the fervor Sylvanis' did. Still, their numbers were overwhelming and many Weres died. There were also losses amongst the Druids. Terrible losses, and ultimately the losses would be the end of the Druids. Their power and influence was so vastly lessened, when the Romans came, they were unable to mount any type of resistance.

"However, I digress." Jackson frowned, thinking about his place in the story. "The true turning point was when Calin defeated Pol and Answi in combat." Leaning forward a little more to accentuate his point. "You see, when a True is killed, all those he has infected are no longer cursed with Lycanthropy. So, when they could no longer be controlled, Kestrel's army dissolved around her. In the end, Sylvanis came for her." Leaning back, he sank into the cushions on the chair.

"My teacher didn't know much about what happened, other than neither one walked away from the confrontation. Word was there was some sort of prophecy promising Kestrel's return. Also, Sylvanis found some way to stop it or counteract it. Not sure. It was never quite explained to me."

"I met some of the Trues, once," Jackson continued after a moment to sip his drink. "It was a few years after the war, and I was finishing my studies as a Druid when Calin and Adonia rode into my village. I remember the expression in Calin's eyes," Jackson said with a faraway look. "It was believed he was in love with Sylvanis, and her loss devastated him. He had the appearance of someone who had lost everything."

75

Continuing to stare at nothing for a moment, he finally shook himself and glanced back at her. "They had come to tell my teacher they were going into hiding, and if we had need of them, they would do their best to return to help. I never saw any of them again."

"A year later, I left my village to see the world. The Romans moved swiftly to eliminate any threats on the isle. I learned later they killed my teacher after some of the villagers turned him in as a Druid." Jackson paused again, reliving the loss for a moment before going on. "I regretted not being there, but I also knew if I was, I would also have been killed. From then on, I hid the fact I was a Druid and traveled extensively. I tried to locate any of the Trues, on either side, but they had either died, or hidden so well I couldn't find them."

"Why have I never heard of this connection before? I realize the Druids didn't keep records, but surely the Romans would have had some records? Stories that were passed down by scholars or such?" Scrunching up her brow. "Why isn't this known?"

Once again, she proved his faith in her with this question. Unfortunately, the only answer he had for her was a theory.

"I believe that someone, along the way, made an effort to eliminate most of the knowledge about Lycans. Who was responsible for this, I was never able to figure out. But you are right, there should have been written testimony regarding the Lycans, and the fact that there isn't any has worried me for some time." He regarded her. " But, that is a mystery for another time."

Jackson slapped his thighs and stood. "Now. What are you planning on doing with this information?"

Sylvia glanced up at him from where she sat.

"Are you kidding? What the hell can I do with this information? I haven't decided if I believe it, and, at least, I've seen one of these things. Who else would believe me?"

Jackson studied her.

"Perhaps it was a mistake to confide this information in you." Jackson turned away from her and made to leave the room. "Please, show yourself out."

Sylvia watched him leave the room and sat there for a while, not sure what to do. She frowned. *What did he want her to do with the information? It's not like it was useful in the here and now. Nobody would believe her if she told it to anyone. The information was useless.* With a shake of her head, she stood and walked to the front door. Glancing around briefly, she saw no trace of Jackson anywhere.

Shaking her head again, she stepped outside. With a quick call to the cab company she started to make her way down the long road from his house. It would be a while before the cab came back so she decided she would put some distance between her and the house.

Halfway down the driveway she moved to the fence corralling the horses and made clicking noises in hopes one of the horses would approach. A tall brown horse trotted over. She had no idea what kind of horse it was; she had never been interested in them, though this one was beautiful. The horse crowded the fence and Sylvia patted its side and thought more of what went on in the house.

He undoubtedly thinks the information he gave me would be useful. Why didn't he just tell me what he wanted for Christ sake! Because you are a reporter, and you should figure these things out for yourself, Sylvia. She didn't know what it could be. Obviously, she would continue to investigate this creature. This half man, half crocodile creature. It hit her. This creature was a man. At least, it had to be most of the time. The cops were searching for a monster, and not a regular guy. Sylvia stared back at the house with eyes of comprehension. *He wants me to find the guy, so he can do something about it!* Sylvia sprinted back to the house.

Jackson was waiting for her at the door.

"I will find him for you Jackson," she told him.

Jackson smiled at her. "I knew you would."

She smiled back at him. "Why didn't you just tell me in the first place?"

"A road without obstacles is one which passes by unnoticed."

"Well, thanks, sensei," she responded sarcastically, but with genuine fondness, since she believed the same way... most times.

Gordon stood with teeth clenched and fists tightened into balls. It had been too long since he had killed anyone, let alone changed into his other form. Gordon didn't like being unable to act on his desires, but it was too risky. He wasn't safe anymore. The police had been by several times with "further questions" for him about Sheila. They were unhappy his responses always were the same. 'He met her at a bar; they went to her place and had sex. He left early and called her the next day to see if she wanted to go out some time but hadn't heard back from her. Yes, he was surprised to hear she was killed, and no, he didn't remember seeing anyone suspicious lurking about. Of course, he would let them know if he remembered anything else.'

Why he allowed himself to get this close to getting caught he would never know. It was stupid and careless. Since it was obvious Sheila was mauled and mutilated by the "monster," he hoped they would cease harassing him. Sitting at his kitchen table, he nibbled absent-mindedly on his toast. It was seven a.m. and he needed to be off to work.

His daily routine was driving him mad. Wanting to return to his life of killing and sex, but with law enforcement keeping an eye on him, he was forced to pretend to be the model citizen, the model doctor. Soon he would return to his real life. He had to be patient.

The last of the toast he left on the plate, grabbed his jacket, and headed to the front door. The door opened, sticking, and Gordon faced a woman he didn't think he would see again. Standing on his door step was the reporter he almost killed and whom had taken photographs of him in his alternate form. She was standing there. Finger inches from pressing the bell. He wondered if he appeared as shocked as she did. He recovered swiftly, but not as swiftly as she did.

"Gordon Sands? Never mind, you don't need to answer, I've seen your picture, so I know it's you," she fired off rapidly. "I have some questions for you."

Studying her, he flashed his charming smile.

"I'm sorry, but I'm on my way to work. I genuinely don't have time, even for an attractive woman as you."

Smiling quaintly, she was not amused at his attempt at flattery.

"Okay, so I guess I will try to get right to the point. When did you first change into the Werecroc? Was it the first time you ever killed anyone?"

The questions hit Gordon like an actual fist. He staggered back. How on earth did this woman guess he and the croc were one and the same? There was no way for anyone to tell! Straightening himself, "I'm not sure what you are talking about miss…?"

"Tyrine. And you know exactly what I'm talking about, I can tell by your reactions. You almost killed me, you son of a bitch! I'm gonna take you down so you can't kill anyone else. I wanted to make sure my suspicions were correct, and by the look in your eyes, and the expression on your face, I see I was right. So, I suggest you call work and let them know you…"

Gordon backhanded her as hard as he could. Her neck rocked to the side and she went flying down the steps. Landing a few feet past the last step, she skidded to a halt a little beyond. Rolling to a crouch, she stared back up at him.

He lost all sight of what was going on around him, his vision tunneled and all he could see was the reporter. All he knew was there was no way he was going to let this woman intimidate him. There was no way he was going to let her expose him. His blood boiled under his skin.

He sensed, rather than felt, his body change form. Absent was the burning pain he normally felt when he changed. Absent was anything but hate and anger. If he had been more aware and not so focused on this woman, he would have heard the screams of terror from the other people standing on the street. He would have realized this woman accomplished what she intended. He was exposed, and now people knew his secret.

None of it mattered. All that mattered was tearing this woman apart. The creature, who was Gordon, moved down the stairs toward the reporter who was only now getting to her feet, hand rubbing her cheek where he had hit her, she started to back away. Gordon was only a few feet from her when the sidewalk below him exploded outward and thick gnarled roots climbed out from the dirt below to begin wrapping around Gordon's legs. Gordon stared at the roots, unbelieving, and glared up at the woman in front of him.

No longer staring at him, she stared off to his right. Peering that way, he saw a strange appearing man. Short and stocky, and yet, standing tall. The man's wild gray hair jutted out at all possible angles from his head. He had a graying beard and was wearing wire rimmed glasses on a sharp beaked nose. The man had his hands out before him and appeared to be chanting something, slowly raising his hands. As he did so, the roots at Gordon's feet moved further up his body, binding him fast.

Jackson Elliot, or as he was once named Seymore Carlson, Johnson Smith, Colin McCready, Julius Privernas, Quintis Volso, and ultimately, his real name, Varden which meant "from the green hill" in Celtic, had lived two millennia. In that time, he had lived as many people, many lives. All separated by centuries of living life as an oak, deep in the forests of England, later Australia.

The ancient magic of being able to shape shift into animals was well versed in Druidic lore. It had many uses. You could shift to a bird, able to fly vast distances and overcome many obstacles. You could become as tiny as a mouse to sneak into buildings and past soldiers. The magic less used was the ability to shape shift into a tree. The uses were limited. The thing Jackson figured out was you could hold the shape almost indefinitely and it was self-sustaining. Light and rain fed you and there was little risk involved.

The true risk was losing yourself in the essence of being a tree. The longer you stayed in form, the more chance you had of becoming the tree, fully. So occasionally, Jackson had to emerge from his tree form and live life again to regain who and what he was. It was risky business, because if you waited too long, you would get to the point where you didn't realize you had passed the point of no return. It was like getting drunk. You keep drinking, and at some point, you lose the ability to realize you've had too much. In the end though, Jackson was always able to realize before it was too late.

He would re-enter the living world and would live a lifetime. Many times, he went to school, got married, owned a business or worked diligently for someone else, all the while knowing at some point, he would be needed again. He held onto the belief, till the fateful day when he read of the first crocodile attack in the city.

It piqued his interest, but it wasn't until he read of some monster attacking people in England, and a giant bear sighted in Illinois, he started to realize these were not coincidences. Weres had returned to the world. The only way for this many Weres to be back was if a Druid was involved. He thought it was impossible, because he was sure he was the only Druid left alive. If there were others, the signs he left, the newspaper ads with the secret symbols, and lastly, the book, would have led them to him. No one ever showed themselves. No. He was alone in this world. He alone had the power to stop these creatures, and he would start with this one here in the place he now called home.

Continuing to raise his arms, the gnarled brown snakelike roots continued their ascent of the Werecroc's body. They were spinning a tighter circle around its abdomen. The thing reached down and took hold of the roots, tearing them apart and tossing them aside like they were play things made of the flimsiest material. The beast strained against the remaining ones holding his legs, as they were thick and heartier. Jackson watched as they gave way. Hurriedly, he cast another spell. Gesturing with his hands, he first threw them out wide and then brought them together in a sweeping motion – the wind began to howl down the boulevard.

The Were was almost free of the roots when the wind slammed into him, and with it, debris and stones from the shattered concrete. Without the ability to use his legs for support against the wind, he was knocked over. Countless little wounds appeared all over the beast's body as he was scoured by the wind and the debris it carried.

The wind subsided and the Were lay still, buckled at the knees. Red blood blossomed from countless cuts and scratches. The red and white of muscle and fascia lay exposed beneath the green-brown scaly hide like some twisted decoration for Christmas. Jackson moved closer, approaching slowly. Stopping several paces away, his mind was so numb he couldn't move. As he examined the body, the skin mended itself, wounds closing before his eyes. The near invincibility of Weres he had heard of, but he thought it tales of legends. Now the tales proved to be nightmares.

Before its wounds were entirely healed, it righted itself. The glare it gave Jackson sent a bolt of fear through him. The Were promptly went back to work trying to free itself from the roots holding it fast by its lower legs. Jackson backed up a few paces and began chanting. It was a clear, blue sky, not a cloud to be found. He needed clouds– at least one. Without, the spell he was attempting would require a great deal of personal strength to cast. Raising his hands high in the air, his voice carried up and down the length of the street. Several hundred people were in the street now, pointing and shouting. Many had cell phones, either at their ear, or held up over the masses to get a picture or film the event.

Jackson continued his chanting, his voice a loud shouting to drown out the crowd. For those who were watching the sky, they would have witnessed a lone cloud, traveling against the wind toward their destination. Jackson, his eyes closed, felt the presence of the cloud as it arrived above him. Lowering his head, he ended his chant, looked back up, and opened his eyes. Black, beady eyes stared at him down the length of a toothy maw. The beast's mouth was inches from his face. Muscular claws grabbed him under his raised arms and lifted him high.

"Jackson!" Sylvia's shout came from behind the beast. He saw her standing there, her face turning purple and swelling up from the blow she had received. The monster began to squeeze his chest. Offering Sylvia a resigned smile, his rib cage collapse under the pressure of the Werecroc. Bringing his hands down in the final execution of the spell, pain enveloped him, he blacked out.

Sylvia watched in desperation as Jackson smiled sadly at her while the monster squeezed the man's chest. She stared in horror as Jackson's torso imploded under the pressure, the man's esophagus and larynx erupted from his mouth, forced out of his chest cavity by the immense pressure. Like a volcano, internal l organs erupted the only direction they could. As they crossed each other inside, ribs pierced skin, and tore through muscle to pass out the other side of his body.

With only a moment to register what happened, she was blinded by an intense white light striking the spot where Jackson and the creature stood. Shielding her eyes, she jumped as the sound of rolling thunder roared above. Windows rattle on either side of the street, like hundreds of individuals stomping their feet. Gazing back, she saw the bodies of Jackson and the Croc lying twenty feet apart from where they had been standing, as if something had exploded between them, tossing them in opposite directions. Blackened concrete now scored the spot where they had stood. As the after image of the lightning strike left her, Sylvia peeked up and saw a lone cloud racing off.

She only gave it a moment's thought before racing to Jackson's side. When she reached him, she had to hold back the need to gag. Not only was Jackson's body almost folded in upon itself, it was also badly burned and blackened, as if cooked too long. There was no need to check to see if he was dead. Nobody could survive what he had suffered. Glancing away from his broken and burned body, a silent sob shook her. She knew him a short time, but Jackson made a strong impression upon her. Her father left her at an early age, and Jackson's demeanor reminded her so much of him, she sometimes thought of him as such. And, now, he was gone. She wasn't sure what to do.

It was someone screaming who snapped her attention back to her surroundings. A teenage girl was standing, about thirty feet from her. She was the one who had screamed. It took Sylvia a moment to realize the girl wasn't staring at her, but past her. A warm, wet breath brushed the back of her neck, accompanied by a low growl. Sylvia closed her eyes and waited for death.

Standing over the reporter's shredded body, Gordon realized he had lost control of the situation quite a long time ago. Standing upon the boulevard. Outside *his* apartment. In his altered form. Murdering two people in broad daylight, in front of multiple witnesses, who were now disappearing from his view. Curiosity gone now he had finished with his victims– the people fled. Glaring over at the charred corpse of the man who had attacked him, he didn't know how the man did what he did. His own flesh was slowly repairing the burns he had received when the lightning struck the two of them.

Gordon knew there had been no clouds in the sky, nor were there any now. So, how to explain the lightning? The roots had wrapped around his body lie broken and burnt around the hole in the concrete. Something had happened here Gordon couldn't seem to get his head around. The man had been chanting, hadn't he? And gesturing, as if casting some sort of spell; like a magician? Yet, this was no parlor trick. This was real. What the man did was impossible. He seemed to have some control over the earth, air and weather, if Gordon understood what he had been hit with.

Sirens screamed in the distance, their droning 'wee woo, wee woo' drew steadily closer. It was time to make himself scarce. Gordon turned and ran down the nearest side street away from the approaching sirens. He needed to change back to his human form. The problem was, he didn't have any clothes as his current garments were shredded. He would have to make his way to one of his safe houses.

Safe for now, anyhow. It wouldn't take the cops long to figure out who had been the attacker, regardless of how crazy it was. They would realize the person who lived in the apartment there was the same one they had interviewed about Sheila's death. They would put two and two together and figure out he was the murderer. They would pull his information and find out where he worked and the other properties he owned. It would still take time, though. He needed to get there in a few hours, but he needed to stay out of sight, too.

As Gordon passed an alley, he noticed an old fire escape ladder had been left lowered. It was enough. Peeling off to the left, he raced down the alley at a swift run, his clawed feet, literally tearing up the ground as he ran. A few feet from the ladder, he leapt, his leg muscles bunching, stretching as he hurled through the air, over ten feet up. His claws grasped the ladder, it shook loose, and dropped sharply, almost jolting him free when it slammed to a halt at the end of its length. Deftly, Gordon spun around it and clambered up the rungs to the first platform. Within seconds, he reached the roof.

Taking a moment to get his bearings, he saw his closest safe house to the south. It appeared like he could get most of the way traveling the roofs. Tracing the route in his mind, he took note of which roof to which roof he would need to cross. As soon as he could make out the last roof he would get to, he bolted for the edge of his current roof and lifted clear of it in a three-stride jump. He landed hard on the roof of the next building. Slamming down, the roof cratered around his impact, his tail lashed out to the right and slammed into a vent pipe, sending it flying away, sheared off at the base. Giving it only a moment's thought, he took long strides to the south west and cleared the space between the two buildings, a grand distance of twenty feet or so. His ankles slammed into the edge of the building, breaking off bricks and masonry which were sent flying down below. Gordon skidded and rolled across the roof, before coming to rest against the ledge of the far end, his momentum so great it took him the length of the roof. Shouts rang out from below where the rocks either hit someone or nearly hit them.

Gordon wasted no time. On his feet again, the pain receding from his ankles where he impacted, Gordon ran back the way he had slid till he was but half way across the roof. Spinning, roof shingles flying, he once again ran to the edge and planted his clawed foot and launched himself to the next roof.

He was making decent time. Never had he tested himself so openly before. This form had immense strength, but he didn't realize how much until he put it in use. Pausing momentarily to get his bearings, he made sure he was still charting the path which would put him on top of the building housing his safe house.

Movement out of the corner of his eyes made him whip around. Some sort of hawk had landed a short distance from him and was staring at him. It was a pretty hawk, red-capped, it had rust colored wings, a tawny breast with black flecks, and a black vertical slash on its cheek. He imagined the bird had never seen anything like him in his domain before which accounted for its curiosity. Giving it scant thought, he launched himself to the next roof.

Two roofs away from his safe house, he again caught sight of the bird flying parallel to him. Not being an expert on birds by any stretch of the imagination, he was still sure this was unusual behavior. Given what he had gone through with the roots and the lightning, the bird was more than a little suspicious to him.

It was time to change tactics. Gordon neared the roof's edge, he didn't leap, but instead stepped off the edge. His bulk descended to land with an echoed boom and crack as the concrete sidewalk shattered on impact. Straightening himself, he peered up to the sky. The silhouette of the hawk against the blue sky passed over the alley. His lips curled a sneer and he turned to continue his way. A man at the entrance to the alley watching him brought him up short. A tall, wiry appearing man, with dark hair and a faintly dark complexion. Perhaps Middle Eastern? The man watched him, but did not approach. Gordon was about to rush and kill him, so he could be on his way, but something about the man gave him pause. It was his eyes, Gordon decided. They held no fear. Gordon was over tree meters of scaly death. The man should be scared shitless. But, he wasn't. The lack of fear worried Gordon. A lot.

Gordon was about to turn and run when the hawk which had been following him landed in front of the man in the alley. The image of the hawk blurred and wavered like a mirage in the desert. When the wavering image stopped, a beautiful woman stood where the hawk had been. She was like him, he decided, except different. Her alteration was something altogether different from what he went through. There was no reconstruction of the body, not an alteration of the physical form, yet altered it was.

Tall as well, though she wasn't as tall as the man. Fair skinned where he was light. Long flowing dark tresses framed her oval face. She was shapely, and naked. Admiring her form, he stood still. The man behind her approached and rested a robe around her shoulders. She pulled it closed.

"Who are you people?" Gordon growled.

The woman smiled, her full lips curling up at the sides.

"We are your friends, Gordon." Her English was weird sounding and it was clear she was uneasy using it.

"We are your friends, and right now it would seem you could use some friends, yes?"

Gordon grunted. This day started out normal and it had gone to shit fast. His whole life was about to be turned upside down, and he didn't know what to do about it. It seemed these two knew what to do. And, she was right; he could use some friends right now.

"Okay. So, what now?" he asked her.

"Now we go to the States. Yes?"

Sure. The states. Why the hell not? Gordon thought.

Samuel sat in a lounge chair aboard his private jet. His long legs stretched out in front of him as he relaxed in opulent comfort. Kestrel was sitting in a seat on the other side of the plane, once again reading some book on history, or perhaps it was on geo-political policies to have shaped the world they currently lived in. Samuel wasn't sure. She bounced back and forth between more subjects than a first-year college student, unsure of their major.

He had to appreciate her mental prowess. Not only was she ruthless when it came to her goals, but she was relentless when it came to learning as much as she could, so she could accomplish her goals. A worthy mistress to serve. While her goals were mostly in line with his, he was not as fanatical as she was. Sure, he believed the Earth was in danger from civilization, and something needed to be done about it. But war? This one? The last one? Would it really accomplish what she wanted? She had not been around all these centuries as he had. Not witnessed the progression civilization had taken. For him, he had been alive to witness all of it. Well most of it. There were times he had to 'sleep' to continue. Missing entire leaps, civilization took. Still, he had witnessed much, and in his way of thinking, all of this was inevitable.

There were two others aboard the plane. The first was a striking looking fellow; a touch above average height with an athletic build. Strong, wide shoulders, and brown hair combed back, but full enough to give it some rise as it swept back, adding a centimeter or two of height. Though the man was in his early fifties, there was nary a single grey hair. Sun-kissed skin made his face a beautiful bronze, which stood out starkly next to his white button-down cotton shirt. Its top three buttons stylishly unbuttoned to show a hairless chest sporting the same bronzed skin.

If Samuel didn't know the man better, he would have thought it a fake tan given how even the tone was, but it wasn't the man's style. He had a strong chin, covered mostly by a finely trimmed goatee. The whitest, straightest teeth known to man, which he seldom hid behind full, soft pink lips. Eyes were bright blue, well at least his contacts were. He made women swoon, even before they realized his net worth. Most men would be jealous of him, but his easy, self-depreciating nature made jealousy seem petty... well, pettier than normal.

Lounging as the man was, Samuel couldn't help but admire the man's taste. The slacks he wore were Gorsuch, the shoes, Mezlan. Expensive taste, for sure, which was precisely the image Samuel wanted the man to have, and he was talented at it. Mr. Ian Kaft. The fourth richest man in the world, according to Wall Street Business magazine. Though in reality, he was the richest man in the world. Yet, he effectively didn't own any of it.

Samuel figured out a long time ago, if you were rich, well then, you were famous. And, famous wouldn't do for Samuel. You couldn't be famous and do what he needed to do, but he also couldn't abide being poor, either. He worked from the sidelines, never the spotlight. Spotlights get you killed. So, he needed someone to be the face of his wealth. Ian was one of many in a long list of people who had been the face of his money.

Samuel would keep them around for as long as was prudent. Sometimes for a few years; sometimes until their death. He had all manner of people play the role. They fit perfectly into it, or they didn't. It should be an easy role to take, one would think. But, there had been those who had tried to expose Samuel for a bigger piece of the pot. Those he had to bury. Others had not known how a wealthy person should act, and so wasn't at all convincing to the public as a wealthy playboy or heiress. Those he made sure they had enough money to live a happy and stress-free life, and they parted ways. Sure, he would keep an eye on them, and if they started saying the wrong things to the wrong people, well, he would have to pay them a visit. Fortunately, he hadn't had to bother...yet. Unlike his Lycan brothers, he didn't have this desire to kill, trying to avoid it as much as possible. Most times it was unnecessary, and it often was problematic.

Most of his money "decoys" throughout the years had handled the job well enough. But, Ian... Ian was in a class by himself. He knew how to spend enough money to stay on people's radar, so they wouldn't start wondering about what he was up to, but not too much as to make a spectacle of himself. He dressed the part, and he managed to spend money on the things wealthy people spent it on. He didn't go on wild spending sprees once he got a few million or so. Joined all the right clubs, schmoozed all the right people, and said all the right things. He was the epitome of how someone who had acquired their wealth through hard work would act. Neither pretentious, nor ostentatious. He bought things of value and of quality, not things for show. Ian understood the value of money, and while he hadn't acquired it himself, he understood he must show the world the appearance of someone who had.

All the while, Samuel sat quietly in the background. Typically, they both did their separate things, but using the private jet required Ian to be present. As part of their agreement, he needed to be available when Samuel needed him, as of yet, Ian hadn't failed him.

As per their agreement, or perhaps because the light did bother him, he wore opaque sunglasses, so he didn't watch anything going on around him while in Samuel's presence. It was probably an unnecessary precaution on Samuel's part, but he hadn't lived this long by not being cautious. Ian had never shown the slightest interest in Samuel's affairs. He was all too happy to play the role Samuel offered him, and he wouldn't do anything to jeopardize it.

Wireless earbuds rested in Ian's ears and his right foot swayed to a beat only he could hear. This was another stipulation for Ian being allowed to be up here, and not in the cargo hold during flights. Hear nothing and see nothing.

When Samuel found Ian, he was full time manager of a retail chain, and a part time day trader. He had done well enough for himself, and with some help, a sudden windfall would not seem out of the ordinary.

The conditions were right for him to fall into the role of someone who had suddenly made a lot of money but had been working his way up slowly the old fashion way, as well.

It was an important quality for Samuel in his candidates, and the understanding they were here for show — to be the face of his money, and not to draw attention to Samuel.

It was impossible for Samuel to avoid all notice, but he was considered a minor player. Some thought him to be a hanger on to someone who had a lot of money, and possibly there to use Ian to further his own prosperity. Their interaction indicated as much. They were not seen in social circles together; parties and the like. No, they were ordinarily only seen together when traveling or involved in a significant business deal. Samuel was there, in the background.

To all who inquired of Samuel to Ian were met with a nonchalant dismissal of the man. Plainly, Samuel was not someone of import to Ian. Just someone he allowed to accompany him on occasion.

Yes, Ian played the part well. So well, in fact, Samuel seriously considered making him a Were. Even before the return of Kestrel, it would have been the first time he had created a Were since his Sundering all those millennia ago.

Samuel thought back to that time. It had been a hard choice to do that, he remembered. To sunder yourself from your Weres was neither easy nor painless. There were few who understood how it worked. He wondered even if Kestrel and Sylvanis, the ones who created the Lycans to start with, understood it. Regardless, it had been necessary. With the defeat of Kestrel and the death of Sylvanis, the war was effectively over. The only Lycans on Kestrel's side still around were the followers of Renwick and himself. Then only his were left after they forced Renwick to sunder his Lycans.

Calin and the rest of the Trues hunted him and his Weres and he was forced into hiding. His followers were hunted and killed, and he knew it was only a matter of time before one of them revealed where he was hiding. How could they not? They could find him easily enough with the link. Luckily, the ones they had found so far had all either fought to the death or refused to give him up. Samuel had little hope his luck would hold out indefinitely. So, given these circumstances, his only hope would be to sunder himself and eliminate the threat all together.

The Sundering didn't require any great ceremony. It was a matter of questing within yourself. Of destroying the parts you found creating the link between you and your Weres. If you had one or two followers, it wasn't as bad, but Samuel, at the time, had hundreds of followers. The questing was exhaustive, and the destruction was painful, and the pain was not something the body found easy to repair.

After he had sundered, the hunting stopped. His assumption they would figure him dead held true. After all, who would freely go through the Sundering?

With Sylvanis' Trues believing him dead, he returned to Crete for a short time. He didn't forget his vow to protect Kestrel. He had learned before he had fled, her body was protected from desecration, and as such, they had sealed and buried the room in which she lay. Because of that, he knew she was not in any immediate danger, certainly not more immediate than the danger he was in. So, he left.

Samuel had always been a forward thinker. He understood because of his ability he would live a preternaturally long life, assuming he could avoid being found by Sylvanis' allies. If he could avoid detection, there was no telling how long he could live. So, to ensure he would live comfortably for as long as he lived, he used his power and influence to acquire the monetary means to do so. He ingratiated himself with those in power and status and used them to further his own goals. Being an expert judge of character and being able to 'read the room' as it were, he could end up on the right side of the conflict and turmoil that was so prevalent in that time of history.

At first, when it became apparent he was no longer a wanted man, he thought to create more Lycans and use them to reacquire his power. He was quickly disavowed of the idea when the Romans began to deal with the Lycans that were left upon the Isle. Their subjugation of the Celts and their systematic destruction through conversion of the remaining Druids was initially met with conflict with the Lycans. Calin and the others were powerful. More powerful than a simple human soldier. The romans weren't simple human warriors, though. They were hardened soldiers. They were trained and efficient in killing, and they were endless. There were skirmishes at first, and when the Romans discovered there were Lycans, there was an all-out quest to purge the world of them. They hunted them down with cruel efficiency and killed them with overwhelming force. The Romans were a tide neither the Druids, nor their Lycans could stem.

As far as Samuel could ascertain, the Romans destroyed every single one of them. Or at least enough they were no longer considered an issue. What happened to Calin and the rest of the Trues, Samuel had never been able to find out. He assumed they were killed, or at the very least, had fled as Samuel had done.

The Roman influence was far and wide, and Samuel would not risk bringing their swift response to any rise of his kind. So, Samuel never dared risk making another Were.

After the fall of the Western Roman Empire, Samuel moved back to the Isle. There was much upheaval during this time, and Samuel maneuvered himself into positions of power in the overflowing political landscape, somehow always floating above the turbulent sea. He danced from side to side, never placing two feet in any particular side, and so, removed himself from political affiliations that would have ended up with him dead.

It was during this time he once more considered recruiting Lycans again, but the rise of Christianity put a stop to that notion. People were killed for far less reasons, and the hint of some sort of sorcery would most likely get him killed, let alone the idea he could shift into a hybrid form of a human-snake.

This had been a difficult time to live in, and so Samuel did what he could to eliminate himself from the scene.

There were areas of the Isles which were seldom visited, or ever traveled. They were either too wild and dangerous, or too out of the way of civilization. Samuel collected all his accumulated wealth, which was quite substantial and left. He found an area undisturbed, and for all intents and purposes, he hibernated. He had learned some of the Druidic spells that would slow his aging and put him into a deep sleep. So, he found himself a deep cave, took with him all his belongings and buried himself inside. Using Druidic spells, he had acquired, he strengthened the walls, sealed the entrance, and put himself to sleep.

He slept for over a hundred years.

When he awoke, the world had changed much. The Roman Empire had all but receded in influence upon what was now commonly referred to as the British Isles. There was much turbulence between the country of England and its neighbors. This ongoing conflict allowed Samuel to once again rise to prominence.

It took him years, though. After exiting his cave with as much of his valuable belongings as he could carry, he traveled towards what was once the closet city to his refuge. It wasn't long before he encountered civilization. It was much closer than it had been. Farms had sprouted up and the forest surrounding where he had slept had been cut back. Dirt roads crisscrossed the landscape and tiny villages had grown around these new bastions of people.

It was during his travel to the nearest city he took the time to find out what had happened during his sleep. His natural charm worked on most who passed by and he was able to gleam a great deal of at least the past few decades. He was adept at getting people to divulge information without it seeming like he was ignorant of what they spoke. He found the language they spoke, while not Italian, it wasn't Celt either. It was a mixture of both. Fortunately, he spoke both and so was able to discern what they said, and they were able to understand him.

He was able to understand the political climate as well and who the principle players were. It was all he needed to get started.

After arriving at the first major town, Samuel traded in a lot of his valuables and procured contemporary attire, both simple and expensive and paid for transport to the capitol. It was true, much had changed since he went away, but people are always the same on the inside. They are all motivated by much the same things, and while those motivations manifest themselves differently in different people, the basics needs and wants are what lie behind it all. Most people say money and power motivate people, but that simply wasn't the case. Money and power are what people use to get what they ultimately want. It is a means to an end.

People's needs are more basic than that. They need love, or at least to feel like they are loved, and are important. They want recognition of who they are, and they want to be accepted by those around them. They want to feel safe, and they want to keep those they care about safe. Sure, there were abnormalities to this basic principle; religious zealots, for instance. There were also those who possessed a singular ego and those who could care less about the viewpoints and opinions of others. Their motivations varied greatly, but one thing could always be certain of them — they are very, very dangerous people. Samuel counted himself among the latter. He had one goal: his continued survival. If he cared anything for those around them, and their opinion, it was only so much as to keep him out of harm's way.

Truly, if he was to be said to care for anyone else, it would be for Kestrel. That, however, was more a matter of duty and a sense of obligation. It was, after all, Kestrel who granted him these gifts allowing him his long life. Though, surely it hadn't been her intent. No. She had created him as a weapon to be used to accomplish her goals. No matter. He had performed this duty for her and although he had abandoned her when she was on the verge of losing, her spell had ensured he would once again, someday, be her weapon, again. So, he did his best to survive. He had no desire to die anyways.

People were still the same. It was a matter of finding out what they needed the most and exploiting it. When you did that, well, they were yours.

Much had changed in the world. The world, the People he had known were gone. Killed, or swallowed up by the power and reach of the Roman Empire and then abandoned to fend for themselves. They had been thrown into a vast mortar and the pestle of the Empire and had changed them forever, so they were no longer Celts, but something altogether different. Now, someone else had picked up the pestle and had begun to once again grind them into a new mixture.

He was an outsider and would not be trusted. Not at first. But, he was smart and attractive in an exotic seeming way, and something else had happened he had expected. He was young. He didn't quite understand it, but he believed the same part of his ability allowing him to heal had also turned back the sands of time in his body. His theory was since aging, in a way, was damage to one's body, when he 'hibernated' it slowed his body's use so much, his ability could heal more damage than his body accumulated. Thus, making him younger. It was a theory, but it made plenty of sense.

Given all he had going for him, he didn't believe it would take him long to rise to prominence within the new hierarchy.

It took longer than he thought it would, but in the end, he rose to a position of importance and power. With power and influence he acquired great wealth. Wealth he knew he would need, for eventually he would need to disappear, again. However, there were two things he needed to accomplish before he could do this. One, he needed to do his best to secure the safety of The Calendar. He had visited the site and the room was still safely hidden under the table. No one knew enough to disturb the site and to dig under the table, so for the time it was safe. Well, safe enough. To accomplish his first goal, he did his best to foment the belief the Calendar was cursed, or at least a site of great magical power. There was enough folklore surrounding the site already it wasn't difficult for this rumor to spread like fire over a bundle of tinder.

To his dismay, at first, he found a sect of Druids. Though these Druids were no longer powerful spell casters. They were simple folk who believed the Calendar was a place of reverence and they used the grounds to pray to Gods who represented nature and the Earth. He befriended a member of their society and subtly made suggestions that would lead them to make part of their spiritual gatherings, elaborate displays. They would wear voluminous white robes, and pray at night, lighting the countryside with fire and torches. He implied the Gods of Earth and Nature demanded sacrifices, and at first, they started with animal sacrifices, he would later hear rumors of human sacrifices being preformed there. The rumor didn't surprise him, since he was the one who started it. But the rumors persisted, and he couldn't help wondering if in the end, there was some truth to them. Either way, the general populace steered clear of the Calendar, which is what he had hoped for.

The other thing he needed to accomplish was to find a place for him to 'hibernate.' He had long ago retrieved all the rest of his valuable from his last site. He considered using the site again, but he had no desire to spend another hundred years or so buried beneath the ground. The problem was, it was the safest way to go. It was true there was very little personal risk if he was found. He wasn't comatose when he hibernated, just a very deep slumber, made deeper by Druidic magic. He could still be awakened. Little risk, but not, no risk, and that was not something the cautious Samuel could live with.

So, he decided to make a compromise with himself. He proceeded to make an underground complex in which he could live, sleep and survive. Even this close to the capitol there were untamed wildernesses, and Samuel went deep into those to find a place to use. He hired poor, unskilled peasants with no families to dig deep into the ground. When they finished their work, he killed them all. When this was accomplished he found masons from outlying towns and brought them to the capitol and gave them room and board. He used them to build his underground home. He paid them well for their work and their silence. He insisted they stay inside their paid for residence until he would gather them to do their work. After the first worker decided to sneak out and go to the local tavern, and never returned, the rest didn't leave.

He paid them handsomely when they finished their work, with the understanding they should not speak of it to anyone. He paid them well and insisted they move on from the city. They gladly took the money and promised they would speak to no one of what they had done, and they left. Samuel hunted them all down and killed them before they could anyways. Samuel was nothing, if not cautious. His underground home was built, and as far as he could determine, no one knew anything about it. Even then, he didn't approach the home for several years. Instead he used another Druid spell he had learned to enlist a sparrow to spy on it for him. Every few days, the sparrow would return to his home in the capitol and let him know if anyone had been investigating his "other" home. No one ever did.

After a few years, he started moving his wealth to his underground home. One thing you learned when you had lived long as he had, there were some things that were always worth something. Precious gems and metals were universally desired. He had, by this time, become vastly rich. He was a hoarder and spent little of his accumulated wealth, only on things that would bring him more wealth, or more opportunity to acquire more wealth.

When he was sure he acquired and secreted the vast amount of wealth, he parted from the Capitol, supposedly to visit family and he was never seen from again.

He woke up periodically as the centuries went by. Not wanting to stay away too long from the Calendar and Kestrel's body. But, each time he found her resting place undisturbed. Each time he would take some time to read the politics of the region, and ingratiate himself into the power structure, he would use the power to procure more wealth, after depleting a large portion of what he had hidden away each time to acclimate himself to society. Depending on the circumstances, he would work to foment fear in the citizenry for the Calendar. Superstition was never in short supply in the uneducated.

When he again amassed enough wealth, secured Kestrel's sanctuary and lived for time in the age, he would vanish all over again.

For many centuries, his first underground home was safe and secure, though in time, like all things, it started to deteriorate and come apart, and he was forced again to create a new underground home. Which meant a new group of widows and orphans or skilled tradesmen, but it couldn't be helped. And to be honest, Samuel truly didn't care. He did what needed to be done. Always. If innocents died in the process to see him safe and secure, he wouldn't concern himself too much about the lives lost, as long as it wasn't his.

Over the centuries, he became practiced at waking, investigating the new time, adapting to it, taking advantage of it, and leaving without a trace. He would sleep for long periods of time, usually a hundred years or so, sometime longer, but never more than two centuries. He found if he rested too long, when he awoke he was by far much younger than the age he had first gone to sleep, and that became problematic to putting himself into a position of power. After the first time of trying this and it taking far too long, and costing a great deal of his cache, he decided he wouldn't sleep as long again. He found one hundred years was usually sufficient to erase the decades he had spent awake previously, but not too much, he would seem, on the surface anyway, to be a youth.

Many things changed when things began to modernize. He could no longer rest like he used to and was forced to spend less time awake as to not grow too old his body couldn't heal itself back enough.

His underground homes became increasingly unsafe to stay in. Man was tearing and digging up the land at a record pace. Kestrel would have been furious if she had witnessed the destruction. Samuel, being less of a fanatic to the cause, was more concerned with being discovered as he slept.

He had to move his homes further and further away from civilized lands. It was also becoming harder to dispose of those who built his homes. There were constables and other forms of law keepers who would investigate disappearances, especially mass ones.

Keeping the Calendar, what was now referred to by most as Stonehenge, safe, had also become very difficult. Man was less afraid of 'ghost stories' and stories of 'witches' and 'sorcerers,' than they had been before. Their curiosity often got the better of them, and at first, Samuel killed any who tried to investigate too closely at the grounds of Stonehenge. This worked for a time keeping others away. Men might not be afraid of ghost stories, but they *were* afraid of the number of corpses of the overly curious found on the grounds.

Eventually, the attention of the government was drawn to it, which had become increasingly more organized and more in control of what happened in the country. It soon became apparent to Samuel he could no longer continue as he had been going. It was drawing too much attention. Instead, he decided to use his ability to infiltrate organizations, as he had done repeatedly with governments age after age and infiltrate the groups who would come to study Stonehenge. That way, he could subtlety move them away from any closer examination of the area around the Alter. And if that failed– eliminate them.

Not for the first time, he began to wonder why he continued to do it. All knowledge of what had happened during that time had either been destroyed or relegated to mythology. The existence of Kestrel and her life all forgotten. Not only that, but if she had been meant to come back, wouldn't she had done it already? The early industrialization had occurred and had been devastating to the planet. Forests cleared without any care to growing new ones, rivers damned without any understanding of the consequences to the ecosystem. Rivers had chemicals poured into them, poisoning the fish and other animals living there.

If there had truly been a time for Kestrel's spell to go into effect, well it was then. Still nothing. Honestly, Samuel had begun to give up hope, if hope was even the correct word. Kestrel was a demanding mistress. Unrelenting in her pursuits, and merciless in her actions. It was possible she would kill him for abandoning her at the end.

On the other hand, he would no longer have to pretend to be other than he was. He would no longer have to create an alternate persona and make his way through positions of power and influence, just so he could do it all over again. While part of him enjoyed playing the con on all those around him, convincing them of who he wanted them to believe he was. It was becoming tiring and tedious. He had been doing it for centuries, and frankly he was tired of it.

It was one of those times of doubt that he sired a child. In all the time he had lived, he had avoided long term commitments with women, not wanting to become attached to anyone for any length of time. He had always been careful not to impregnate anyone, or if he did, he would ensure the child was not born. That had happened only a dozen or so times in the millennia he had lived.

When one of the women he had been with became pregnant, it had been during a time when he truly believed Kestrel would never return, and he was wasting his life constantly trying to keep her safe. So, why shouldn't he have a child? Someone to teach, someone to carry on businesses while he was 'away' sleeping?

So, he allowed the child to be born. A boy. Samuel named him Cirrus. The mother increasingly became demanding of him and his time and so he took the child and told the woman to never come back. She did, of course. She would not give up her son. So, she suffered from an 'accident' and the boy was his, and his alone.

It was awkward at first. He knew nothing of raising a child and was forced to hire a nanny. It didn't stop him from spending as much time with the boy as possible. He didn't fail at anything, and he wouldn't fail at this, no matter how uncomfortable it made him. He was not a compassionate person. He was not expressive with his feelings. A child expresses these things naturally. Samuel taught him through his own actions to be cold and aloof. Cirrus learned swiftly, and soon became like his father, passionless and emotionless.

In time, the nanny was dismissed, and Samuel was able to take care of Cirrus on his own. In part, because Cirrus required very little in the way of parenting. He had become very self-sufficient and showed a maturity well beyond his years. Several months after Cirrus' sixteenth birthday, Samuel got a call from one of his informants about an American woman who had begun poking around Stonehenge.

This came as a bit of a surprise to Samuel. It had been decades since any in-depth investigation into Stonehenge had occurred. It was believed, that what was to be discovered about Stonehenge had already been discovered. It was part of the reason Samuel had felt comfortable and guiltless about not taking a more active role in keeping Stonehenge free of interference.

With knowledge that his abandoned role of protector of Kestrel's resting place was being tested, Samuel had no other choice but to resume it. If Kestrel was found in her resting place, her body would be disturbed, and possibly destroyed. Then all his earlier work would have been for naught. He would not have that. As much as he wished to be finally free of this obligation, it was a failure he could not accept.

He contacted his informant to locate where the woman was conducting her research, and after finding out it was at the Institute of Historical Research, he created a new background for himself as a Professor and used his influence and considerable money to gain a position at the Institute. He would need to keep watch over this woman, and steer her away from finding anything of importance about Stonehenge.

The problem, of course, was he couldn't do this with a kid in tow. He would need to deal with Cirrus, keep him out of the way, and cut ties with him. The boy was sixteen now. When Samuel was sixteen, he had already done so much in his life, but times had changed, and the expectations on the youth in this age were minimal.

Cirrus, of course, was different. Samuel had made sure of it. He had done his best to train him to be self-sufficient. Not only self-sufficient, but also a highly trained and skilled individual. He had Cirrus trained in fighting, both martial and with weapons. He had educated the boy and trained his mind to think way more analytically than a child his age would normally be capable. Samuel had trained him in tactics, and warfare as well. Trained him in survival, wilderness and city. Cirrus could make snares to catch prey and make bombs to kill a different type of prey.

And, as with all children of Trues, he carried lycanthropy. Though it only manifested itself in rapid healing. He would never be a real lycanthrope, only a dormant carrier. That wasn't true. He could one day be a real lycanthrope. If Samuel were to die and Kestrel returned, then Cirrus would have it awakened in him.

When Samuel realized this, he realized he needed to tell Cirrus what he was, well, what he could someday be. Cirrus already understood he was different. He had noticed his rapid healing and knew it to be unusual. He hadn't been prepared to hear the truth of it, though. Samuel remembered the day vividly.

Samuel had returned home later in the evening than usual to find his son, Cirrus, reading. Cirrus was bent over a book, sitting on the green plush sofa prominently placed within their home's great room. The sofa faced a massive cobblestoned fireplace, the stonework framed the open hearth and traveled up the wall above it all the way to the ceiling. A second plush sofa faced the fireplace at an angle, across from a black recliner, also angled to face the fireplace. The fireplace was cold now, it being mid-summer and there being no reason to have the extra heat. To a visitor, this room would seem peculiar to most other homes for its absence of a television. It wasn't as if Samuel didn't like to watch TV. He did. He felt it important to keep up with the news, no matter how dodgy it sometimes was. He also made sure Cirrus was kept apprised of current events as well. Both of their bedrooms sported state of the art televisions which would make any AV enthusiast giddy. He didn't feel it belonged in a social room as what he considered the great room to be. That room was meant for conversing, interaction, or if there was no one about, then quiet contemplation, and of course, reading.

Samuel entered the great room and approached Cirrus. His son was like him in many ways. He shared Samuel's olive-tinged skin and dark hair. Though, where Samuel was gangly,

Cirrus was proportionate. He didn't share Samuel's long limbs. His body was more equal in size and shape. At sixteen, Cirrus was shy of Samuel's height, making him tall, indeed. Whether finishing puberty would put him taller, they would have to wait and see. Years of martial training had also seen him fill out more than Samuel ever was. Samuel always avoided fighting if he could, and so he never tried to make himself a stronger person. With his enhanced strength from being a True, he could out-match pretty much anyone alive today. His son would not have supernatural strength, so Samuel did his best to make sure he had his own natural strength to help him.

"Hello, father," Cirrus said, without glancing up from his book.

"Good evening, Cirrus. How are you today?" They both knew it was a meaningless query.

"All is well, father." Cirrus answered distractedly, still not removing himself from the book.

"There is something we need to discuss." Samuel made sure to impart the importance of the comment in his tone, and Cirrus closed the book immediately, not marking the page. Samuel knew the boy's memory was almost equal his own, and he could easily pick up the book in a couple of months and know exactly which page he had been reading. Cirrus set the book on one of the end tables flanking the sofa and looked at him.

Cirrus had a humble face. It lacked the length of Samuel's and was fuller and rounder. Flat-nosed and full lips made him appear a little bit like an oaf. His eyes were sharp though, close examination of those would quickly clue you to the intelligence of the boy. Samuel thought back to the day Cirrus complained about his facial features and how they made him seem stupid. He had assured Cirrus it was a blessing. If people thought you were stupid without knowing you, you will always surprise them. And a person surprised is a person vulnerable. Intelligence should never be underestimated, and when it was, it became as powerful as a loaded gun.

Cirrus waited patiently. He had learned early on that to try and rush Samuel with harassing questions swiftly led to punishment. And, it was punishment Samuel doled out quickly and effectively. Even rebellious as children usually are could not last long under the unforgiving lessons Samuel imparted without remorse or restraint.

"There is something I need to tell you. Something which might be of import later in your life." Samuel began, taking his suit's jacket off and folding it carefully before putting it on the edge of the sofa.

"It is possible this will never happen, but in case it does. I would be remiss to you, and to Her, if I didn't explain some things to you." He knew he was being purposely vague, and in part, it was because he was unsure of how to explain this, or how it would be taken.

Cirrus continued to wait patiently for him to get to the point. It was a testament to the lessons he had learned that the boy had yet to interrupt, though there were clearly questions he would already have forming in his mind. Not least of which was, why it appeared his father was undressing in front of him, as Samuel had proceeded to also remove his dress shirt.

"You are aware of your ability to heal at an accelerated rate?" Raising his eyebrows in question, Samuel folded his shirt, awaiting a response.

Cirrus nodded, his eyes following Samuel's movements.

"Are you aware we share the ability?"

Samuel asked this not truly knowing the answer. To his knowledge, he had never been injured in front of Cirrus, so it shouldn't have been apparent. However, there were other aspects of the healing Cirrus might have clued in to. If he was very observant, and very intuitive.

Cirrus nodded again, and Samuel smiled in pride.

"Good." Samuel began to remove his belt and he allowed his trousers to fall to the ground where he collected them and proceeded to fold them. He felt odd, doing this in front of his son, but he assumed his son would not believe him when he told him and would therefore be forced to shift to prove it, and he didn't want to destroy a fine suit.

"The reason we have this ability is because we are unlike other people. We carry something within our bloodstream others do not.

This is why I have told you under no circumstances should you ever go to a hospital. A hospital would find out about this, and you, and me would not be safe."

Cirrus watched him raptly. Clearly interested in where this was going, yet still refraining from asking questions that must be running through his young mind.

"What we carry in our bloodstream is known as Lycanthropy." Cirrus started at this. He clearly recognized the word, and since the world had distorted the reality of Lycanthropy over the years, he could understand his son's reaction.

"It is not what it has been portrayed as in the movies and in literature, son. Lycanthropy is not a madness, nor is it a 'disease' as well. It was something created and gifted to a chosen few.

"What you have, is a dormant form. You can't shift into a Were-form. In fact, you will most likely never transform… ever. The only way it would ever happen is upon my death, and the awakening of the one who created it in the first place. Neither of which has happened in two millennia."

Samuel paused for a moment and watched as what he said dawned on Cirrus. When Cirrus raised questioning eyes to Samuel, he nodded his permission for him to speak.

"So," Cirrus began. "You mean to tell me you have been alive for 2,000 years? How is that possible? And who is this person who created it, and why and how would this person be awakened? And why are you nearly naked?"

Samuel quirked a smile at his son. All excellent questions.

"The answer to your first question is yes. I have been alive for over 2,000 years. How is it possible? Well, that is harder to explain." Samuel sat down and took a moment to collect his thoughts on how best to say it.

"When a body ages, it does so because the cells in the body break down, they are slowly destroyed. Our ability to heal rapidly, offsets this damage slightly. You less than me, for reasons I will come back to. Our body's cells break down naturally over time, but also partially because our body is active."

Samuel paused for a moment to study his son. He was clearly paying attention, but given the quick intelligence he had, it was obvious this still made little sense to him. So, Samuel tried a different track.

"Think of it as a car. A car will break down over time. It will break down quicker if it is used more. The more wear and tear a car goes through, the faster it will reach the end of its life. Now, if you were to keep the car in storage, and only use it occasionally, it would take a lot longer to break down, right?"

Cirrus nodded.

" Okay, well now, imagine if while you put that car in storage, anything that was damaged, or worn out while you did use it was repaired and fixed. You would essentially have a car that would never die. That is how my body works. Now, there are, of course, other things that happen to people, like disease or sicknesses, but as you may or may not have noticed, those do not happen to us. Our bodies do not suffer natural maladies, as others do."

Cirrus nodded his head slightly in understanding. The analogy made sense to him.

"So occasionally, throughout the years, you 'rested'? Somehow, slowing your metabolism to a point it was slower than the speed of your healing?"

Samuel was once again impressed by his son's ability to reason things out.

"That is correct."

"As to the person who created this, well, it was a long time ago... a different time. Kestrel was a Druid. Not like those supposed druids you might read about that gather at Stonehenge these days. These were the spiritual leaders of the Celts. They were powerful, and they had powerful spells. They used their power and their spells to protect nature, and the Celtic way of life. Kestrel believed civilization was a plague, if allowed to spread would harm and eventually destroy nature. Much like the environmentalist of today.

"Her beliefs were not shared by many, including the Elder. Knowing the longer it took for her to convince the others of the truth, the more damage civilization would do. She took matters into her own hands.

"She created the first Lycans, the Trues. These she used to create an army of Lycans and went to war. A war she lost. However, before she lost, she used a spell which would ensure she would come back, and when she did, the descendants of the first Trues would once again become Lycanthropes. It's rather a complicated story, but since it has yet to happen yet, and possibly never will, is part of the reason you will most likely never be a true lycanthrope. Also, since I am still alive, if she was to come back now, I would already occupy the role, and as such, you wouldn't change.

"As to how she would be awakened? Well Kestrel put a contingency into her spell that when the last of the stones of Stonehenge were to fall, she would be awakened."

Cirrus stared at him for a moment before asking.

"So why have you not toppled Stonehenge?"

Another excellent question, Samuel thought. Of course, he had thought to topple Stonehenge and awaken Kestrel, but part of the spell stated, '...nature will make the call..." Nature will make the call. Not him. He couldn't risk it. If he toppled Stonehenge, and it didn't work, there would be no fixing it. She would never be able to return. No, he couldn't risk it.

"It wouldn't had worked, Cirrus. There were aspects of the spell preventing tampering. It must happen naturally. And so, we wait."

Cirrus examined him closely before saying more.

"While this all seems plausible the way you have said it, father. It seems complete and thorough, and reasonable. It still is impossib…"

Cirrus didn't finish, as right before his eyes, Samuel shifted. His body took on a more rounded form. Skin transformed to reptile-like scales. Samuel's physical form elongated, torso stretching, merging with, and extending behind, to form a tail. Neck melded with body and head, arching forward into snake-like head. Within seconds, a hybrid, part snake, part man towered over Cirrus.

"…ible." Cirrus managed to finish finally, staring with a mixture of wonder, fear, and disbelief.

Samuel knew it would take this to convince his son. He couldn't have shifted right away, though. He needed to set the groundwork for understanding in his son's mind. Without the background, both the history and the science of it, his son would have most likely run from fear, or attempted to attack him when he had shifted. Now, his son understood what he was seeing, and why he was seeing it, which in turn would help him understand it.

"That…that is incredible." Cirrus stammered. "So, you are a Were-snake? I have never heard of that type. Werewolf, obviously, I have heard of. I have even heard mention of bear and tiger. But, never snake."

Samuel frowned. Even though he had gone to great lengths to erase information about himself, it still irked him the lycans people knew about still were Sylvanis' lackeys. The victors truly do write history.

"Yes. Well. There were others, as well. Eight total. Four of us fought for Kestrel. Four for the opposing side." Samuel shifted back and began to put his clothes back on.

"Understand this, Cirrus. If I were to die, and Kestrel were to return afterwards. You will become like me, and it will be your duty to find Kestrel, and join her, help her continue her fight. That is your legacy.

"I know you didn't ask for this, and as I have said, it will most likely never come to fruition in your lifetime, but I felt it imperative I inform you, in case it did." Samuel finished dressing and scrutinized his son. It seemed he was taking this information in stride. He had faith his son would come to grips with this shortly. It was true he was an intellectual, but he was also young, and so unburdened by much of the hard truths of life. The cynicism and the rigid thinking came with adulthood. As such, he should be able to accept this, though it was fantastical, and in many ways unbelievable, regardless of what he saw Samuel do with his own eyes.

Cirrus eventually relaxed in his seat, the tension of the moment had passed, and acceptance had creeped in. To Samuel's surprise, Cirrus looked at him, nodded, picked his book back up and returned to reading. The matter was closed.

That was a year ago when he got the call from his informant. A year since he left his son. He hadn't left him alone. He hired a handler. Someone to stay and watch over Cirrus for as long as the person felt it was necessary. At which point, he would contact Samuel and explain why he felt Cirrus no longer needed minding.

Samuel, time permitting, checked in on his son. Though, he did it in a manner, so Cirrus never knew he was there. He couldn't. He utterly and completely cut ties with his son. Accounts were set up, with it a trust for him which would become his when he turned eighteen, or when the handler felt he was capable of living on his own. If he used it wisely, there was more than enough money to live a life most people only dreamed of. Also, he was armed with the knowledge, at some point, there was always a possibility he might become a full Lycan. Samuel hoped Cirrus would continue to keep himself in top shape, both physically and mentally.

Since the day he told him he was leaving, he hadn't spoken to Cirrus. There were no tears, no yelling. It was clear, while Cirrus was not happy about it, he accepted it. In part because he was aware, no matter what he said or did, Samuel would still walk out the door, and any amount of debasing of himself would only make him appear weak in his father's eyes.

This wasn't the first time he thought about Cirrus since leaving, and now, more so since Kestrel's awakening. He assumed when she awoke, because he was still alive, Cirrus would be unaffected, but he couldn't be sure. The spell was old, and he doubted it had been crafted with the idea one of the original Trues would still be alive.

Contacting the handler, he asked if anything strange had occurred. The handler informed him everything was fine and not to worry. Something in the man's voice left Samuel with an uneasy feeling. Unfortunately, things moved along steadily with Kestrel, or he would have checked on things himself. He sent one of his informants by the house to check on things. The informant told him he saw the handler several times, come and go from the house, but not Cirrus. He told Samuel while he hadn't seen Cirrus, the handler did not appear to be distressed or upset, and everything, for the most part,

114

appeared to be normal. Samuel decided to evaluate this information later, but he hadn't had a chance, yet.

He wondered if he should tell her about Cirrus. Truth is, he didn't wish her to know about him. While Cirrus' and his relationship was never one of closeness, he still felt the need to protect his son in some way. And, keeping him away from her plans was the best way to do this. Samuel glanced Kestrel's way, she was still engrossed in her books. No. He didn't think he would tell her of Cirrus. As far as he could tell, Cirrus was still a carrier of Lycanthropy, but not a lycanthrope. She would have no need of him. There was no way to turn him into a full lycanthrope. Since he carried it, he couldn't contract it. For all intents and purposes, Cirrus would be useless to Kestrel for her plans. His eyes roamed the cabin once more, stopping to examine Gordon again, then back to Ian, who was still taping his feet to some unheard music.

Ian rested in the soft comfortable chair of the airplane's cabin, eyes closed as electronic trance music thrummed in his ear. He was aware of eyes on him, but was unsure of whose — probably Samuel, or whatever his name was. Ian was smart enough to realize most of what the man had told him was a lie, which included his name. Not that it mattered overmuch to Ian. He had thrown his lot in with the guy, and it was best not to worry too much about things he couldn't change.

He doubted it was the new guy on the plane. Gordon Sands, Ian had caught his name. Gordon and he had a lot in common, as Gordon was wealthy, being a doctor, they both were well dressed and attractive middle-aged men, but that was where the similarities ended. Gordon was congenial and friendly, but Ian could tell it was a fake smile the man hid behind. It scarcely hid his superiority complex or his masochism.

What scared him more was what they had discussed. Oh sure, he never listened to them when they spoke, but long ago he became curious of Samuel and his dealings. Whenever he could, he would record conversations held around him when he was 'not listening' by totally immersing himself in music. Putting on earbuds and playing music, he made it obvious he was listening to music. All the while, the wireless microphone in his watch, and a recorder in his pocket, recorded the conversations. Most times, when he would play back what was said between Samuel and whoever was with him on the plane, it was business.

What Ian heard Samuel and the woman discuss was not business. It was insanity. Some of it he didn't understand at all. Talk of Trues, and animals. The talk of finding some girl and killing her he understood all too well. This woman they sought was a Druid and a little girl now, a baby, and others would be searching for her as well. He sensed the man, Gordon, was going to help them get this girl. Why they would need a man like Gordon, a doctor from Australia to do this, he wasn't sure.

They also talked about someone else they sent to Chicago to kill a wolf. A wolf? In Chicago? None of it made sense. Frankly, the whole thing made him wonder if it was time to get out of this business with Samuel. He had completed his job and done it well. Convinced the world all this money, all this wealth, was his. The world watched him, and ignored Samuel, the way it was supposed to. He had done it well for many years. If he left, he knew it would be with a sizable stipend for continued silence about the arrangement. At least, he believed that was what would happen. After hearing the conversation between Samuel and the woman, he was no longer sure. It seemed Samuel might be the type of guy who

116

understood the only way to ensure silence was if the person could no longer talk.

He could try to disappear. It wasn't like he didn't have enough money. The problem? He was well known. Everywhere. It would only be a matter of time before Samuel could locate him. It would be easy enough. If he disappeared, his location would be a hot news story to anyone who ran into him, no matter how remote. They would know the information to be valuable. He couldn't run, and he no longer believed he could quit. He could, however, ensure his ass was covered which meant recording as many of these conversations as he could.

Keeping a record, so when the time came, and the authorities were alerted to what Samuel was doing, he could distance himself from the man and provide evidence he wasn't involved. It was the best he could do. Anything else could put him at the mercy of Samuel, or worse, the woman, which was something he most definitely wished to avoid.

Chapter 5

"Does love always feel like this?" Jason Randal asked his buddy, Mike.

"Lust you mean?" Mike smirked back.

"I'm in love, you idiot."

"You don't know her, Jason. I mean…really know her. You have been staring at her since what? The third grade? Have you ever talked to her?"

"I mean, first, it was grade school, and then it was the same high school," Jason went on, ignoring what Mike had asked. "Then the same college. It must be fate, right?" Jason glared over at Mike. "What?" Noticing for the first time Mike's expression of frustration.

"If it's fate, why the hell haven't you gone over to her and asked her out? Do you know how annoying it is to hear someone drone on and on about the love of their life for ten years or more?" It was obvious Mike was a little ticked off. "You're an adult now, for pity's sake, act like one. Go over to her and ask her out! Or I'll do it!"

"You'd ask her out for me?"

"No, you idiot. I would ask her out for ME. She is rather hot, and if you are gonna sit on your ass and not do anything about it, I might as well have a shot at her."

"You wouldn't?" Jason demanded, eyes widening to never before seen heights.

"Why not?" Mike shrugged. "It's not as if you are ever going to do anything about it."

Jason was about to respond, his mouth opening a little. He snapped it closed. Mike was right about one thing. He hadn't done anything about it.

He watched Stephanie Boles who sat across the student union at Tennessee State. The room wasn't at all crowded right now since it was late in the day and most people took classes earlier. He had a clear shot of her. A tiny thing, perhaps five feet tall in heels, she barely weighed one hundred pounds. Lithe and yet, she still appeared feminine, like a miniature version of a runway model. She had all the right curves in all the right places. Rusty brown hair was cut short, a little above her shoulders, and she had part of her bangs teased down in front of her left eye.

She had a pale complexion, but not so pale as to be white. Just pale enough to show some slight freckles, like fading stars in the early morning light. Eyes were a light brown, almost amber, and always sparkled when she laughed.

Jason had loved Stephanie since grade school. In the third grade, she sat in front of him and she would always smile at him when she took her seat. His heart was claimed by that smile and had been ever since.

Mike was right about something else. Stephanie and he maybe exchanged a half a dozen sentences in the past decade. Jason was extremely shy and apart from saying hi and hello, he did nothing but stare at her, as if willing her, by mental force, to come over to him and say something. She never did.

Jason had been a dorky looking kid, at least in his opinion, taller than most in his grade, not filled out, just tall and gangly. The over-sized tortoise-color framed glasses with wide thick lenses sat awkwardly on his face.

A lot less dorky now, he still felt he appeared a little dorky. In junior high, everyone caught up to him and passed him in height, so he was no longer taller than everyone. He was average height for a man, thin with a little bit of a gut from college drinking. His hair was cropped short, almost army cut. He was a somewhat average looking guy, nothing striking about him in any way.

Because of all of this, he knew there would be no way Stephanie would be interested in a guy like him. Of course, it's not like he knew what kind of guy interested Stephanie, but he was sure it wouldn't be a guy like him. Irrational he knew, yet it always stopped him from trying to talk to her. The sad thing is, until two years ago, she lived only eight houses from him. This year she moved in with her friend, Beth, somewhere here on campus.

He kept staring at her till she glanced in his direction, as soon as their eyes met; Jason quickly glanced away, back to his buddy Mike, who was staring at him like he was some pathetic loser… which he was.

Mike stood up.

"What are you doing?" Fearing Mike at long last had enough of his stupidity and was going to go over to ask her out.

"Calm down, Casanova, I've got a class to get to." With that, Mike left Jason alone.

Jason peeked back over at Stephanie who was still gazing at him. Jason glanced away and pretended to scan the rest of the student union as if he was people watching and not purposely staring at her. He still glanced at her out of the corner of his eye, though, and watched as she gathered up her books and slipped them into her blue and gray backpack. Standing, she slung the backpack over her shoulder and made her way to the exit, once again, walking out of Jason's life.

Enough! Not this time, Jason decided and gathered up his books, and headed for the exit. Walking briskly towards where he had seen Stephanie leave. She had rounded the corner up ahead and would leave the building through the glass doors at the entrance to the student union. Yet, when he turned the corner and saw those doors, frantically scanning outside, he didn't see her anywhere.

"You know," came a voice from his right. "I wait here every day for a minute to see if you would try to catch me."

Jason turned to see Stephanie leaning up against the wall, next to a glass trophy case where she couldn't be seen by someone coming around the corner.

"Well, almost every day." She peered out the double doors. "Sometimes I am too late for class and I can't wait. I always worried it was going to be one of those days you'd chose to try and catch me, and I wouldn't have time to let you," Stephanie said, glancing back at him.

She smiled at him, eyes slightly cast downward. His heart skipped a beat.

"Umm...ah...I wasn't, I mean, I didn't...umm. You were waiting for me?" Jason sputtered out.

Stephanie giggled a little bit. It was the sexiest thing Jason had ever heard, he ignored the fact she was giggling at him.

"Yeah, I was. It sure took you long enough. I thought you would have said something our junior year of high school."

"Truth be told, it would have been third grade."

"Wow." Eyebrows raised, mouth parted slightly, Stephanie took in this information. "I started to notice your interest in high school. Wow. You're way shyer than me. I didn't think it was possible." Stephanie gazed at him still leaning against the wall.

"It would seem, it is," Jason said smiling, rocking slightly from foot to foot.

They stared at each other for what was like an eternity. Neither of them knew what to do with the acknowledgement of their interest in each other. Jason was going to be damned if he was going to let this moment pass. Since the third grade, he had dreamed of this day.

"So... Do you have some time to talk? Or do you have to get to class? It's okay if you do, I understand. We can always talk later," the words, scrambling to get out of his mouth, spilling out like an open firehose.

"I do have to get to class," she said with a frown, angling her body towards the door.

Jason deflated in front of her, shoulders sagging and head drooping slightly. He felt as if he was losing his one chance with her.

"But..." She turned back towards him. "I would rather talk to you than go to class, so let's go back inside!"

"Really?"

"Really." Approaching him, she linked her arm around his and turned him back towards the Union.

They made their way back to the table he had been sitting at, since hers was now taken.

"Third grade, huh?" She peeked up at him with her amber eyes.

"Yeeeeaaahhh...umm," Jason replied while glancing down and peering away.

Stephanie giggled again, and Jason's heart melted a little more.

They reached the table and Jason sat, Stephanie sat next to him, not across from him as he had expected. It was an unexpected delight.

"So, what took you so long?" Stephanie enquired.

"I don't know," Jason told her. "Well, not entirely true. I do know. I thought you wouldn't be interested in a guy like me."

"Why? What's wrong with *a guy like you*?" A little peeved at his answer.

"I don't know," Jason shrugged. "I am a bit of a dork."

"Maybe I like dorks. Did you ever think of that?"

"Oh, come on. You are beautiful, sexy and amazing. Why would you be interested in dorks when you could have any guy you wanted?" Jason asked her.

Stephanie searched his eyes for a moment, finding nothing but innocent sincerity.

"First, thank you for the compliments," she told him with a smile. "And secondly, why do think because someone can have something, they are going to want it? I also discount your belief I could have any guy I want. I'm not *that* beautiful. I'm too short. I don't like to wear girly clothes or makeup. I like to keep my hair short, not flowing like some Barbie doll." She ranted for a moment as her voice got a little louder as she spoke. "Did you ever consider just because you seem to think of me as beautiful, doesn't mean every other guy does?"

"I don't understand what you are saying," Jason told her flatly.

"Are you telling me you have never seen some hot girl with some ugly guy and wonder what the hell does she see in him?"

"Are you saying I'm ugly?" Jason teased, knowing now where she was going with her point, but couldn't pass up the opening she had left.

"No... That's not what...I wasn't saying that," she stumbled over herself to explain to him, and saw the small smirk he was trying to hide and slugged him in shoulder.

"You know what I mean!" She yelled at him, trying to sound put out, but hiding a laugh.

Jason rubbed his shoulder where she had slugged him. He didn't have to feign hurt, she packed quite a punch.

"Yeah, I know what you mean, Stephanie. Beauty is in the eye of the beholder, right?"

"More or less. I think people are attracted to different things. I don't think because you appear a certain way you are attracted to those types of people."

Pondering this for a bit, Jason had to admit she had a point. Unfortunately, it meant he had wasted all this time when he could have been with Stephanie since the third grade, or at least high school.

His expression sank, the muscles in his face slackened, his lips dipped downward at the corners. His sadness must have been noticeable, for Stephanie seemed to understand what it meant, and took his hands in hers.

"It's okay, Jason, we have from this moment on. We might not have been ready to meet before this point. Maybe there were things we had to experience in life before we experienced this."

Jason smiled. He also believed sometimes things in life don't work out because we try them too early, or perhaps, too late. If we don't experience certain things at certain times, they are doomed to fail. Glancing over at the girl he hoped to be with all his life, sitting there holding his hands in hers, and gazing into his eyes, he was happier than he had ever been in his entire life.

"Would you like to go out on Saturday?"

Her smile lit up his heart. "I would love to, Jason."

Stephanie Boles applied lipstick to her upper lip and pursed her lips in a kiss towards the mirror. Her round face was almost doll-like. Taking a moment, she examined herself in the mirror. She was a small girl; she always thought she appeared like a gymnast, though she was shapelier than one. Gymnast tended to lack the curves of a woman, and she wasn't lacking in that department.

She had full B-cupped breasts which were perky, her body thinned down to her waist with a slight flaring out at the hips. Her ass was heart shaped and firm, since she spent hours in the gym to make it so, and the legs were shapely and slight. Freckles dotted her cheeks and upper chest, but they were faint and hardly noticeable, she considered them highlights.

Tonight, was her first real date with Jason.

Of course, they talked every day on the phone and met in the Union between classes. It drove his friend Mike nuts. They were practically fawning over each other, she knew, but she couldn't help herself. Every time they would say sweet stuff to each other and Mike was there, he would groan or make gagging sounds. Jason and she laughed, but they toned it down till Mike left for a class.

It was amazing, after all this time of being near someone and never *really* meeting, you could find your soul mate. It sounded stupid, even to her, to say, but she honestly felt an amazing connection to him, as if they were meant to be.

"If you glowed anymore, we'd be able to save money on the electric bill." Beth said, stepping in lightly from the bathroom doorway.

Stephanie looked at her and smiled more. Beth had been her friend since the first year of college. She was quite different from Stephanie in many ways, she was tall, light skinned, for a black girl, but still darker than Stephanie. A shapely girl as well, but where Stephanie was thin and shapely, Beth was a bit fleshier. The only down side was Beth's long face. It gave the impression of a high forehead and a long chin. She was good-looking, not beautiful.

"If the light bothers you, there is a pair of sunglasses in the drawer," Stephanie told her and smiled, yet again.

Beth walked to the counter and began applying a little mascara to her eyelashes.

"This Jason better be nice to you lil' sis."

125

Little sis was the nickname Beth had given to her when they first met, when some guy at the bar was trying to be funny and asked if they were sisters. Beth glared at the guy and told him off.

"Right, this is my lil' sis. Now get lost." They laughed over it and became fast friends. From then on she was Beth's lil' sis.

"You don't need to worry. Jason is a fantastic guy and so terribly in love with me there is no way he would ever try to hurt me."

"Well, he better not, or I'll have to take him out back and whoop his ass."

Stephanie laughed, only because she was sure Beth could most likely whoop Jason's ass. It wasn't as if Jason was a wimp. He just wouldn't do anything to hurt anyone, even if he was getting his ass whooped.

"Don't worry, if for any reason, Jason hurts me, there won't be anything left for you to whoop. I'll have torn him to pieces," Stephanie assured her.

Beth smiled at her. "I'm happy for you, I honestly am, lil' sis. I know you have been diggin' on this guy for quite some time, I'm glad he at long last made a move on you."

"Me, too. I didn't know if he was ever going to. I didn't think he was interested in me, and I was beginning to think maybe he thought I was freak, which was why he kept staring at me. I mean, he never really made eye contact. If I glanced at him, he would glance away, so perhaps he was disgusted by me."

Beth snorted. "You realize you were telling yourself that, so you wouldn't go over and talk to him, right? It was your rationale, so you never had to risk putting yourself out there and converse with the guy?"

"Well, I know now..."

"Bullshit. You knew it then. You kept ignoring what you knew was the truth cuz you were scared. After all, you are hot girl. Who the hell would be disgusted by you?"

Shyly, Stephanie glanced down. Beth was right, she should have gotten up the guts months, no, years ago, to go over and talk to Jason. She always tried to be in the places he was, waited for him to say or do something. Going to Tennessee State, in part, was because she knew he was going here. Though, that was one fact she would never tell anyone. If anyone found out, especially Beth, they would throttle her.

It wasn't like she couldn't get the education she needed here. She could. It was a fine school. But, she was an excellent student and could have gotten into a much better school. It was Jason who made her decide to come here. In the end, it seems, it worked out for the best. She was doing quite well in school, and she now had a date with Jason.

Now she knew he was as shy as her and had been hoping she would make a move. She wished she had. Even though she told Jason it might have been because they weren't ready, she still longed for all the possible time they could have spent together. She shook her head to clear those thoughts. *There was nothing she could do about it now*, she thought. *The past was the past.*

"You're right, Beth. It was a silly way to handle myself. I should have asked him out a long time ago, but there is no reason to beat myself up about it now. After all, I have a date to get ready for."

Beth smiled again at her. "That's right, lil' sis, you get ready and go out and have some fun. Don't do anything I wouldn't do," she told Stephanie as she turned and smacked Stephanie on the ass as she left.

Stephanie gave a little yelp and tried to kick Beth as she scooted out of her reach.

"Maybe, if you had some length to those legs you might have got me, midget," Beth shouted back to her.

127

"Bitch!" Stephanie yelled at her with a smile.

Stephanie could think of nothing but love for Beth. In many ways, she was Stephanie's big sis. Stephanie never had a big sister, and never knew what it was like to have an older sibling. Beth was always looking out for her, and was never afraid to tell her the truth, no matter what.

Stephanie finished her make-up and took care of getting dressed. A green spaghetti strap blouse and black slacks which fit her ass like a glove. Glancing at herself in the mirror, again, she was finished and had to admit she looked damn hot.

Jason was due any minute, and she was sure his jaw would drop when he saw her.

There was a knock at the front door and she heard Beth shout she would get it. Stephanie hastily made sure her hair was in order and she didn't have any of her make-up smeared so she could get out there fast. The last thing she needed was Beth threatening to whoop Jason's ass if he did anything to hurt her.

Everything appeared to be in order. Making her way out to the living room where she assumed Beth and Jason would be, she heard voices. Her worst fears were realized.

"...She's like a sister to me Jason, so if you do anything, and I mean anything at all to hurt..."

"Hi, Jason," Stephanie blurted, hurriedly interrupting from the hallway.

Jason turned toward her and stared. His mouth parted as if to say something and his eyes opened a little bit more, as if he could fit more of her in his vision by doing so.

"You look...unbelievable." He managed to say after a few seconds.

"Thank you, Jason. You look quite nice yourself," she told him. Which he did. He was wearing a pair of khakis and a blue button-down shirt. His hair was spiked up a little and as

she moved a little closer, she could catch a little whiff of cologne –
sexy.

A small smile crept up on her lips, and she received one in
return. He couldn't keep his eyes off her. Feeling flushed, her eyes
widened by the expression of desire in his eyes when he stared at her.
Taking a deep breath, she tried to slow her heart racing.

"Shall we go?" he asked.

"Yeah. Let's leave before mother threatens you anymore." She
glared at Beth to make her point. Beth tilted her head and shrugged
unapologetically in response.

Seeing the exchange, Jason turned, and approached Beth.

"I understand your concern, Beth, but believe me, I would
rather die than do anything to hurt Stephanie. But, if I ever do hurt her,
you have my permission to kick my ass till I can't walk and have to eat
through a straw for the rest of my life."

Stephanie would have laughed at this comment normally, but
Jason said it with so much seriousness, she couldn't do anything but
stare at his back.

Left dumbfounded by his statement, Beth finally recovered
enough to nod her head to him. Jason took this as agreement and
turned back around to Stephanie. Stephanie saw Beth peek at her,
mouth a 'wow' and smile. Jason approached and took her hands in his
and raised them to his lips.

"Let's go have some fun," he told her and walked her to the
door.

Stephanie never had so much fun in her life. They went out to
dinner first at a nice restaurant and talked about everything you could
think of. They had many things in common, from philosophies of life

to dream vacations and hobbies. It almost scared her how much they had in common. She never shared this much with anyone.

After dinner, they went to see a movie which they both wanted to see, but none of their friends wanted to see. Now, they were making out in his apartment he shared with his friend Mike, who conveniently was staying with a friend tonight. The fact that he orchestrated some alone time with her didn't upset her, she was excited by it and was wondering if this would go all the way. She knew she shouldn't have sex with him on their first date, but she was so into him. If he tried to take it further than making out and some touchy feely, she wasn't sure she would try and stop him.

Kissing her neck, his hand cautiously slid under her blouse to slip inside her bra. His fingers brushed against her nipple and she pushed them against his hand and leaned into his kisses. His fingers pinched her nipple and she gasped. He rolled it softly and suddenly she was awash in pain. Doubling over, she rolled away from his hands and onto the floor. A cry escaped her lips as pain lanced up and down her body, a thousand slashes of heat and agony.

Her mind was numb and muddled, thoughts flew from her like a hundred birds spooked by a loud noise. She could scarcely hear Jason shouting at her, asking if she was alright, yelling he was sorry, he didn't mean to do anything to hurt her. If she could have laughed, she would have at Jason for thinking pinching her nipple would cause her to writhe in pain. However, she couldn't laugh. Could barely breathe. Never had she felt anything so painful in all her life. The sound of cracking, like the breaking of sticks, as her bones broke throughout her body reached her ears first, before she felt them.

What was happening to her, she didn't know, but she knew Jason needed to get out of here as soon as possible. For some reason, she was afraid for his life. It didn't make any sense. She was the one who felt like she was dying, why would she worry for him? But, worry she did. Rolling over onto her hands and knees, she peered up at Jason. Tears pooled in the corner of his eyes, and his lips quivered as his eyes darted, questing her from head to toe.

"Run, Jason," she forced out, teeth clenched as pain racked her body.

"I'm not leaving, I need to call the paramedics, and you need some help."

"I need you to run, Jason. RUN!" Shouting, finally unable to control her panic.

"I'm not leaving you, Stephanie," he screamed back at her.

"You are in danger, Jason. Please," she sobbed through the pain. " Please, run."

Unable to comprehend her wishes, he moved to the floor and held her in his arms.

"No." she cried, not for the pain, but because she sensed Jason was going to die because of her. It was at that moment the bones in her face shattered and she blacked out.

Holding Stephanie tighter in his arms, Jason had no idea what was happening. Bones moved under her skin, like writhing snakes. Rightly, he was afraid for himself, but was more afraid for Stephanie. He promised he wouldn't leave. If she was going to die and it brought about his death, so be it.

Staring at her face, he saw it collapse as the bones broke all at once; he saw her head lull to the side, either from dying or falling unconscious. Bringing his fingers up to her neck, he checked for a pulse. His eyes widened when he felt her pulse. It beat with strength and purpose.

Glancing back up at her face, he saw it begin to elongate out into a snout, the nose flattening and turning black. The rusty brown color of her hair reddened, as similar hair began to push its way out of her skin all over her body. Even her face was sprouting reddish brown

131

hair, except along her mouth and neck where the hair was white. Her skull flattened some, pushing her ears to near the top of her head. The head took shape by curving towards the front, canine-like. Red hair covered the ears as well as they swooped up, elongating above her now flattened head.

Bones began to settle, but her body was not done changing, it inflated somewhat, and her clothes split at many of the seams to compensate. Muscle formed along her body where his hands rested, her body firming up under his touch, becoming hard and defined. Similar changes were occurring in her legs as he watched the opening of the ripped seams in her slacks.

Jason freaked out. Was this going to kill Stephanie? He had every intention of keeping his promise of staying with her. At least, he did until he felt something digging into his leg. When he glanced down he saw the hand she had resting in his lap had elongated and sharp claws were growing from the ends of her fingers. One claw pushed its way into his leg. Watching in fascination, it punched through his khakis and slid easily into his skin. Crying out, Jason scrambled away.

With some distance between them now, he could take her all in. Her face had taken on a canine aspect, but it wasn't bulky, it was sleek and slight. The reddish hair covered everywhere as far as he could see, except around her lower jaw and down her chest where it was white. Black hair erupted along the tips of her ears jutting high above her head. It took Jason a moment to figure out what she resembled. It wasn't that she appeared canine-like, she appeared foxlike — like a red fox. Blood ran down his leg where her claw punctured his leg, a slow and steady river of lifeblood. The thing emitted a soft rumble of a growl. At that moment, he decided to take her advice, and ran.

Bolting through the doorway and into the hall, the pain from the wound in his leg throbbed with every step he took. Jason made it to the bottom of the stairwell when he heard a crash of something big breaking upstairs, presumably from his room. He thought about calling the police but discarded the idea. The thing was Stephanie, and there was no way the cops wouldn't open fire on it and kill her. Once outside his apartment complex, he stumbled into the night.

The parking lot was virtually empty, being a Saturday night, everyone had somewhere else to be. Jason turned to glance back up at the window in his apartment. There was nothing to see except a shadow moving about. Jason continued to stare.

Until the shadow disappeared, he figured he was in no real danger, since it meant she was still in there. Something smashed through his apartment window, and he realized his mistake. A huge form sailed over his head. Spinning around the moment before the thing hit the ground, he saw it land and pivot to face him. It definitely was foxlike.

It was humanoid, standing on two pawed feet. Its legs were thin, yet muscular, and partially covered by shredded black slacks. A bushy tail swept down from behind it to curl around its right leg. Little of the thing's torso was visible as it was still mostly covered by the blouse Stephanie wore. Reddish-brown hair covered her muscular arms. White fur coated the underneath of her sweeping neck and elongated jaw. Its snout was thin, like a fox, and ended in a black canine-like nose. Black, beady eyes stared down at him, for she was now taller than him. Jason watched as the thing's lips peeled back into a growl and took a step towards him.

"Stephanie, please don't," Jason said as the thing lunged for him. He brought his arm up in front of his face, but the attack never came. Jason lowered his arm and peeked out above it. The creature scrutinized him with its head cocked to one side. It appeared it was trying to figure him out.

133

"Stephanie, it's me, Jason. I know it's you. Can you hear me? Do you understand?" Jason took a step towards her. She continued to peer at him and he could see the confusion in her eyes. After a moment, the thing examined itself, as if seeing for the first time what it appeared like. When it gazed back at him, he thought he could see recognition, but before he could ask any more, the thing turned and ran off. It moved like lightning and was out of his sight in seconds. It was a moment before he realized how close to dying he had come.

The first thing Stephanie remembered after she blacked out was seeing Jason standing before her outside his apartment complex. Looking and smelling of fear and blood. Blood stained his left pant leg and he was covered in sweat, his blue shirt to sticking to his chest. Wondering why he appeared afraid, she realized something was wrong. She was staring down at him, which was odd, as he should have been taller than her. Something was very wrong. It was at the same moment she noticed she was peering down a long snout, ending in a black nose. Raising her arms, she examined them.

Instead of her thin, pale-skinned arms, she saw a muscular arm covered in red fur which ended in a clawed hand. The other one was the same. Not taking the time to see the rest of her body, as she assumed it appeared somewhat similar, she needed to get out of here. She needed to get away from Jason whom she had already hurt and who knows what would have happened if she hadn't regained consciousness. Glancing at Jason, she turned, and ran.

When the panic subsided, she realized how exhilarating it was to be running this fast. Darting everywhere, she swiftly made her way into a local park to hide. She hoped Jason could forgive her for what she did. *"Who am I kidding? I'm a monster, why would he want to have anything to do with me?"*

Running a little bit deeper into the forested area of the park; she could hear animals scramble out of her way, their mad dash to safety audible to her as if they were only mere inches away. The thing scaring her the most, though, was the fact she could also smell them. There was a pair of squirrels skittering off to her right. A bunny was sitting perfectly still to her left, hoping she wouldn't know it was there, but ready to bolt at the slightest sign she did. Catching a whiff of deer from up ahead, she could hear the pair of white-tails run away from her.

When she was deep into the forest she stopped and took a moment to come to grips with what had happened. Which would have helped if she had any idea what the hell had happened, she told herself. Evidently, she had turned into some sort of creature. The what and how were questions she didn't have an answer to. Lowering herself onto her haunches, she rocked back and forth.

Again, she took a moment to examine herself. It was odd, she shouldn't have been able to see herself at all, given the fact there was only a sliver of a moon and plenty of tree cover, but she was able to see almost perfectly. Sure, the colors were muted, but she could see the redness of her fur, though she knew it was redder than it appeared right now.

The sounds of the forest were beginning to resurface after they had gone silent because of her mad dash through the thicket. It was odd, she could pick out all the sounds and was sure she could point to each one individually.

She had bulked up from her lithe body size. Taller than Jason now, her body, was a mass of muscles. Flexing her arms, she was amazed to see muscles hard and defined. Judging by how fast she fled from Jason's apartment, she had a clear idea of how strong her new leg muscles were.

135

If the rest of her muscles were as capable, she was formidable, indeed. She also was the proud owner of a semi-bushy tail, evidently. *The only problem, if you could say there was only one problem*, she thought, *was she looked like a monster*. As such, she would be most likely hunted down and either killed or captured.

Jason was probably talking to the cops right now. Frankly, she wouldn't blame him. Blood had soaked his leg, and she knew it had been her who caused it. The desire to kill faded when she came to her senses, but she remembered. The expression on Jason's face told her everything she needed to know. If she hadn't come around, he would have been torn to pieces, and she would have done the tearing.

The thing she needed to deal with now, was what to do. Going back to her apartment wasn't an option; neither was going home to her house. Since the cops were going to be searching for her, she was sure any of her old haunts were not an option. In the form she was in, anywhere in civilized society was now off limits. *What the hell am I going to do*, she thought. Her life, as she knew it, was over. The fact was slowly seeping into her head. It was strange, because she knew she should not be handling this as easy as she was. It was as if her brain had always known this was going to happen, so it was prepared to handle it. She thought about how she crammed last minute for an exam she knew she was going to do horribly on and how it typically brought her to tears. "*Yeah, I'm handling this damn well.*"

She needed to know if Jason was alright though, and how long before the police started to search for her. Standing, she felt the blood flow back into her cramped-up legs. With a slight hop, she bolted back the way she came. This time she allowed her vision and her amazing quickness and dexterity to control her movements as she whispered through the forest, only disturbing animals she happened upon directly. The desire to hunt pulled upon her, a force as strong as gravity that held her to the earth, and she had to fight it as she went. The feeling was strong, especially as rabbits tore from her path. A flash of white from their tails and her eyes would lose focus a little and her heart would race, but through sheer force of will she stayed the course. In the end, she got clear of the forest and back to Jason's apartment speedily and undetected.

There was a small stand of trees near the parking lot where she could get a decent view of Jason's apartment without being seen. The lights were off, which was weird. There was no sign of Jason, or the police. The cops would have still been here, if they had been called. This was a crime scene and they would have done some investigating and collecting of evidence before they left. After all, it typically took fifteen minutes for them to write you a speeding ticket, and it had only been about forty minutes since she left.

Was it possible Jason hadn't called them? But why? She had attacked him, had no idea what she had been doing at the time, no control over herself, but still, she hurt him and almost killed him. Could it be he loved her so much he didn't tell on her? It seemed impossible, given what she turned into, but she could figure out no other explanation.

Stephanie waited another half an hour before deciding nothing was going to happen. Returning to the forest, she wondered at the amazing possibility Jason chose not to tell on her, even though she was a monster. She, unfortunately, would never be able to thank him for not turning her in and devastating her family and friends with the news she was some monster.

She hoped he wouldn't get into any trouble, since she disappeared after going out with him. Beth, she was sure, wouldn't drop it. Thinking he was responsible for Stephanie's sudden disappearance, she would go after him with everything she had. Stephanie was going to have to find some way to let Beth know she was fine and she had returned home for personal reasons or some such.

Beth was the only one she was going to have a problem with. Jason would know why she had disappeared, which would cover most of the people who cared about her enough to wonder why she was missing. Her father wasn't expecting her home, so she wouldn't worry about it, if she ever did. She still wondered how Jason was doing. Hopefully, he went to the hospital since he had lost a lot of blood.

Returning to the same area of the forest she had stopped at earlier, she sat. The first thing she was going to have to handle was Beth. If she didn't return tonight, she knew Beth would have assumed she spent the night at Jason's and not think overly much about it. Oh, she would be a little judgmental, but that was Beth.

Somehow, she would have to figure out a way to call or leave her a note, both of which were a little impossible now. Long, sharp claws would make it difficult to dial a phone, let alone write something down with a pen. Not to mention her cell phone was in her purse which was still in Jason's apartment. So, calling Beth was going to be next to impossible. No paper or pen, either. This was starting to give her a headache.

So, after she figured out how she would deal with Beth, she would have to find a way to see if Jason was okay. Again, that meant either figuring out how to use a telephone or talking to him directly. It was possible she could talk to him directly. After all, he knew what she was, so he wouldn't be as surprised when she showed up. At least, she hoped he wouldn't freak out too much. Perhaps he could tell Beth to meet and she could explain a little about what had happened. Who was she kidding? How was Jason going to explain her best friend had grown a foot taller, was covered in red fur, and had some dog-like nose? Not to mention a tail!

The shear task of what she was going to have to try to do was daunting. It was too much to think about, her brain was starting to short-circuit. She needed to sleep this off. Tomorrow she would be able to tackle this again, and hopefully, have some better ideas as to how to move forward like this.

Jason hoped against hope Stephanie was alright. There was no telling what was going to happen to her if she was spotted and pursued by law enforcement. He would be damned if they found out anything from him, though. The drugs they were pumping into his system were starting to take the edge off the pain radiating from his puncture wound in his leg. He had driven himself to the hospital after wrapping his leg up.

He had assured his one neighbor nothing was wrong and to not call the police. The sound of breaking glass he had heard was a stack of beer bottles which fell over and Jason also told his neighbor he had cut himself when he had slipped and knocked the bottles over. In a college town, it was a likely excuse and his neighbor nodded while offering to drive him. Jason declined, because the last thing he needed was his neighbor to step outside and see the broken window shattered all over the front walkway. He would know Jason lied and might decide to call the police.

Jason got a hold of Mike and asked him to go back to the apartment straightaway to clean up the glass. When he got back from the hospital, he would explain everything, he assured Mike. It took quite a bit of convincing to get Mike to go to the apartment instead of here, but in the end Mike agreed to go clean up first, before he came to the hospital.

Laying on the bed, Jason watched the small TV on a stand attached to the wall in the corner, angled to give the patient the best view. Watching the news all morning since he woke up, he hoped nobody saw the thing Stephanie turned into. It still frightened him to think about it. He was sure he had been close to being torn apart.

Somehow, he had gotten through to her, to Stephanie, and it saved him. Yet, there was nothing about any monster sightings — just story after story about the earthquake in England and the destruction of Stonehenge. It seems Stephanie got away undetected. And now she was gone. Life was so cruel. After nearly a decade of pursuing the love of his life, he at long last gets to be with her and she is taken out of his life. It was a sick joke, for both. For at least five years now she had been interested in him, she confessed. It was like an old Greek tragedy, including the horrible monster.

What had happened to her? It was like she was a werewolf from the movies, except she wasn't a wolf, she was a fox. A chuckle escaped his lips. *She was a fox, indeed,* he thought. *Oh, man. What the hell am I going to do? How am I going to explain this...to anyone?*

They weren't playing the news he feared to hear on the TV, so he shut it off. Moving his finger onto the remote controlling his bed, he lowered it down flat, so he could concentrate on figuring out a clever lie to tell everyone. There was no way he could tell the truth. Even if someone would believe him, he couldn't do it. It would only cause problems for Stephanie, and he couldn't do it to her. She was going to have enough problems without him making it harder for her.

The pain was almost gone in his leg, but for some reason his left arm was tingling like it was going numb. The numbness spread up his shoulder and started across his chest. Jason panicked, he grabbed nurse's button and pressed it. Pain in his chest shot through the numbness, and he gasped.

"Can I help you?" The voice asked from the speaker beside his bed.

"Yes," Jason gasped out. "I think I'm dying."

Everything around him faded.

Cold was the first thing Stephanie noticed. She shivered as the heat stealing tendrils of morning mist caressed her body. Another thing she noticed was she was uncomfortable. Something was digging into her back and her legs itched. She had a moment of vertigo as she opened her eyes; trees crowded her vision against the back drop of moving clouds. She was in a forest. She remembered. Hurriedly, she scrambled to her feet and examined herself. Relief flooded over her. She was herself, again. If it wasn't for the shredded slacks and torn blouse she would have thought someone ruffied her drink and dumped her out here. Vaguely, she remembered falling asleep, being woken up in overwhelming pain, so overwhelming she must have passed out all over, again.

The previous night's events flooded back, a mental onslaught of confusion. Still, she was at a loss as to what the hell happened, or what had happened to her, specifically. Somehow, she had transformed into some sort of monster. It was like a bad nightmare, or some sci-fi movie, or a bad nightmare of a sci-fi movie. These things didn't happen in the real world. Only in the *Enquirer* do things like this get reported. Something insane happened, but now it was gone. She was in the middle of the woods, her clothing ripped to shreds and no easy way to get home without drawing attention.

Making her way out of the forest, she reached the edge, and paused. There was a gas station up the road. If she could call Beth and have her pick her up, it would save her a lot of trouble. The problem was, she was showing a lot of flesh through all the rips and tears in her clothes, the cops would undoubtedly be called. Not to mention, she was covered in dirt from sleeping on the ground in the forest. She couldn't see herself, but she was sure she must appear a mess. She didn't have much choice, though.

It was early morning and there wasn't much traffic as she ran behind the gas station. There was one car getting gas which she waited to leave before heading around to the front of the building. Glancing through the window, the teller was nowhere in sight. Hastily, she ducked inside and made her way to the bathroom.

At first glance at herself in the mirror, she thanked her lucky stars no one had seen her up to this point. Her short hair was dirty; its rusty brown muted by a soft gray from the dry dirt she had been laying on. A thin layer of it stained her right cheek and nose where she had rested her head. Leaves and pine boughs were stuck to her clothes like some third grader's art project. Her clothing, if it could still be called clothes, was covered in dirt as well. For the next twenty minutes, Stephanie stripped down and attempted to bath herself in the gas station's bathroom using paper towels and water from the sink.

When Stephanie finished washing, she blotted herself down with the paper towels. After, she proceeded to clean the dirt off her clothes. Most of it brushed off, but some she needed to use water to get it off. Her slacks were torn down most of the seams on both sides. Ripping off the legs, she made them into shorts, really short, shorts. By tucking a strip of cloth into the tops on both sides she was able to cover most of the split running up to her hip bones. Taking another strip, she ran it around her chest to cover her breasts which were occasionally peeking out between the rips in her blouse when she moved.

Checking herself once again in the mirror, she appeared like she was dressed like one of the extras in Michael Jackson's *Thriller* video, but, she considered the image passable. Chances were, her shorts were short enough to distract the attendant, so he wouldn't ask too many questions. Especially like why she had been in the bathroom for a half an hour and how she had gotten there.

Stephanie stepped out of the bathroom and made her way up to the counter. The attendant was a college-aged guy whose eyes hadn't left her since she stepped from the bathroom. She couldn't blame him; she was showing more leg than a Rockette dancer, and without the stockings. At least she knew she would be able to get him to allow her to use the phone. Guys were so predictable.

Fifteen minutes later Beth came speeding into the gas station. Stephanie waited around back. Beth pulled up right next to her. Before Stephanie took a step to the car, Beth was out and around the front of it, red-faced and yelling at her.

"Dear lord, Stephanie, what did the asshole do to you?"

"Calm down, Beth. Jason didn't do a damn thing to me. I did this all to myself."

"What do you mean, you did this? You left with the guy and I find you out here miles from where he lives, half-dressed. And you say it was your fault? I know you like this guy, but don't let him get away with something like this. I'm taking you to the police right now, and you're going to tell them what happened." Beth was in her face at this point, upset with her apparent self-blame for some apparent attack made by Jason.

"They wouldn't believe me if I told them. Or, I'll be locked up for the rest of my life. Is that what you want, Beth?"

"What are you talking about, lil sis? The guy assaulted you, and if you aren't going to do anything about it, I'm gonna go and find the fucker and kick his ass."

"Well, you will doubtless find him at the hospital," Stephanie told her.

That stopped Beth's tirade. "What?"

"You will find him at the hospital since I hurt him. I almost killed him, Beth. In fact, I would have if he hadn't gotten through to me."

"Well, good, little sis. I'm glad you showed him he couldn't treat you like that. I'm surprised you had it in you, though."

Stephanie glared at Beth with as much of a chastising air as she could muster.

"Beth. I'm only going to say this one more time. I hurt Jason and I ran from his apartment. This current state my clothes are in is totally my fault. If you would take a moment to inspect me, you would see not a single scratch, not a single bruise. If I was assaulted, don't you think it would have left physical marks — somewhere? Only my clothes are shredded to the point of uselessness. Speaking of which..." Stephanie stepped past Beth and got into the car. She had enough of standing outside appearing like a stripper. Beth was left standing there, open mouthed for a moment until she also got into the car.

Once inside Beth regarded Stephanie.

"Okay, so he didn't assault you. So, what *did* happen, lil sis?"

"Take me home, Beth."

"Then you'll tell me?"

"Then I'll tell you. You won't believe me, but I'll tell you."

Stephanie didn't tell Beth right away. Instead, she went to her room and changed into some sweat pants and a t-shirt. After getting dressed, she realized she hadn't eaten since yesterday evening and it was coming up on ten in the morning. Grabbing a bowl of cereal, she went to sit in front of the TV and watched the local news. Beth seemed to sense Stephanie was going to need some time before she would be able to talk and watched her quietly from the sofa.

Watching the news intently, Stephanie bounced between the three majors to see if there was anything about the incident last night. To her amazement there was nothing about it at all. So, Jason hadn't called the police. Or, at least, they were keeping quiet about it. Well, they would have been waiting here for her to return if they knew anything about it, so she guessed she was safe – for now.

Finishing her bowl of cereal, she set it on the coffee table in front of her. She thought about the best ways to tell Beth, and yet, she still didn't know. Anything, and everything she would say would seem like a made-up story. It was unbelievable to her, and she was the one who lived it!

Beth sat quietly, hands clasped in her lap, waiting for the explanation.

"Beth. I don't know what to tell you. If I told you the truth, there is no way you would believe me."

"Try me."

Stephanie smiled faintly at Beth.

"You have no idea what you are in for, Beth. I'm talking X-files with a little bit of B-movie mixed in the bunch."

"What? Are you going to tell me you were abducted by aliens?"

"That would be a little more believable than what I'm going to tell you."

Beth laughed for a moment and stopped when she realized Stephanie wasn't laughing. In fact, Stephanie seemed serious.

"Okay, lil sis. I'm listening."

"Alright," Stephanie began. "Everything was going terrific with Jason. We had an amazing time together and in the end, we went back

145

to his place for some making out. It was going super, until I was suddenly struck with the most excruciating pain I've ever experienced in my life. It was like having cramps times a thousand, and all over my body, not just the abdomen. It was so painful, I lost consciousness. When I came to, I was standing in front of Jason, outside his apartment. He was bleeding and was backing away from me. He was frightened. It was then I realized I had changed into something."

"Wait. What do you mean changed into something?" Until this point, Beth had been riveted to the story. Now she had a perplexed expression on her face.

"I'm getting there, Beth. Just give me a second." Beth's face reddened slightly, chastised. "I never got a good view of myself to tell you exactly what I appeared like, but I turned into some kind of monster. I was almost six feet tall and covered in red fur. I had sharp claws, which is evidently how I wounded Jason." The moment of sadness she had for hurting Jason was suddenly replaced by excitement as she leaned forward, eyes shining.

"You wouldn't believe the speed I had, Beth. When I was running it was like I was flying. Oh, and I could see in the dark like it was day. Only the colors appeared washed out, like on an overcast day. My senses were amazing, as well. I could smell animals and could have walked right to them following their scents. It was *amazing…* and frightening." Stephanie watched Beth for her response.

Beth sat there for a moment, staring at her.

"Did you hit your head?"

"Beth, I'm telling you the truth."

"You can't be, lil sis. What you are saying isn't possible," Beth told her.

"Yeah, I know. It shouldn't be possible, but it happened."

"Alright, Stephanie. It's obvious you suffered some sort of trauma. Your brain must be trying to compensate by imagining these things." Her concern was obvious. It was clear the attempt to convince Beth what happened wasn't working.

Stephanie sighed. This was going nowhere. It hit her. The only way she was going to convince Beth what happened was to have Jason tell her the same thing.

"Fine, Beth. I'll get checked out, but first, I want to go see if Jason is okay."

"You want to go see the guy who assaulted you? To check if he is okay? You are messed up." Beth shook her head.

"Look, Beth, you can go with me. Just drive me to Jason's apartment to check to see if he is there and check on him, and then you can drive me to the hospital to get me checked out."

Beth stared skeptically at her, as if trying to figure out if she was being scammed. Stephanie tried to hide the fact she was absolutely scared to death about going to get checked out. Afraid they would be able to figure out what happened and lock her away. Luckily, she was sure once Beth saw what she did to Jason, and when Jason told her what he had seen, Beth would have no choice but to accept the story Stephanie was telling her. Hopefully, Jason would see her after what had happened.

"Fine. I'll drive you," Beth agreed. "But, there's a chance I'm gonna kill Jason myself."

Stephanie smiled warmly at Beth. She knew Beth was all talk. Well, she hoped at least.

Stephanie knew there was something wrong when they pulled into Jason's parking lot. Mike, Jason's roommate, was running down the stairs at full speed carrying a duffle bag. When he saw her in the car, he dropped the bag and headed right for Beth's car. Beth had to stop or run over him. Mike went around to Stephanie's side of the car and opened the door.

"What the hell did you do to him?" he shouted. "What the hell happened to my apartment?"

"Is Jason alright?" Stephanie managed to get in amidst Mike's interrogation.

"Is Jason alright? Is Jason alright? He had a heart attack. He almost died. Is he alright?" Mike's eyes were wild, and his words tumbled out in an angry hurry. "I get a call from him early this morning asking me to come home and clean up the mess in and outside the apartment. My apartment is a wreck, the window is broken, and there is a blood stain on the carpet."

Beth had gotten out of the car and moved around from her side and slid between Mike and Stephanie.

"Now hold on here," Beth interceded. "Calm down and start making some sense."

Mike glared at Beth for a moment, took a deep breath, and turned back to Stephanie.

"I've been cleaning up here for hours, and then I get a call from the hospital, seems I'm Jason's emergency contact number. Anyway, I get a call from the hospital. Jason went into cardiac arrest. They have no idea what caused it, since he only suffered a puncture wound in his thigh — not anything to have caused heart failure. They brought him back, but since they didn't know the cause, and whether he might go into it again, I should perhaps call his next of kin and get down there myself. That's what they told me." Mike glanced back towards his car and the bag lying beside it. "I packed up some things so, at least, he could have some change of clothes and his tablet to play on." He glared back at her. "What happened, Stephanie? What did you do to him?"

This was Stephanie's worst fear and she couldn't contain herself anymore. A sob broke loose, followed by another. She couldn't stand the thought of having hurt, let alone kill Jason. The fact he was still alive was the only reason she hadn't collapsed into a heap on the pavement.

"I'm sorry, Mike. I didn't mean to do anything," she told him. Mike stared at her, his features softening under her obvious distress. Beth, however, stared intently at Stephanie. It seems this wasn't what she had expected to find at Jason's apartment. Her expression implied she was starting to suspect what Stephanie told her, no matter how unbelievable it was, might be the truth.

Stephanie got herself together enough to tell Mike they were going to go and see Jason.

"Oh, no, you aren't. You did this to him. I'm not going to let you anywhere near him."

"How do you know she did this to him?" Beth asked.

Mike spared a glare for Beth, who didn't back down and glared right back.

"Well, for starters, she damn near apologized. Also, when I asked Jason what happened, he wouldn't tell me. When I asked about Stephanie, he wouldn't say anything, either." Mike glanced back and forth between the two girls. "Now, I don't know exactly what happened, but it is obvious it involved you, Stephanie."

"Look, Mike, I am not going to tell you the reason Jason is in the hospital didn't involve me. Or what happened in your apartment didn't involve me, either. What I can tell you, nothing is quite what it seems, and if Jason didn't tell you what happened, it means he doesn't put the blame on me, or he would have said it was my fault. Now, unless you are planning on physically stopping me, I am going to go see Jason." Stephanie shut the car door and waited for Beth to get back in.

For a moment, it seemed as if Mike might decide to take her up on using physical force, but Beth said something to him, and he changed his mind. Stephanie watched as Mike stormed over to grab the duffle bag and head to his car, glaring at her over his shoulder. Beth got into the car and spun the car around to head to the hospital.

"You got an explanation for this?" Beth side-eyed Stephanie.

Stephanie shook her head. Why Jason had a heart attack, she had no idea. You would assume if it was from stress, he would have had it when he was face to face with her when she had transformed into a monster, not hours later. It was a decent chance his heart attack had nothing to do with her at all. Possibly he had an allergic reaction to something they gave him. Or, he had a weak heart and it happened to give out. For some reason, she didn't believe any of her possible answers. For some reason, she knew she caused it.

They arrived ten minutes later and parked. Wanting to get in there and see Jason before Mike arrived, Stephanie jumped out of the car before Beth had it fully parked.

"Hey!" Beth shouted at her and swiftly followed.

Running inside, Stephanie got to the elevators. All the elevators were many floors up and she didn't feel like waiting. A couple of strides took her to the stairwell.

Beth came around the corner as Stephanie darted into the stairwell, taking the stairs two at a time. She would have taken them three at a time, but with her short legs she would have eventually stumbled. Not for the first time did she wish she was taller, so she could run these damn stairs quicker.

Glancing behind, she saw Beth down a flight of stairs from her. Even though Beth was much taller than Stephanie, she was having trouble keeping up. Stephanie opened the door to level three. Taking a second, she yelled into the stairwell. 'He is on level three — take a right out of the stairs.' Proceeding down the hallway, she passed eight rooms, before stopping outside the door of the ninth room. The name on the board beside the door read Jason Randal.

Standing in front of the door, she realized Mike hadn't told her the room number, yet she knew exactly how to get here. Somehow, she knew Jason was here. Level three could be considered an educated guess given he was a recovering patient, but to know to turn right out of the stairwell and to go eight rooms down and stop right in front of the door... was a little too farfetched.

"Come in, Stephanie," she heard Jason call from inside.

Staring at the door, Stephanie wondered how Jason knew it was her outside, or that there was anyone outside his door. Glancing down the hallway, she saw Beth emerge from the stairwell and glance her way. Before Beth could stop her, she opened the door to Jason's room and entered.

Propped up in bed, Jason watched her as she entered. Her heart hiccupped for a moment upon seeing him, wondering how he would react to seeing her. He broke into a huge smile.

"I am so glad you're alright," Jason said. "After what happened, I wasn't sure... "

Mouth stuck open, she stood frozen for a moment. He was worried about her? She had almost killed him, and he was worried about her?

Running over, she hugged him, hard.

"I thought you wouldn't want to see me, again." She buried her face in his shoulder.

"I love you, Stephanie. Why wouldn't I want to see you, again?"

She pulled away from him.

"Umm, I don't know, Jason, perhaps because I turned into a huge monster and almost killed you."

Jason laughed. "Yeah. Well, all women turn into monsters once a month at least, you're just a little extreme." He smiled. "Oh, hello, Beth."

151

Peeking over her shoulder at the door, she turned to see Beth there staring at them.

"So, what she told me is true, Jason?" Beth watched his face.

Jason studied Stephanie for a moment, searching her face for some hint of how to handle this.

"Yeah, Beth. It's true."

"I need to sit down." Beth moved to the corner where a cushioned chair waited and slumped into it.

Almost instantaneously she sat up straight. "How did you know he was here? The whole time I was following, I kept wondering how the hell you knew where you were going. I never heard Mike tell you Jason's room number."

"I don't know, Beth; I was wondering myself. It was as if I knew he was here. I could almost sense him." She turned to Jason. "How did you know I was outside your door?"

Jason cocked his head. "It was weird. I felt you approaching. Ever since I woke up from my heart attack I had a sense of you. It's the best way I can describe it. I had a sense of where you were, like in the back of my mind. When I thought of you, I could get a stronger sense of where you were. Does that make sense?"

Allowing herself to feel with her senses, she could sense Jason's presence. If she closed her eyes, she could easily point to him in a crowded room.

"Yeah. It makes sense. I can sense you, too. I think I could before, but was so stressed out over everything happening, I didn't let myself be aware of you." She smiled at Jason, her face reddening. Jason returned it.

"Wonderful," Beth moaned from the chair. "Now you guys are more attached to each other. It still begs to reason why all this is happening, whatever *this* is."

Beth had a point and Stephanie didn't have an answer for her. At the moment, she was too happy to care. Jason didn't hate her. In fact, he said he loved her, despite the fact she almost killed him as a monster. Jason took her hand in his.

"Do you understand anything about what happened to you?"

Shaking her head, she squeezed his hand.

"Well, I can tell you what I saw happen and we can go from there."

Striding into the room, Mike entered, with the duffle hanging from his right shoulder. Taking one glimpse at Jason, his eyes traveled to Stephanie and Beth in the corner. Sensing something important was about to be said, he dropped the duffle and shut the door behind him. "Okay. Let's hear it."

Jason peered up at Stephanie, again. It warmed her heart he would check with her if it was alright to divulge her secret with Mike before saying anything. Mike needed to be told. He wouldn't let this go. If she and Jason were together, he would always imply something happened last night which defied explanation. Nodding to Jason, she let him know it was okay.

"We were on my couch when you doubled over from pain. I watched you as your body shattered and remade itself." Shaking his head. "At least, that is the best way I can describe it. I didn't know what to do. I could see how much pain you were in, but there was nothing I could see I could do. I tried to comfort you on some level, but you screamed at me to get away from you. You told me to run, I was in danger. At first, I didn't listen and tried to stay with you." Jason gazed into her eyes. She could see how hard it had been for him to leave her.

"It's okay, Jason. I told you to leave for a reason," she told him.

"When you say, remade itself, what do you mean, Jason?" Mike asked.

"You saw the movie *American Werewolf in London*, right?"

"Yeah. Wait. Are you saying she is a werewolf? Come on man." Mike was incredulous.

"Not a werewolf, because she didn't appear like a wolf, she appeared more like a red fox."

Mike gawked at him and broke out laughing. "Are you kidding me? Is this a joke? Am I on camera or something?"

They didn't answer him, only regarded him straight-faced.

"You're not, are you? You're serious?"

They both nodded at him. Standing there for a moment, he raised his hands in defeat, and motioned for Jason to continue.

"I didn't run at first, as I said. I tried to hold you and help you through the pain. When you grew claws, one of them punctured my khakis and my leg. I ran. When I ran outside, I was staring up at the apartment window. Suddenly, you came flying through it, landing behind me. When I turned to observe you, I saw you, as some sort of humanoid fox. You were covered in red fur, except for your chest and abdomen which was white from what I could tell. You were taller than me, and frightening." Shrugging. "Sorry." Jason smiled apologetically up at her. "I thought you were going to kill me. All I could think of was to try to reach you. I called out your name, hoping you would recognize me."

"Just when I thought you were going to slice me into little pieces, my words must have gotten to you. You stopped, and it was like you saw yourself for the first time. Then you ran away. Man, did you run. I don't think I've ever seen anyone move so fast in my life." Jason took a deep breath. "It was the last I saw you."

"From there I ran to the park and into the forest," Stephanie said, taking up where Jason finished. "I didn't know what to do, but I was worried about Jason, so I came back to the apartment, but the lights were out. It seemed like you were gone." She glanced to Jason for confirmation.

"I drove myself to the hospital after wrapping my leg." Jason informed her.

Stephanie continued. "Seeing no one was home, I went back to the forest and eventually fell asleep. I remember waking up at some point to incredible pain, but must have passed out, because the next thing I knew, I woke up, and I was no longer in that form. I was back looking like I normally do."

"Okay," Mike began. "Let's assume for a moment what you are saying is true, and I'm still not entirely convinced it is, but let's say it is, for the sake of this argument. If you were some sort of were-creature like a werewolf, only a fox instead, how did you change. It wasn't a full moon, yet. You still have a week or so before it gets here!"

"Well, Mike," Beth spoke up. "First, since none of us, and I think I speak for all of us here, have ever heard of a werefox before, let's assume everything we think we know about werewolves isn't true."

"Fair enough. I'll grant you that." Mike conceded.

"Now, I don't think it's a coincidence after she injured you, Jason, you guys can somehow sense each other," Beth interjected.

"What do you mean?" Mike glanced over at her.

"Well, this is before you got here, but Stephanie walked right to this room. I mean, she didn't ask anyone for directions or a room number. She bee-lined it right here. And, it appears your buddy here could sense my girl standing outside his room without seeing it was her."

Mike stared at them both, and as one, they nodded their agreement.

"Well, I think you guys need to tell the doctor or something," Mike told them.

"Are you nuts, Mike?" Beth walked over to the bed, in a form of support. "They will stick them in a lab somewhere. Run some tests for who knows how long. That is, of course, if they don't throw us all in the loony bin for trying to tell them this story." Beth shook her head. "No. The best thing for them to do is to get out of here as fast as possible and go on with their lives."

"Okay, you got a point," Mike said. "But, I also don't think they can go on pretending this didn't happen, or it might not happen, again. What if Stephanie is sitting in class and she changes into this creature. Who knows what sort of devastation she could cause. Just because she could stop herself from killing Jason doesn't mean she would be able to stop herself, again." Turning towards her. "No offense, Stephanie, but I don't want you at the apartment, again. I'm not gonna risk my life because Jason cares for you."

"Now hold on a minute, Mike..." Jason began.

"No, Jason," Stephanie broke in, "it's okay. I totally understand what he is saying and respect it."

Stephanie wasn't upset at Mike. She understood what he was saying. It was clear she needed to avoid people as much as possible, but she didn't know what she was going to do either. There was no obvious reason why she changed into the creature, and without some sort of clue what had triggered it, there was no way to predict if, and when, it would happen again.

"I'm going to go back home. I live on a farm. I can easily get away from people if I need to. I think it's for the best," she said.

"Nonsense, Stephanie, there is no point in not living your life. You don't know if it *will* happen again," Jason said to her. "Are you going to live the rest of your life in solitude? There has got to be a better way." Jason was regarding all of them in turn, searching for suggestions. None of them had any. Jason sighed.

"Well, there is one thing I agree with Mike on in this. We should get out of here right away." Jason swung his legs off the bed and started to get up.

Stephanie placed her hand against Jason's chest and pushed him back down.

"Your injured, and in no shape to go home, buddy."

Jason smiled. "That's the thing. I wasn't feeling pain at all anymore in my leg. So, I took the liberty of checking..." Lifting the bandage of his thigh where his puncture wound had been; showing them. It was gone. Stitches were stuck to the gauze as if they had been pressed into it. The leg wasn't red or swollen at all. It was like he never was injured at all.

"You see. I think it would be a terrific idea if we got out of here. I don't think I want to try to explain my miraculous recovery to any of the doctors. Not to mention, I feel fine. In fact, I feel better than fine. I feel better than I've ever felt in my entire life." With the giant smile still on his face, he stood up.

Stephanie frowned. She didn't disagree with his statement about getting out of here, but about him saying he felt better than he had ever felt before. Because, it was how she felt. Never had she felt more alive, more vigorous, and stronger than she did today. She was sure this was a by-product of the change she had gone through last night. If Jason felt that way now, as well, not to mention their strange connection they had, it was possible he was somehow changed now as well.

It was too much to take in, either way. The first thing they needed to do was to get out of here. Stephanie went to the bag at Mike's feet and grabbed him some clothes and tossed them over.

"We'll wait outside." She kissed him. "Make it quick."

Mike, Beth and she stepped outside the room and waited for Jason to get dressed. She didn't think they would have too much

157

difficulty getting out of here with Jason dressed. It was the patients trying to leave in gowns they would frown upon she imagined.

It didn't take too long for Jason to get dressed and he was with them shortly. They made small talk as they walked down the hallway, keeping Jason on the far side away from the nurse's station. They ducked into the stairwell and made their way out. They agreed to meet at Stephanie's and Beth's place, so Jason went with Mike who followed Beth there.

When they were all in the apartment it was Mike who had come up with a new idea and started the conversation.

"So, Jason and I were talking on the way over, and we are in agreement, you have some form of lycanthropy." Stephanie and Jason sat together on the couch and Mike took the recliner, while Beth occupied the ottoman.

"What is lycanthropy?" Beth asked.

"Lycanthropy is basically what makes a werewolf a werewolf," Jason chimed in. "It was supposed to be some sort of blood disease which caused people to take on the form of a wolf, or in this case, a fox. Which is why, I believe, I almost died."

"So, it *was* my fault?" Stephanie cast her eyes downward in shame.

"Not really, sweetie. It was more mine than yours. You told me to get away, and it was I who didn't listen. I held you so I was close enough for your claw to dig into my skin. You weren't conscious at the time." Jason tried to convince her.

Feeling a little bit better, Stephanie asked. "So, why did you almost die?"

"Well," Jason began. "Well, lycanthropy is supposedly a blood disease. So, when you cut me, you infected me. I believe my body attempted to fight it off and failed. So, in response, it shut down, instead. However, the hospital was able to revive me, so I survived the infection... basically."

"So, that means, what?" Beth asked him.

"It means I am now, most likely, the same as her," gesturing towards Stephanie. "I am now also a werewol...er fox."

"Oh, god," Stephanie groaned out. "I am so sorry, Jason. I didn't mean for any of this to happen."

Jason patted her hand. "I know you didn't, Stephanie. You had no control over the situation. What I don't understand though, is where you got it from and what triggered the change, since it was not a full moon which caused it." He was doing a fantastic job at making her not feel like a total monster. Even though she was sure this meant she had destroyed his life. No matter what he said, she didn't think she would forgive herself.

"I wish I could tell you something to explain it, Jason. But I have no idea how or why I would have this lycanthropy. I don't think I've seen a red fox, and I'm positive I have never changed into this thing before." Shaking her head, she was frustrated she didn't have any answers.

Mike leaned forward. "Have you ever been hurt, Stephanie? Or sick?"

At first, her response was to say of course she had been sick. But, it occurred to her, she couldn't think of a single time she had been sick. Perfect attendance all throughout high school and there was no time in grade school which came to mind. Never got hurt, either. In of itself, it wasn't odd. Lots of people go through their entire life without breaking anything. She had cut herself a few times, but those had always healed up nicely. In fact, she didn't think she had a scar.

"I've always had this disease!" She realized. "It's why I never got sick. It wasn't until you asked, Mike, I also realized I had never broken anything. Plus, anytime I had cut myself, I never scarred and always healed rapidly. But, why haven't I changed until now?"

159

No one gave her an answer. After a moment of silence, Jason spoke up.

"The nice thing is, I don't think we need to worry about anything until there is a full moon."

"Why?" Beth asked.

"Well, it would be the mythology of lycanthropy, right? We must assume since evidently, lycanthropy is real, the mythology holds a bit of truth. I can't speak for last night, other than perhaps it happens for the first time is when you reach a certain age, or certain part of the season. One could never know. But, what is commonly agreed upon is, when it comes to lycanthropy, it commonly occurs on a full moon." Jason continued, "So, I believe we are safe from any changing for a week or so."

Stephanie wasn't convinced. "Can we risk it? This is all supposition. We have no idea for sure about any of this." She threw her hands into the air. "Hell, I could be moments away from changing again and killing all of you." That got their attention. "We don't know. And I, for one, am not willing to risk your lives, or the lives of other innocents on a guess."

So excitedly sure of himself, Jason deflated under her rationale.

"So, what are we going to do?"

"I told you. I'm going to return home and try to stay as far away from people as I can."

"What about me?"

"What about you? Jason, I almost killed you the last time I changed. I can't bear the thought of causing you any pain, let alone killing you. I can't risk having you near me." She pleaded with him. Hoping he would understand. The expression in his eyes told her he wasn't going to give up.

"Stephanie. Even if you don't believe you have lycanthropy, you should at least believe whatever you have, I

160

now have. There is no other explanation for the fact my wound disappeared. So, whatever you do, I am doing it with you. If you are going home, I'm going home with you."

She wanted to argue with him, but the truth was, she felt alone. Realizing she wasn't like everyone else now, and although she had terrific friends, there was no way for them to understand what she was going through. Hell, she didn't understand what she was going through. She needed Jason. Not because she needed a friend now more than ever, but she needed someone who was going to be experiencing everything she went through. Someone who would understand. In the end, she decided it was best not to argue with him on this and nodded her agreement he could accompany her to her home.

Smiling at her, Jason squeezed her hand. She turned to Beth and Mike.

"You two on the other hand, I need to say goodbye to now." Raising a hand to forestall Beth who was about to say something. "Now, don't argue. It's all nice and well to assume we are all safe till a full moon, but as I mentioned before, we have no proof. I will not risk your lives on a guess, no matter how logical it is." Stephanie stood up. "Jason and I leave tonight. If you could make yourself scarce, in case I change in the next five minutes or something?"

Standing, Beth nodded slowly to her and was suddenly hugging her hard. "You take care of yourself, little sis."

"I will, big sis."

"You better," Beth insisted as she disengaged herself.

"Or what? You'll break my legs? They will heal right back up." The joke rang a little hollow, since she wasn't quite used to the idea yet. Beth smiled at her all the same.

Beth turned to Jason. "And you! That's my little sis over there, and if you allow anything to happen to her, I will get a gun with a silver bullet and shoot you myself!"

161

Gazing at her, Jason just smiled then hugged her as suddenly as she had hugged Stephanie. At first Beth was stiff in his arms but hugged him back.

"I will do my best, Beth, I promise," Jason whispered and released her.

"Well, okay," Beth told him.

Stepping around Beth, Mike held out his hand for Jason. Jason took it and shook it vigorously.

"You're a decent man, Jason, try to be careful. And, good luck."

"Thanks, Mike. You've been a terrific friend. Don't worry, you guys, we'll keep in touch. We'll call you when we get to Pennsylvania," Jason told them.

๑
๛

A day later they were in Brookville, Pennsylvania. A few hours north of Punxsutawney, the town made famous by the Bill Murray movie *Groundhog Day*. Stephanie remembered when she was younger making the drive down there for Groundhog Day to see Punxsutawney Phil. It was one of her fondest memories she had of growing up.

They stopped attending the event after her mom died. Her mother had drowned in the farm's lake when Steph had just turned ten. It was hard after that. Her father had never been a loving dad. A farmer, he worked hard and long. He didn't have time for her or her sister which was what wives were for. It was the kind of mentality which didn't surface much anymore, but her dad was old-school.

He left them alone to raise themselves, and to deal with the grief of the loss of their mother, as well. Her sister, Caroline, was only seven, so it was up to Stephanie to take care

162

of things. Teaching herself how to cook, she made sure Caroline and she ate well. Her father, she left to fend for himself; after all, it was what he was doing to them.

It wasn't the taking care of them which hurt Stephanie the most. It was dealing with the grief which was the hardest. It was why she always resented her dad and why she left as soon as it was obvious Caroline would be okay on her own.

Working hard in school, she received a scholarship, including boarding. The day before she left for school, she told her dad where she was going. She remembered it vividly.

Sitting on the sofa, her dad was watching TV. Having come in off the fields, he was falling asleep with a beer in his hand. Her father was a rough seeming man. Dark tanned skin, creased and marked by age lines from too many years in the field. He seldom smiled, though she always believed it was because of his bad teeth more than he was never happy. Stubble covered his chin and cheeks. It appeared he never shaved, but she knew he had; only it was so early in the morning, by the time his work was done at the end of the day, he needed to shave again. Stretched out on the sofa, he sat with his long legs sprawled out before him. Some might say her father was lanky, though to her, lanky always meant weak. Her father was not weak. It was true, he was tall and skinny, but his biceps were corded lumps which stood out, even at rest. He was all skin and muscle, not an ounce of fat on him.

Sparing her a glance when she sat, he looked back to the TV. She let him know she was leaving in the morning for the University of Pittsburg where she would be staying and going to school. She wasn't sure when she would be back.

She remembered his reaction like it was yesterday. Taking a sip of his beer, his eyes never leaving the TV, he told her, " Well, good luck."

Stunned, she sat in the chair for a moment before slowly going up to her room. Packing all her clothes, she cried the entire time.

Morning came and when she went to leave, she saw her father out on the fields working. Hugging her sister long and hard, she told her to find a way out as soon as possible.

To her credit, Caroline nodded and hugged her back. Stephanie felt she was abandoning Caroline, but there was no help for it. She had to leave. Her friend, Clea, gave her a ride into town where Stephanie boarded the bus to Pittsburg. In the two years she was at school, she hadn't been back. Until now.

As Jason turned on the road which would lead them to the driveway of her home, she felt a moment of panic. Caroline had left for school in the early fall, getting away from here. Only her father was at the farm; her father who had so coldly said goodbye when she left. Hell, he didn't say goodbye, just wished her luck. She wasn't sure what she was going to say to him. How she was going to explain to him why she was there. Wasn't sure he wanted her there. Stephanie hadn't bothered calling, either. Just showing up with her boyfriend after two years...

"Let's go somewhere else, Jason," she uttered when they pulled into the driveway of her childhood home.

She felt Jason's eyes on her as she stared down the long driveway to the house. Bringing the car to a halt, he turned off the radio.

"Okay, Stephanie, what is it? You have been quiet most of the way here and frankly, I could feel the tension elevate the closer we got. You worried about seeing your father?"

Stephanie stared out the window at the fields. She didn't want to talk about it, and yet, she desperately needed to.

"I'm sorry," Jason said after a moment of silence. "Hey, never mind, if you don't want to talk about it, it's fine. Just know, I'm here if you want to talk, okay?"

"No." She considered him. "It's okay. You should know a little about what you are getting into."

She told him everything about her mother's death, and the years afterwards leading up to her leaving home for college.

"So, you see? I'm not sure he is going to welcome us home. Plainly, he didn't want me here before I left," she finished.

Jason let out a long sigh.

"Well, I'm not sure what to say about all of that, but I think after coming all this way, we should at least stop by."

Thinking long and hard on it for a bit, she decided Jason was right. She at least owed her father that much. Nodding her assent, he continued down the drive.

As she neared the house, all the comments Caroline made to her the last few years before she left started to come to mind. She had dismissed them because she still hurt and didn't want to hear anything about her father, but they ran straight to her thoughts the moment they came close to the house.

It appeared dilapidated; as if no one lived there. The windows carried a sheet of dust from the fields so thick as to make them opaque. Shutters were either missing or almost falling off. Weeds and vines choked the landscaped bushes marking the front of her home, leaving them brown and skeletal. The front door screen was ripped from one corner and draped over the rest of the door, fluttering when the wind blew.

Caroline tried to tell her how bad it was getting at home, but Stephanie ignored it, not wanting to hear. Caroline tried to tell her how little their father did to maintain the house; even how bad he maintained the fields.

She glanced at the fields. Most of them were barren and appeared untilled this year. One section of the farm held some crops, and it appeared paltry, at best.

The car stopped, and she saw the front door open. Her father stepped out onto the front step, shading his eyes, trying to make out who his visitors were. It was strange to see him at the house during the day time. He was either out in the fields, or in the shed working on the equipment, never at the house till dusk, or later.

At first glance, he appeared much like he did when she left, tall and thin, skin worn and leathery. At closer inspection, she saw how sunken his eyes were. He didn't stand as straight as he used to. Now, he hunched over as if beaten into submission and forced to bow and scrape. His hair, which had never been neat, was wispy and disheveled. Several days of growth spread uncomfortably up from his chin to form a patchy, salt and pepper beard.

This was not the strong man she knew. This man appeared as if he had nothing left worth fighting for. For the first time in her life, her father seemed weak to her.

She stepped out of the car. Her father lowered his hand from his eyes and stared at her. They stared, unmoving, glaring at one another for what seemed like an eternity. She couldn't take it anymore.

"Aren't you going to say anything?"

When he heard her voice, he dropped to his knees and let out a loud sob, burying his face in his hands.

Stephanie stood there for a moment, dumbfounded. She never heard her father cry — not even at her mother's funeral. Standing there, frozen, she was unable to move. The moment passed, and she crossed the distance to her father. When she approached, he threw his arms open wide. Barreling into him,

166

he wrapped his arms around her and continued to cry against her stomach.

Stroking his hair, she held him. It took her a moment to realize he was uttering something, almost unintelligible. She strained to hear him, and when she at last did make out what he was saying, she began to cry as well.

He kept repeating "I'm so sorry."

"So am I, Dad. So am I."

Jason watched from the car as Stephanie and her father hugged each other and exchanged words. He felt it wouldn't be right to interrupt the reunion as it appeared to be an emotional one. He inhaled deeply, contented, figuring the moment would be, and it was.

When Stephanie told him the story of her childhood, he knew she misunderstood her father. Stephanie and her sister lost a mother they knew for a decade. He lost his wife, friend and the partner he knew for twice that time– at least. He knew many times children consider their parents as larger than life. As if the things which affect us, don't affect them. We expect them to act above everything. Sometimes, when we are disillusioned with the belief, it can be painful, as it was with Stephanie.

Somehow, she expected him to be unaffected by her mother's death, and yet, be sensitive to it with them, when in fact, he was devastated. Doubtless, he felt he had lost the one person who sincerely 'got' him, the one person who he had shared his life with for many years. Her father was only human, after all, and he couldn't be expected to continue with his life as if nothing happened.

Jason didn't excuse his actions, though. The man had two daughters who needed him. He should have done his best to deal with his grief and move on as best he could and take care of them. No. Jason didn't excuse it, but he understood it.

Stephanie was waving for him to get out of the car. Joining her and her dad, he could feel her father's eyes on him, weighing him. Jason met the man's stare and her father's features softened. He knew he had lost the right to judge any man Stephanie brought home a long time ago.

Jason stuck out his hand.

"It's splendid to meet you sir, I'm Jason."

"So, Stephanie tells me." Taking Jason's hand and shaking it firmly. "You can call me Jack. I haven't had anyone call me sir in a long time, and I've gotten used to being just Jack."

"All right, Jack. Well, I'm glad to meet you," Jason told him, smiling down at Stephanie.

"Likewise, though I didn't know there was a possibility I would meet you."

"Yeah, I apologize, Dad." Stephanie stepped in. "I should have called. But, I didn't know what to say. And, I don't know how to ask you this, so I'm just gonna ask." Stephanie was uncomfortable. "Can we stay here for a while?"

"Can I ask why?" Holding up his palms apologetically, he continued. "I'm not saying I don't want you to stay, or you can't. I'm just saying I haven't seen you in two years, my fault, but there it is. Two years and nothing, then you show up with some guy and ask to stay for a while." He eyeballed each of them in turn. "You had to know I would want to know why."

Stephanie stared at her dad for a long while before answering.

"Can we go inside? This is going to take a bit to explain."

Jack stared at them both for a long time when Stephanie finished her story. Stephanie's father was thoughtful before he broke the silence. "I wonder if you got this from your mother?"

Stephanie was taken aback at this possibility.

"Why would you think that?" Stephanie peered at her father quizzically.

"Well, I always found it odd your mother never got hurt. Perfect health and she always mended right quick." Shaking his head and chuckling softly as if something funny had occurred to him.

"I remember one time hearing her cry out from the kitchen. I ran in there as fast as I could, and your mother was standing over the sink with a towel wrapped around her finger. There was so much blood, the towel was soaked through and I had only been a moment reaching her." Clicking his tongue, he peered at them, winking one eye.

"I thought for sure she had cut the tip of her finger off. It had to be the only way there would be that much blood. Waving me off, said she just cut herself a little, nothing a Band-Aid and some time wouldn't cure."

"I remember insisting we go to the hospital and get some stitches," he continued. "It was the first time I ever remember your mother getting angry. Yelling at me for suggesting it and accusing me of thinking she was dainty flower who couldn't handle a little cut."

Shaking his head, again. "I was so surprised at her attitude, I stammered an apology and left her there."

"Thinking back on it now, I wonder if it was what she intended. To upset me so much I wouldn't question what I thought I had seen. I assumed I was wrong, though I had seen someone cut the tip of their finger off before and seen how much blood was lost. You can't compare it to a cut which doesn't require stitches." He was lost in thought for a while, remembering the past.

"She wore a bandage for a week or so and when she took it off there wasn't a scar."

Shaking his head, yet again. "Apart from that, there is nothing else similar. I'm sure I would have noticed any...umm...changes, if they occurred. It seems logical she also had this...err...thing you have as well. But for some reason yours is a ..." Again, he searched for the right words. "An advanced form, or whatever."

Stephanie nodded. It was nice to hear stories of her mom. She remembered her of course, the way she looked and special moments they had shared together or as a family, but there hadn't been many of those. Then she died. Afterwards, her father never spoke of her, until tonight. It was weird to hear her father speak of her mother now and show some emotion in remembering her. She wasn't sure she understood the transformation her father had gone through, but it was nice.

Perhaps once Caroline left, and he was all alone, he had time to think about what he was like these years, to sincerely face his demons and cast them out.

"Well, Dad, if we could stay here for a while, till we figure out exactly what is happening to me… us." She smiled sheepishly as Jason, who smiled back re-assuredly.

"We can stay out in the loft above the barn so we're out of your way," she finished, but Jack was shaking his head.

"Nonsense. No daughter of mine is going to sleep out in the barn like some kinda wayward drifter. You can stay in your old room, and Jason can stay in Caroline's room." He glared at Jason, whose smile slipped a little.

"Dad!" Stephanie exclaimed. "We are both adults; if we wish to stay in the same room, we can do so."

"Of course you can Stephanie, just not in my house." Raising a hand to forestall her comment. "I'm not naive enough to believe you haven't stayed in the same room, but please, respect an old man's sense of propriety."

Thinking to argue, she decided it wasn't worth it. Jason and she had spent the night together before, but not the way her dad undoubtedly thought. It wasn't too difficult for her to agree to the stipulation, though something still bothered her.

"The thing is, Dad, I don't know if I am going to change again, or when, and your life could be at risk."

He gave her a gaze meaning he understood the risks, but he still wanted her to stay in the house.

"Okay, Dad, okay." She dodged his chastisement. "We'll stay in the house and in separate rooms, but promise me this, any sign, any indication something bad is about to happen, you run from here as fast and as far as you can go. Okay?"

He seemed reluctant to agree but did.

"From what Jason has guessed, it seems logical there will not be another change until a full moon, but we are not certain. You will also be gone that night as well, Dad. No arguments. There is too much risk. I won't have me be the cause of your death."

"It's fine, I will stay at the inn in town. There are some people I have lost touch with for many years, I might wish to call on them as well."

They stared at each other across the table.

"It's good to have you back, Stephanie."

"You, too, Dad."

Four nights passed without incident. At long last, it was the night of the full moon. Jason and Stephanie sat on the grass by the small lake located on the property. The cool grass was a comforting blanket, lying softly beneath them. Her father had left hours ago, and they decided to move outside to minimize any damage done to property. Wearing loose fitting clothes, as Stephanie suggested after her experience with her last transformation, they sat and watched the sky. The full moon was slowly climbing up into the sky on a relatively cloudless night, its luminesce bathing the night in a surreal glow.

Despite the bright shine of the moon, several stars were visible the further away you gazed from the moon, slowly fading into nothingness if your vision strayed too close to the moon. There was a bite to the air, Stephanie was bundled up and pressed against Jason whose arm was wrapped around her shoulder, comforting and giving warmth. Crickets and frogs sang a surprisingly calming, but divergent melody. The lake's surface was flat and still, broken only by an occasional fish trying to nab a low flying insect or a surfacing minnow in its hopes to escape being eaten.

To Stephanie, these sounds were all calming, and she felt sleepy. There was an initial scare when the moon first crested the horizon. They clung to each other expecting to go under their metamorphosis right then. Nothing happened. They waited till the moon cleared the horizon to begin its journey across the sky, a slow march almost imperceptible in its movement. Again, nothing happened. They realized it either wasn't going to happen, or it would happen when the moon reached its zenith, around midnight. It was a waiting game. They talked of many things, mundane things, as if not wanting to discuss the most serious matter for fear it might trigger the shift.

Feeling obligated after she had divulged hers, Jason told her of his childhood. It was a stark contrast from hers. He was the third child of four — three boys and one girl. His sister, Telly, was a year and half older than him, and always been protective. First from their older brother, Jim, who loved to try and torture his younger siblings. Later, it was from the older boys at school who picked on him. His sister had meant well, but her standing up for him to the older boys only made his abuse much harder.

He never told her because she always was so happy to stop them, and he managed well enough with the harassment. His mother and father were successful lawyers with his mother a senior partner at a law firm. His father was a civil trial lawyer. When they started their family, his father decided to do contract writing so he could stay at home and raise the kids.

His father was a caring and patient man who routinely used logic and reasoning to teach his kids how to do the right things. Never raising his voice or punishing them overmuch, he simply explained what they did wrong, asked them questions to get them to think through why it was wrong. After, the children seldom did the same thing wrong twice — unless they wanted to cause trouble, just to cause trouble. When they did, he laughed it off and made light of it, and so it never was worth it.

His mother was wonderful, except she worked too much, often getting home at seven or eight at night, an hour or two before they went to bed. She didn't get to spend as much time with them. The time she did spend was terrific.

When Jason realized Stephanie appeared to be upset, he stopped talking.

"Oh, I'm sorry, Stephanie. I shouldn't be going on and on about my happy childhood. I know yours wasn't always the best, by far. I don't want you to think I'm trying to rub it in or anything."

"It's okay," she said. "I'm not upset at you telling me about your life. I'm upset because of what I did to you. You may have difficulties with your family from now on."

"Nonsense. Why would I have difficulty with my family?"

"Jason, sometimes you are such a dope," she chastised him. "You turn into a monster, and you may or may not be able to control it. Plus, you have no idea when it might happen. What are you going to do? Drop by for a visit, and maul your family?"

He had the good sense to blush.

"You're right," he told her. "I keep forgetting all of this. Perhaps, because, as of yet, it hasn't happened to me."

"Well, you will know after tonight," she reminded him.

"Possibly." Jason glanced out over the pond.

She could do nothing but nod. Here they were sitting together, waiting for the impossible to happen. Not impossible it would happen tonight, just the impossibility of the whole idea. What happened to her, and what may happen to them tonight was, well, impossible.

Hours passed in silence, and despite her feeble attempts at staying awake, Stephanie fell asleep against Jason. Unsure of what woke her, she awoke, bleary-eyed as she glanced about her. Jason had also fallen asleep and had slid away, lying angled off from her. Slowly, she stood and brushed her hands down the sides of her legs to brush away any dirt or grass which may have hitched a ride. Again, she glanced about. It was quite bright given the moon's fullness, she was able to see as if it was day.

Crickets sang softly off to her right, they were the only sound audible around her. She forgot how quiet farmlands can be in the dead of night. No car noises, no sounds of people

174

partying or conversing loudly over their cellphones, as if it wasn't the middle of the night and people were sleeping.

Suddenly, she remembered why they were out there and gazed up at the location of the moon. It hung ominously overhead, as if waiting for the cue to drop right on top of her. It had to be close to midnight and she fished into her pocket for her cellphone. Turning it on, it read 11:59. It changed to midnight as she watched.

Jason cried out. She whirled around. Turned from her, his back was arched in pain, hands clenched so strongly they stood out bright white in the moon's glow. She only had seconds to take this in before the moon finally made its plummet to the earth to land on top of her. Crumpling into a heap, she collapsed as pain wracked her entire body. Whimpering softly, she clenched her teeth. Vaguely, she remembered what happened the last time, when she had lost consciousness. This time she avowed she would remain conscious. She needed to, because Jason needed her.

Snapping bones, he cried out as the transformation began. Needing to help him, she cleared her mind. Pushing the pain back, she managed to stand. Focusing hard on not transforming, to stay as she was. Focus was a goal she raced hard for but seemed forever further away.

Picturing herself as she was, she focused on the image as a life vest to keep from sinking into the pain. It was then she felt something lock within her brain and the pain ceased instantaneously. No longer was she transforming. It was amazing. She had stopped the change from happening. She only had a moment to marvel at this fact before she saw the thing which had been Jason rise before her.

Though she never considered foxes as intimidating, an over seven-foot-tall, muscular one with gleaming sharp teeth behind peeled back lips was a little disconcerting. A low growl emanated from the thing and Stephanie reminded herself it was Jason, and not some monster. Hopefully, he would remember as well. The thing took a step toward her.

175

"Jason? Can you hear me? It's Stephanie. Please, Jason, listen to me."

The thing which was Jason slowed his approach and cocked his head in a canine like way.

"That's right, Jason. It's me. It's going to be alright. I think I know how to get you back."

Watching, she saw him begin to examine himself. Holding up his muscular arm in front of him, long claws extended from the tips of his fingers. Squeezing his fist closed, he flexed his forearm, making his muscles bulge beneath the rusty red colored hair. Black eyes returned their gaze to her. They were deep and piercing. Taking a step back, despite herself, he was an imposing vision. The thing stared at her for a moment, nodded its head, which she took as Jason understanding her.

"Picture yourself as you appear in human form. Picture it in your mind and focus."

The thing continued to stare at her for a moment, and she thought it got a faraway look in its eyes. Moments later she heard the first snap of bone and the creature snarled. The transformation went rapidly this time. It was over in seconds and Jason stood before her once again, his baggy clothing a little worse for wear.

Glancing down at his hands first, he gawked back up at her in astonishment.

"How did you know how to do that?"

"I somehow figured it out. When you started to change, I felt so compelled to help you. I needed something to focus on, to ignore the pain so I wouldn't lose consciousness like last time. So, I formed a picture of myself as I normally am and focused on the image to block out the pain. As soon as I did, I felt something... I don't know how to explain it."

"Lock?"

Stephanie regarded Jason and smiled.

"Yeah. Lock. You felt it too?" He nodded. "When that happened, I ceased changing. I guessed if it could stop me from changing, perhaps it could also change you back." She shrugged. "It worked." Smiling again at him, he smiled back.

"This is amazing Stephanie. It was amazing. I mean, it hurt like hell, but after the transformation — I have never felt so alive!"

"I know the feeling, Jason. It was how I felt, too."

"I want to change, again. I could sense things better. The colors were brighter, the sounds louder, and more distinct. I could smell things!"

Jason couldn't control his excitement. Feeling less enthused by the idea, she felt more alive in that form, but at what cost?

"I wonder," Jason interrupted her thoughts. "I wonder if what we did to stay or change into human form would work in the opposite?"

"What? You mean like form an image of what we appear like in the other form?"

"Exactly!" Jason said, his eyes wide and a huge smile on his face.

"Well, we could try, I guess. Not sure I want to go through the pain again."

"There was something I noticed about the pain," Jason told her. "It lessened after I pictured the image of myself. So perhaps, the change will be less painful when we do it this way? And quicker?"

Stephanie shrugged.

"Okay, I'll try first," Jason volunteered.

"I don't know, Jason. It doesn't seem like a safe idea."

Cocking his head, he gave her a small smile.

"Look. We were searching for a way to control this, right? If forming an image of ourselves in one form or the other works, isn't it what we wanted?"

Not waiting for her response, he stepped back from her and closed his eyes. She waited, because there was nothing else for her to do. She didn't have to wait long. Almost instantly Jason gasped as pain wracked his body. Bones began to break. But, not like before. They broke systematically before, as if dealing with one part of the body at a time. This time they broke all at once, yet less audible, a muffled cracking. Red fur sprung from out of the pores in his skin to coat him almost instantly and wholly. It was painful to watch, especially when his face changed. It was as if someone shattered his skull and put it back together in an instant, only this time in a more canine shape.

The change was over in seconds. It was obvious what Jason had surmised was correct. The change was definitely quicker. She wondered if it was less painful. It sure as hell didn't seem like it.

In his new form, he towered over her. Again, he marveled at his new form, his gaze roaming his newly shaped body. After a moment, he turned to her.

"Did it hurt less?" she questioned him.

"Yes." Jason answered her, but it didn't sound like Jason. It was his voice, but deeper, rougher. It would take some getting used to.

"You try now."

Stephanie wasn't sure she wanted to, was more interested in being able to stay in her human form. Not wanting to become the monster. Afraid she would lose herself.

The problem was there being no way of telling if she would be able to control the change next time. It worked this time, but what about the next? She couldn't risk not being able to control it, for fear of hurting someone. Or worse, making them like her. The best way to deal with this is to learn control through practice. *Oh, what the hell*, she thought and pictured the image of herself in the fox form.

Suddenly, the agony lanced through her entire body. Bones snapped and elongated or shortened as necessary, she could feel her skin breakdown in some areas and form up in others. Her entire skin tingled as red fur erupted from her pores. As swiftly as the pain came, it was gone, leaving an emptiness in its wake. She stood taller and firmer, she was instantly aware of the sounds and smells around her. The way the breeze brushed against and rippled her fur. She could smell Jason. She felt…Invigorated! Scanning the area, she was amazed at how crisp and clear her vision was. With the full moon, she could see well at night, but this was different. Like full daylight. It was amazing, but it scared her as well. She liked this too much. It was too strong, too amazing.

About to change back, Jason interrupted her thoughts.

"Hey. Race you back to the house?"

"Wait… What?" she asked, but he had turned and took off running. His speed was amazing.

Thinking for a moment, she took off after him.

They ran fast and wild. It was as if there were no obstacles in their way. Slowing, Jason allowed her to catch up. They traveled in a roughly straight line, jumping logs and bales of hay. As they neared the house, they traveled at an amazing speed.

As they approached the fence, Jason pulled ahead, his longer legs eating up the ground before him. The fence was only four feet tall, and was something she couldn't jump normally, even with a running start. Jason took it at full speed and leaped a decent four feet or more over it. So startled by the leap, she almost forgot to jump herself. Bunching her legs, she leapt when she was nearly on top of the fence, clearing it easily. Hitting the ground running, she took off after Jason.

Slowing a little to let her close some of the distance between them, he was still around the side of the house before her. There was a loud booming noise and a flash of light.

179

Rounding the corner, she watched as Jason's body hit the ground. Fleetingly, she scanned the area. With his shotgun, smoke tendrils sliding out of the barrel, twin ghosts escaping their haunts, her father stood on the porch. Eyes wide, he hurriedly pumped the gun and shakily leveled it at her.

"Stephanie? If it's you, and you understand me, please say something."

"You shot Jason, Dad!" Her voice sounded strange to her and by the expression on her father's face, it sounded strange to him, but something about it was familiar enough, he lowered the gun.

"I'm sorry. I heard something running hard in the fields coming this way. After all the warnings you gave me about how dangerous you might be, I thought it best to prepare myself in case what you said was true. The last thing I wanted was to have you come upon me in my sleep."

Hardly listening, she moved over to Jason, picturing herself as a human in her mind. Absently, she felt herself go through the change. She felt next to nothing.

"Good god." She heard her father utter.

Jason was covered in blood, holes perforated his loose t-shirt, his chest fur matted and sticky.

"Jason? Jason?" She bent low over him.

Laying there, unmoving, his eyes finally fluttered opened.

"Ow. That fucking hurt."

Jason moved to get up.

"Oh, no, you lay back down. You had buckshot blown into your chest. It's amazing you're still alive, Jason." It was. Very amazing. Considering how much blood there was.

"It is amazing, isn't it?" Again, trying to stand.

She pushed him down, but he used it to his advantage and pulled himself up on her.

As he stood she heard a couple of thuds hit the ground. Jason must have heard them, too, because he bent down to pick whatever they were off the ground. Several more thuds accompanied him as he leaned over. Watching, she saw him pick several things off the ground. Holding his hand out to her, she opened her hand to catch what he was dropping into them.

Three heavy objects drop into her palm. She examined them. They were small pieces of metal, almost like mangled lead balls. Glancing up at Jason, she noticed he was in the middle of changing back to his human form. The end of his transformation was punctuated by the sound of dozens more buckshot striking the ground.

"Good god," her father muttered, again.

Glancing up at her father. "Sorry for scaring you, sir." Jason apologized.

"Sorry for sca…," her father sputtered, mortified. "You're apologizing to me? I'm the one who shot you!"

"Well, that is true," Jason began, "but you wouldn't have done so if I hadn't come around the corner so fast and looking the way I did." Jason barked a laugh. "I would have shot me, too."

Her father appeared like he was going to pass out, his face pale, almost white in the moon's radiance.

Jaws clenched and her hands on her hips, Stephanie lashed out at her father. "What are you doing here, Dad? You were supposed to be gone, remember?"

Her father lowered his head.

"I'm sorry Stephanie. It's just, I thought you might need me. Also, I didn't know if when you guys changed if you would be able to change back." He gave a sheepish grin. "There are some decent people around here I didn't want to see get hurt."

Staring hard at her father for a moment longer, her countenance softened. He did the right thing she decided. Stupid. But right.

"Why don't we go in and sit," she suggested.

Glancing at Stephanie and giving a curt nod, he turned and made his way inside.

Stephanie stared at Jason. It seemed impossible he was standing there as if nothing had happened, though he had, a minute ago, been blasted off his feet by a shotgun.

He smiled at her. "I'm all right, Stephanie. Trust me."

Frowning at him, she was not sure if she believed him, but could see no evidence to the contrary.

Continuing to smile at her, he moved to take her hand. Taking his, they went inside.

They each gave their account of the night's events to her dad and answered his questions as best as they could. They changed forms several times to let him watch. Stephanie was exhausted. It had been a long day, and a long evening with some stressful events. She had a great deal to think about.

They discussed returning to school. At first Jason was all for it, but she convinced him they should wait it out for a bit. Just to make sure they had control over this thing. Capitulating, he agreed she had a point. Quite honestly, she was scared. This thing scared her. It also excited her at the same time.

Several hours later in the wee hours of the morning, Jason and Stephanie finally retired.

They spent a few months at her father's place learning what they could of their new forms and helping her father resurrect the farm. They found after a few more changes, the transformation became almost instantaneous, and nearly painless. Though, there is only so much pain you can ignore of your body being dismantled, stretched, and fused back to a new body.

There were many things they learned. Their senses were more acute than before. Their sense of smell and eyesight were especially keen. The ability to see almost perfectly at night was amazing, as well as their increase in strength and speed. In time, Stephanie became comfortable with the changes happening with her and suggested to Jason they return to school.

Although both had contacted the school and requested a medical leave of absence, the schoolwork must have been piling up, so Jason readily agreed. They said their goodbyes to her father and headed back to school.

Leaving was tough. During the last month, her father and she were able to heal much of the damage caused during her childhood. They were starting a new relationship which promised to be special. As their relationship healed, it brought new life back to her father. Every day, with their help, he worked tirelessly on the house, exacting repairs and much needed maintenance. Returning to the fields, he planted new crops of corn. When she left, they shared a long and warm hug. She knew he would be okay. When Jason and she backed out of the driveway, she could see tears running down his cheek. She knew she would be okay, too.

Chapter 6

Returning to school was easier than she had expected. Beth was ecstatic she was back and wanted to know all about what happened. She asked Stephanie to change for her, because she had never gotten a chance to see it. It was a little awkward to be asked to do it, like she was some kind of circus freak or something. But, she knew Beth wasn't like that, so she changed for her. She was a little worried Beth might be a little weirded out by the whole thing, but she took it stoically.

Everything was going well at school and with Jason, as well. It was a nice thing she liked him so much, because she could sense him wherever he was. Everything was going as well as could be expected, and for a while it was like the transformation thing was only a dream.

Sitting next to each other at the kitchen table in the apartment she shared with Beth, they worked tirelessly on their homework. Months had passed since Stephanie's initial shift. Life had returned to relative normalcy of classes and schoolwork.

It had been a long night and their eyes drooped and their thoughts grew sluggish, but they were trying desperately to finish up the last of the schoolwork they needed to get done for tomorrow's classes. Stephanie stared blankly at the calculus problems, trying hard to convince it to solve itself, but to no avail. Math was hard enough when rested.

Pressing pencil to paper to try for another go at it, she felt her mind lurch. It was as if someone had grabbed her whole body and yanked in one direction. It was a clumsy grab, heavy handed. The strong pull lessened, and she felt her muscles ease, though she didn't remember clenching them. There was still a pull, but less than before. Staring off in the direction it came from– north, maybe northwest, out of the corner of her eye she caught Jason also staring in the same direction.

"Did you feel it, too?"

Turning his head, he gazed at her, his body still facing the pull, and nodded.

"What do you think it is?" The question was left unanswered. Though they both knew they needed to find out.

Hank and Simon sat around the fire outside their cabin, cooking up a deer they hunted down earlier. They ate half of it while in bear form but saved the rest for the evening's meal which they chose to cook over the fire. While hunting and feeding in their bear form was exciting and freeing, they both realized the risk of getting carried away in the power of their Lycan body. Though they could hunt and feast in bear form, they chose to do so only occasionally, relying on more mundane methods most days.

They appeared different than they had only a few months ago. Hank let his beard grow out and it was now full and scraggly. His hair was longer as well, now reaching his shoulders. Sim had filled out as well. It appears, along with the extra strength, came the muscle shape as well. Facial hair had started to grow on his face, but it only came in at the lower jaw line and the upper cheek, leaving the middle somewhat sparse.

These past few months had been wonderful for both Sim and him. With the situation they were in together, they couldn't help but grow closer. They shared something like no other two could share. They could always sense the other's presence, an unspoken acknowledgement of the other's importance.

They sat in silence around the fire, neither needing to speak. A weird tingling crawled up Hank's neck. It was like someone dragging a string up his neck. The string dragged from the back of his skull and out the front. It dragged his head around to face south-west. It unraveled inside his brain as it traveled south, to reach its destination and grow taut. He could feel a slight pull on him in that direction. Sim, he noticed out of the corner of his eye was standing, staring off in the same direction.

He wasn't sure what it meant. But, he knew it must have something to do with them being lycanthropes. As strange as it seemed, he could sense no hostility from the feeling. If anything, it brought a sense of peace to him.

"Sim?"

"Yeah, Dad?"

"It's time to go." Standing, Hank walked to the house.

"Right behind you, Dad."

Chapter 7

Sylvanis knelt in the garden behind her latest home. It had been a tumultuous time these last eight month. Harder for her parents, she knew. The moving, searching for new jobs, and the separation from their families, all to raise her. And yet, they had no idea as to whom they were raising.

In many ways, she didn't know who she was — a child of this world and this time or a woman of the past? Her memories, though spotty at times, were of someone from a time long ago and far away. Now she understood why she was here, alive now which was what mattered. Her power was returning to her, a dribble at times, a rush, overwhelming her, at others. There was an urgency to it which frightened her. She learned long ago to trust her power, and when it was urgent, something important was coming. She only hoped she lived long enough to find out what it was.

She had gambled, and her life was the wager. But, the bones were cast; it was only a short while till they revealed their roll.

Her parents, if she could still call them that, had left. They had suffered profoundly for what her essence had been forced to do. They essentially lost their child upon her arrival, though she promised herself she would endeavor to be a daughter to them. She smiled. *You shouldn't promise things you don't know if you can accomplish,* she chided herself. After all, she might not live through the night.

Shaking off her doubt, for it was the doubt of the child she was. Regardless of the age of her memories, she was still, in some ways, a baby. Sylvanis hoped her gamble paid off, because there was much to do.

There was a shuffle off to her left, a presence on the wind confirming she was no longer alone in the garden.

"You are slipping, Sylvanis." Kestrel's voice was still shocking to her, for when she drove the knife into the woman's heart, she thought for sure it was the last time she would hear it. Rising, she turned to face the woman.

"Have you lost the old ways?" Kestrel's eyebrow arched. "You neglected to hide your presence from me... I could sense you from the other side of the world."

Kestrel moved into the light from the porch. Sylvanis gazed at her. Kestrel, of course, was unchanged. Tall, regal, and beautiful. Yet, cold and hard, like the alabaster her skin resembled. Black hair flanked her face and flowed down over her shoulders. She wore a dark green robe of what Sylvanis believed to be silk, given its reflective quality. It was hitched in the front with a belt, looped over twice, enough to keep it snug to show off her curvaceous body.

Never one to be jealous of Kestrel's beauty or shape, she felt a little envy rise inside her now when she considered her own shapeless body. Pushing down those thoughts, they were the child's in her head, not her own. This was going to be difficult if these thoughts continued to push their way forward.

"Good evening, Kestrel. I see your spell worked well. Although vile in nature, it was a creative way to escape your punishment."

Anger flashed briefly across Kestrel's face but fled promptly as she smiled.

"Your counter spell was equally creative, Sylvanis. To be honest, when I woke, I was quite astonished you had the nerve to conceive of such a response. I see your essence has made its mark upon the body of the one you confiscated." Her lip curled in a sneer. "Yet, you still have not answered my initial question. Have you lost the old ways? By not hiding your presence, you must have known I would find you?"

"I wanted you to find me."

Kestrel, who had been moving closer, stopped, wary.

"What do you mean? You wanted me to find you?"

Sylvanis took in a deep breath and released it slowly before answering.

"I was hoping you would join me."

Kestrel barked a laugh. "Join you? Join you for what? Tea?"

"Join me in the work we began long ago, sister."

"Don't call me that!" Kestrel snarled at her. "You turned your back from the right path long ago, Sylvanis. When that happened, you ceased to be my sister. You were unable to do what needed to be done. You failed to do your duty as a Druidess."

Sylvanis could do nothing but shake her head.

"It was you who turned from the right path. It is not our place to decide the direction any one animal species should go. Our duty, our calling, is in teaching, and healing. Our job is to teach mankind how to live with nature, not to force them."

Kestrel moved forward again, stepping within an arm's length of Sylvanis.

"You are wrong. They are destroying this Earth. Haven't you sensed its pain? It cries out in suffering, suffering caused by mankind and its unrestrained desire to expand at any cost. If you had let me do what needed to be done centuries ago, our Earth would be joyous!"

Sylvanis shook her head as Kestrel spoke. "Oh, Kestrel, you hear what you want from the Earth. Don't you understand? It is always in pain. It is not done growing, yet. It's like a child going through growth spurts, and it can be painful. You would understand if you *listened* to the Earth, not just heard it.

"There is still time to correct your course, Kestrel. Work with me. Help me guide this age in how to live *with* nature. They have made vast strides from where they were a few short decades ago. Together, we can teach and heal as we were meant to." Even as Sylvanis finished, she knew Kestrel's answer. She would never change. She would continue to fight and attempt to control mankind, to ensure it would not damage Earth anymore. For those she couldn't control, she would destroy.

"Enough of this pointless conversation, Sylvanis. Your arrogance in believing I need you for anything is humorous." Turning from Sylvanis. "I might have one day said this was going to pain me. That I would grieve after you were dead, but since you stabbed me in the heart, I feel less remorseful about it."

There was a loud thud from near the fence behind her. Turning, she couldn't believe her eyes.

"Syndor?" Impossibly, the man she would have assumed dead centuries ago, stood before her. "Did you also cast that vile spell as well?"

A slight smile crept up on Syndor's mouth.

"It's Samuel now. I wondered how your spell would play out." He examined her. "The same, yet different, fascinating." He shifted, cobra form, neck flaring.

Sylvanis had gambled poorly it seemed. By allowing her presence to be felt by others, she knew it would allow Kestrel to find her. If Kestrel had come alone she could at least hold off any attacks, if not defeat her. Figuring Kestrel knew this as well, she would wait till she could round up some of her minions. Hopefully giving her time for hers to arrive. She never believed for a moment Syndor would have found a way to survive. He must have been waiting for Kestrel's spell to activate, and then it was a matter of showing up at the Calendar.

She didn't think she could take them both. She was sure she couldn't. She needed to act, and act now.

190

"*Coirt*," she whispered, and her skin transformed into a rough, thick bark. Syndor started toward her.

"*Talamh titim.*" The ground beneath Syndor's feet drop away as she uttered her spell. He fell, his momentum slamming him into the far wall of the pit she opened beneath him. Turning towards Kestrel, who surprisingly hadn't made a move, made her hesitate.

"My Lady, what do you wish me to do with these two?" A voice called out from behind her, near the house. A sense of dread creeped into Sylvanis as she saw the wicked smile twist upon Kestrel's mouth.

Sylvanis turned towards the voice.

Standing near the house was a Werecroc. Not Answi, he at least, had died at Calin's hands a long time ago. Clearly a descendent though, whose lycanthropy had been passed on to him by his bloodline.

She was doomed. Foolishly, she had believed, she might be able to defeat Syndor and Kestrel. It wasn't the addition of this new Were which doomed her, though. It was what, or rather, who, he held. Hanging limp from each of his upraised arms were her parents, trussed up and gagged, which was the only way she could tell they were still alive. She closed her eyes.

"Did you think I wouldn't cover all my options, Sylvanis? I am not going to make a mistake like you did when you killed me. No. You will surrender yourself to me, and I will take your life. Your fight is at an end, or I will have Gordon over there kill your parents. He is fond of human flesh it seems. It happens sometimes among the Weres. Once they taste it, they want more and more of it. I'm sure your parents will make a nice meal for him, unless you give up now."

Sylvanis was trapped. If she gave up, Kestrel would indeed kill her, and she held no doubts about the real fate of her parents, regardless of what Kestrel claimed. Unless...

Straightening, she turned back towards Kestrel. "Your oath?"

"My oath on what?"

"You will allow my parents to go, and you or your minions will never harm them if I surrender."

The expression on Kestrel's face confirmed her fears of Kestrel's intent. Kestrel smoothed her face, and nodded, reluctantly.

"You have my oath; they will not be harmed."

A low growl came from behind her and Kestrel turned to the Were with a glare, whose growling swiftly subsided.

"There. It is done." Kestrel pulled a dagger from a sheath resting in the small of her back.

Sighing, Sylvanis stepped forward to approach Kestrel when she heard two thumps and a loud grunt from behind her. Kestrel's eyes widened and Sylvanis knew something happened. Kestrel lunged at her desperately with the dagger. Diving to her left, she felt the dagger score off her barked skin harmlessly.

Rolling, Sylvanis sprang to her feet to take in the scene. She couldn't help but feel a little bit of joy at what she was seeing. Her gamble may have paid off after all.

The Werecroc was on his knees in the grass, his hands pressing against either side of his back, pain was evident in his eyes. On either side of him, a short distance away, setting her parents down in the grass were two Werefoxes, a male and a female. They straightened almost synchronously, and faced off against Kestrel who, when she lunged at Sylvanis, made her stumble closer to the scene.

"I'm not all too sure what the hell is going on here," the female fox said. "But I'm going to suggest you and your crocodile friend here leave."

When Kestrel re-acted, Sylvanis was waiting. She knew her too well.

"*Tine!*" Kestrel shouted, pointing at the bodies of her parents.

"*Uisce!*" Sylvanis' hands shot out, fingers spread. Just as fire erupted from the ground around her parents, water doused them, putting the fires out.

"That was a mistake, lady," the male fox stated, and both foxes started towards Kestrel.

They were closing the gap when Syndor, totally forgotten, leapt out of the pit where he had been waiting patiently, landing between Kestrel and the two foxes. His tail swung out and wrapped around the ankle of the female fox, pulling her from her feet.

A loud growl escaped from the male fox as he charged Syndor whose neck flared. Syndor spat at him. Syndor was an old blood True, he had fought other Weres before, and was skillful at it. The spit hit the fox square in the eyes, blinding him and bringing him to a stop, trying to wipe the stinging spit from his vision. A tail slap from the Werecroc, who had regained his feet and entered the fray, sent him flying. The male fox slammed through the fence on the far side of the yard, tossing wood everywhere.

Meanwhile the female fox pounced to her feet and avoided a tail attack from Syndor, deftly moving behind him, leaping onto his back, her teeth burying into the back of Syndor's neck. Thrashing about, trying to throw her. Sylvanis watched as the Werecroc moved towards the fence to finish off the male fox.

"*Balla Cloiche*" palms out, Sylvanis called upon the power of earth, as dirt and stone erupted from the ground before the hole in the fence, creating a barrier to slow the Croc.

Sylvanis narrowly got out of the way as Kestrel launched another attack upon her. A snake like column of stone slammed into the spot where she had stood. She watched as Kestrel lifted her hands and the column rose back into the air, like a giant stone snake, to swing sideways toward her. She wasn't quick enough this time; the column slammed into her. Barked skin was the only reason her ribcage didn't break when it hit her. The stone snake carried her a short distance through the air. The column stopped. She didn't. Airborne for a little bit more, she hit the ground, hard, tumbling to a stop.

Stephanie held on as long as she could, but the Snake was skilled. He managed to throw her, but not before she tore a sizeable chunk out of his neck, which oozed blood into her mouth. Spitting it out onto the ground, she knelt on one knee, one hand pressed to the ground and the other pressed against her elevated knee, searching for another opening. The Snake faced her, a small distance away.

She hoped Jason was okay. That tail had given him one hell of a hit. Glancing in the direction he had flown, the Croc, who was momentarily thwarted by a dirt and rock wall, moved to the side of the wall and was beginning to rip the fence apart to reach Jason.

Out of the corner of her eye she saw the blonde girl get slammed by some sort of flying stone column, sending her airborne. This was not going well. Returning her attention to the Snake, she saw what seemed like a smile creep up on his face, as if he was aware of what transpired behind him, and knew it was only a matter of time before this fight was his.

The problem was, Stephanie was afraid he was right. She had never been a fighter. This was not something she was prepared for. Of course, she had increased strength and speed, but evidently so did the Snake, so her advantage was negated by his equality to her in attributes. Worse, he knew what he was doing, which meant he was going to kick her ass.

Who was she kidding, this wasn't a playground fight, this thing wasn't going to beat her up and leave. He was going to beat her up and kill her. Wishing Jason was here, probably the two of them could take him, but she had a feeling when the Croc got to him, Jason wasn't going to last long, either.

The column of stone curled upwards almost straight into the air behind the Snake. It was then she saw the black-haired woman, her arms held upwards, facing the column. It occurred to Stephanie the woman was in control of the stones. Maybe she couldn't take the Snake, but she sure as hell could take that bitch.

Charging the Snake, she used her new-found speed to get to him as swiftly as possible. The moment she saw him brace for her attack, she increased her speed and dodged around him, heading straight at the black-haired woman.

Glancing to her right, she saw the column hanging over the blonde-haired woman, who was slowly lifting herself off the ground, shaking her head, as if trying to clear her thoughts. It was clear she wasn't aware of the impending threat, literally looming over her. If Stephanie could reach the woman in time, she might be able to stop the attack from happening.

Stephanie was a few feet from the black-haired woman. Launching herself into the air to tackle her, she felt a scaly tail wrap around her midsection and slam her into the ground – just out of reach of the woman. The woman gazed down at her and smiled. Stephanie could only watch as the woman's arms swept downward. The column descended.

Consciousness returned with the sound of nearby wood being torn asunder. Jason, his vision blurry, climbed to his feet. He could feel his body knitting his broken bones… an unusual feeling. Glancing down at a throbbing pain at his side, a piece of wood jutted from his abdomen. Its splintered end was soaked in his blood. Grunting, he reached around at the end puncturing his back and pulled. It eased out of his body with a sickening sucking sound.

Jason knew he only had a few moments to gather his wits. Glancing towards the sounds which had awakened him, he saw the Croc pulling out the last plank of wood preventing his passage through the fence. Curiously, Jason noticed the dirt and stone wall blocking where he knew he had broken through. Promptly dismissing it as irrelevant to his survival, he turned to the now emerging Croc.

Everything happened so quick back at the house when he and Stephanie arrived, he never got a decent view at the thing. He did now. It towered over him by a foot and a half, possibly two. Where Jason's body was muscularly defined, this thing was bulging with muscles, corded, under scaly skin. Jason was dead meat, and he knew it. So did the Croc.

"I've never had fox meat," it growled. "But, I bet it's tasty."

"I hope you choke!" Jason shouted at him in defiance, and moved in to attack. Launching several punches on the softer underbelly of the Croc, it grunted with each hit, then chuckled at Jason.

Two massive clawed hands slammed into either side of his head, causing him to black out momentarily. He was lifted into the air by his head. The croc turned and slammed him into the stone wall, not letting go. Jason clawed at the Croc's arms holding him, gouging them severely, but the thing wouldn't drop him.

"When I take my first bite out of you... Scream... Please?" The cruel light in the Croc's eyes and the prospect of being eaten alive frightened him more than anything he had ever encountered in his life.

The Croc lifted him higher and Jason watched in horror as the thing turned its head, its maw opening to rip into his midsection.

The right hook which hit the side of the Croc's head was so forceful, Jason could hear the Croc's jaw break, and its head snapped back by the force of the blow. The Croc stumbled back, releasing Jason. Landing on weak legs, the reality of how close he came to dying, sank in.

Jason turned towards his savior. A large Werebear stood before him, rubbing his sizeable paw with the other one to rub out the pain from the impact with the Croc's jaw. The bear eyed him up and down.

"I'm not sure whose side I should be on, but that thing appears a hell of a lot meaner than you." The bear watched him warily.

"Thanks, I'm Jason, and yeah, if you want my opinion, he is one evil son of a bitch."

"Simon. And you're welcome." Simon turned, the Croc who was watching both, warily, resetting its jaw with a popping sound.

"Now," he began moving toward the Croc. "Let's take care of this thing."

The column descended and there was nothing Sylvanis could do about it. She had lost this time. Kestrel would declare war on civilization and there would be nobody with the knowledge and the ability to stop her. Curling herself into a ball, she waited for the column to crush her. Suddenly, something bulky loomed over and covered her. A hairy form enveloped, shielding her. She could still feel the impact of the column as it slammed into the guardian's body above her with a grunt. After a moment, she opened her eyes and she peered at the face of a Werebear.

"You okay?" he asked in a low rumbling voice.

"Me? You are the one who got a ton of rocks dropped on him!"

"Yeah, and believe me, it hurt. I hope you are worth it." Before she had time to retort, he was off her.

Sylvanis rose to her feet. The column of stone lay upon the ground, shattered at the point where it had impacted upon the Werebear. Kestrel stood facing her with her arms at her sides, stunned disbelief evident on her face. The Werefox was lying on the ground almost at Kestrel's feet, Syndor's tail still wrapped around her waist. Both watched her, as well as the Bear. The whole scene seemed frozen in time, with no one making a move.

The silence was interrupted by a loud roar from the other side of the fence where the Fox and the Croc had gone. They all turned towards the sound as the Croc came diving through the hole he had created a short time earlier. He was followed shortly by another Bear and the Fox.

Everyone was brought up short as the newcomers took in the scene before them as well. It was obvious the odds had shifted. Sylvanis turned back towards Kestrel. The fury showed livid upon Kestrel's face. She glared at Sylvanis.

"This isn't over, Sylvanis. You may have won today, but when we meet again, you will die!" Her arms shot skyward, palms up. *"Brocamas Stoirm!"*

The ground erupted over the entire yard. Dirt shot skyward, filling the air with dust and debris, making vision negligible. Everyone fell into a fit of coughing as they inadvertently inhaled the dirt and dust. By the time Sylvanis got a breath in and cast her spell to send a strong gust of wind to blow the dirt away, she knew it was too late. Kestrel and her minions were gone, leaving Sylvanis alone with her new-found companions. Taking a moment to study them, they did the same, two foxes and two bears. It was a start. She wondered where the other two might be?

Sylvanis stared off in the distance. There were others missing from Kestrel's group as well. Hopefully, their line had ended a long time ago.

"These two are alive, but still unconscious." The female fox called from where Sylvanis' parents lay.

Sylvanis breathed a sigh of relief. The last thing she wanted was her parents to have come to harm. It was bad enough they had effectively lost their daughter.

"Please, take them inside. You have questions, yes? I have answers. Not all of them, but a start."

"*Mín Craiceann*," Sylvanis ended her bark skin spell, her body reverting to its original flesh. The two foxes picked up her parents and moved inside. The bears she noticed reverted to their human form.

One was a hulking man, over six feet, broad of shoulders and back, heavily muscular, genuinely a bear of a man, as well. Long dark brown hair framed a rough, chiseled face with a blunt nose and bushy eyebrows over soft blue eyes. He felt like a man she could trust implicitly. Next to him was a young man, tall, but not as tall as the man.

Their demeanor together suggested they were father and son, but the looks told a different story. Apart from the height, they had almost no resemblance. The man was all hard lines and where he wasn't exactly attractive, he was distinct. The boy was plain, with fleshy, almost plump cheeks, and thin lips. He had brown, wavy hair, where the man's was straight and without form. The boy was fit and well proportioned, but nothing like the man who was in remarkable shape from a long life of doing manual labor. Approaching them, she greeted the man first.

"I wanted to thank you. I do believe I would have perished if not for your actions."

"Well." He appeared uncomfortable with the praise. "If it had been the other one about to be smashed, I perhaps would've intervened for her. It was a lucky guess of the circumstances to see me save you."

He shuffled. "I could sense you to some extent but couldn't discern which one of you was drawing me."

Cocking her head, she considered. "Yes, of course. This close to Kestrel, and with both of us emitting power, I could see how it would have been confusing for you. Well," she smiled at him, "I'm glad you made the choice you did." Her smile included both.

"My name is Sylvanis. As I said, you must have questions and I will do all I can to answer them. However, I would suggest we move inside. It is likely the noise we made will draw snoops."

"The name's Hank. This is Sim, my son. And yes, we have a lot of questions."

Nodding, she beckoned them into the house.

When they entered, a man and a woman were descending the stairs. The woman drew Sylvanis' attention first, short, with a well formed feminine body. She was fair of skin, with delicate features. Short rusty brown hair encircled a round pixie like face, with soft thin lips and a small nose. Sylvanis could make out some freckles lightly touching her features. She was the obvious True in Sylvanis' estimation. The other would be her Pure, from the transfer of lycanthropy.

Next to her, walking down the stairs by her side was a man who was taller than her, but not as tall as many men. Average looking, with short cropped brown hair, and an oversized nose on an otherwise plain looking face. Average build, he carried a little paunch.

When they reached the bottom of the stairs they turned to see the three of them watching them descend.

"We put your parents in bed. They were still unconscious. I hope you don't mind?" The girl motioned absently up the stairs with one hand.

"No. Thank you. You have both been most kind. Please, sit, all of you." Indicating the available seating in the room they used to watch TV. A beige couch and love seat faced off against a flat screen TV. Hank and Sim took the couch and the others took the loveseat. Sitting close enough to leave no doubt they were in love.

Sylvanis turned to the two of them.

"My name is Sylvanis. I am a Druidess. I would know your names?"

The man eyed the woman with a silent question, which she answered by glancing to Sylvanis to answer her question.

"My name is Stephanie. This is Jason," she indicated the man next to her who nodded.

"I am Hank; this is my son, Simon. It is nice to meet you." Hank added from across the way.

"Hi, Simon," Jason piped up. "Once again, thanks for saving my ass out there."

"Hey, no problem, Jason." shrugging off the thanks. "I'm sure you could have gotten him yourself."

"Yeah," Jason replied, meeting Simon's eyes. Jason broke out laughing. He couldn't help it. They both knew the Croc would have devoured Jason if Simon hadn't showed up. But, he was trying to help Jason save some face in front of his girl. Jason was not one for false bravado, so he was okay with admitting he would have been done if not for Simon's intervention.

Staring at him for a moment, Simon started laughing as well. They shared a laugh as the others watched, some amusement in Stephanie's case and bewilderment in Hank's.

Their laughter subsided after a moment and Jason waved Sylvanis on.

"Sorry, please, continue," he told her.

Sylvanis snapped her jaw shut. The laughter had caught her off guard. It was a real pleasure, though. What they faced tonight was as close to dying as any of them had most likely ever been. The fact they felt comfortable enough with each other to release some of their stress openly was delightful. It boded well for an agreeable working relationship, which they were going to need. They were going to have to learn to trust each other and to work together. She had no doubt what Kestrel would do next. Though, if Syndor had been alive all this time, he must be aware what Kestrel would want to attempt would be difficult to execute in this age. A confrontation would occur, she knew, but she was certain it would be when Kestrel felt she was ready. Plus, now she knew Sylvanis was no longer alone, confrontation may be a long way off.

Sylvanis cleared her throat.

"As I said, my name is Sylvanis, I am a Druidess. The woman you helped drive off is known as Kestrel. She is also a Druidess. This is not the first time we have fought. The last time, however, was many centuries ago on the land you know now as England. I defeated her, or at least I thought I had.

"She had cast a vile spell triggered upon her death. It removed her essence from her body, not allowing it to move on, and put her body in a form of stasis to wait for her essence to return. That event would be triggered when the last stone of the Calendar, what you know as Stonehenge, fell. Some of you may remember about eight months ago, an earthquake, located near London, caused the last of the stones of the Calendar to fall." Glancing around for confirmation, they all nodded their heads. They remembered.

"When it occurred, her essence returned to her body. Another aspect of her spell would awaken within the descendants of the Trues, the ones who were loyal to her, the ability of lycanthropy." She gazed around at all the faces watching her. In Hank and Simon's face she saw some understanding of what she was referring too. They must have done some research into lycanthropy and understood a little

202

what she was referring. The other two appeared a little confused.

"Any questions so far?"

Jason raised his hand. "What does this have to do with us?"

"Well, Jason, and you don't need to raise your hand, we aren't in school." He dropped it in his lap, chagrined.

"When I realized what she did," she continued. "I cast a counter spell, one allowing my essence to be reborn when it was needed, the moment being when Kestrel returned to her body. I also made it contain the same provision, to awaken the descendants of the Trues who were loyal to me. Those descendants are you Hank, and you Stephanie.

"I am honestly sorry for the upheaval this must have caused you in your life. But I assure you, the need is great. Even now Kestrel will be attempting to reach the other Trues who were loyal to her, the boar and the rat. There is no way to know if their line continued, but those who are carriers of lycanthropy, whether they can change or not, are not easy to kill. So, we must assume they are out there, and she will find them." Hank wanted to interject something, and she indicated with a nod he could talk.

"You said the need was great. What need?"

She knew she was going to like Hank. Thoughtful and straight to the point. She liked that.

"Kestrel is a Druidess, like me. For those of you who don't know what a Druid is, it is a kind of priest of nature. We were in power around 200 B.C. We tasked ourselves with the preservation and conservation of the natural world. She was under the belief nature would never be safe if civilization was around. It was her personal quest to thwart civilization wherever possible.

"To do that, she felt she needed to subjugate mankind. To do this, she created the first Trues, which she used to pass lycanthropy on to others; many times, by force. She created an army of Were-beasts." Sylvanis recalled all of this as if through another's eyes. Though they were hers, they were also someone else's.

"I was left with no other choice but to create my own Trues."

"I'm sorry, I don't mean to interrupt," Simon said, "but you keep referring to Trues. I think I know what you mean, but could you clarify?"

"Of course, Simon, my apologies, sometimes you assume others understand your terminology, when there is no way for you to know." Sylvanis paused to clarify the explanation in her head before she went on.

"Trues is a term we used when we refer to the first eight who were given lycanthropy. Then there are the Pures. Those which were given lycanthropy directly from Trues. The rest are considered Weres, or those who got it from Pures. Got it?"

Glancing around, she was looking at a room of confused expressions.

"Okay. Think of it like this. Trues are like grandparents, Pures are like parents and Weres are like grandkids."

Again, she gazed around, this time though, she saw comprehension.

"When I created my Trues, I tasked them with creating an army with which to fight Kestrel's. I would not allow force to be used to recruit, which in some ways put us at a disadvantage. In other ways, it was a boon."

"Well, to make a long story short, we were able to defeat Kestrel's army, mainly by killing some of the Trues."

"How did that help?" A voice from the back of the room made Sylvanis and the others turn.

Standing at the back of the room were two individuals. The male was tall, lanky of form yet muscular with broad shoulders. Brown unruly hair covered his head and a face which was angular with a squared chin, rounded on the edges. The woman was a touch shorter, a fighter's body with slim but muscular arms, not a shred of fat existed on her body as far as

Sylvanis could tell. Short cropped tawny red hair stood upright topping a long attractive face. She gave the impression of feminine brutality– a strange contrast. It was the male who had spoken though and was waiting for her response. He appeared ignorant of the group occupying the room, some of them rising to their feet in anticipation of violence.

Sylvanis noticed the female was aware of the possible danger and had changed her stance to square her body off towards Hank, whom she must have assumed was the worse threat. Smart girl, Sylvanis thought.

If she wasn't missing her guess, this was Wolf and Tiger. Hands clenched tightly into fists, the Wolf stood erect and his eyes were cold rage.

"Once killed," Sylvanis offered up. "All Pures and Weres who are recipients of his or her lycanthropy, whether directly, or indirectly, lose their ability to shift and become non-weres."

Tension left the Wolf's body.

"I need your help. I need to kill the Boar, he infected my girlfriend."

The others relaxed audibly, and perhaps for the first time, the Wolf became aware of the others in the room.

"Ah, so the Boar has awoken." Sylvanis mused, not liking the idea that perhaps all of Kestrel's minions' scions were alive. At least all of hers were, it was a start.

"I will do what I can to help release your girlfriend from the Boar, though it will not be easy. Right now, Kestrel will be tracking him down, if she wasn't the one who sent him after you in the first place. It would be like her."

The man appeared confused. "Kestrel?"

Sylvanis closed her eyes and sighed. She had always been patient, but she found in this body things grew tiresome fast. Summarizing, she told him what she had told the others, though she didn't elaborate as before.

205

"That is what we are up against," she told him. "Kestrel will begin using her Trues to start gathering an army. Fortunately for us, but unfortunately for those who she comes across, the survivability rate is low when exposed to lycanthropy. Most perish when their bodies start to try and fight off what they believe is an infection, which ordinarily leads to heart failure."

It was Simon who spoke up at this point. "How is it, of the two of us here who were exposed, we lived?"

"One thing Kestrel never knew, and we never told her was the bond between the two involved in the transfer somehow seems to increase the rate of survival. Also, if the person is agreeable to becoming a lycanthrope, it also increases their likelihood of survival. Or, so we believed. It was how it worked out, anyhow." She shrugged, a slight gesture.

"So, you see? Your relationship to your father and Jason's relationship to Stephanie was what saved you."

Sylvanis stopped to consider something she hadn't thought of yet and gave voice to the troubling thought.

"Of course, this was before we had real doctors and defibrillators. I am not sure what will happen now that these things are in existence. It may be possible to ensure everyone who gets lycanthropy survives."

Sylvanis straightened her back. This was the part she dreaded from the first. She was not like Kestrel. Did not demand obedience. If these people were to help her defeat Kestrel, it would be on their terms, not hers.

"Now, here is the thing. I cannot make you help me. Nor would I want to. If you choose not to help me, I will bid you farewell, and you may go. I can tell you this, though. If Kestrel creates a strong enough army, there will not be many places to go to get away from her. So, in the end, you will have to fight or die. At least now, at this point, we have an excellent chance to stop her before she gets too strong. So, I beg of you. Please, help me defeat her."

Taking a moment, she studied each of them, trying and make a connection, and to hopefully transmit wordlessly her dire need for their help.

No one moved. It was clear they were all digesting the information she had dumped on them and trying to make up their minds. Out of the corner of her eye she saw Hank gather himself to stand. She had faith he, at least, would help her. Before he could stand and speak, the man at the back walked forward to stand before her. The intensity in his eyes startled her, and strangely, reminded her of Calin.

"My name is Clint," he told her, loudly for the rest of the room to hear him as well. He gave her a slight smile taking the fierceness out of his eyes. He turned to the rest of the room.

"I am also begging you for help. The woman I love is now being held against her will." Glancing at each one as he spoke. "The only way I can save her is to defeat the monster who gave her lycanthropy. To do so, I must help defeat this Kestrel. So please, join us." He turned back to her and moved to stand behind her, hands clasped behind him.

Hank again made to stand after lowering himself when Clint began to speak. And once again he didn't make it up before someone else spoke up.

"Well, hey," the woman who had come in with Clint spoke up. "I saved your ass once, Clint. I can't have you go off by yourself and get killed now, can I?" She moved to join them. "You can count me in."

Clint smiled at her as she approached. "Thanks, Kat."

Sylvanis nodded at Kat as she passed her to stand next to Clint at her back.

She watched as Hank made a rush to get to his feet, determined to not let anyone speak again before him.

"Dad and I are in as well," Simon said as Hank got fully to his feet. Hank glared down at Simon who smiled up at him mischievously. Hank snorted.

"Yeah, as Sim said, we are in," sitting back down unceremoniously.

The room turned as one to gaze over at Stephanie and Jason, who shrank back under the scrutiny.

"Stephanie. Jason. As I said, you do not have to do this. No one will think ill of you. We all understand other people's lives are involved, families, school and the like." Mentioning it mainly to remind the others so they would not be angry if the two decided to go.

Stephanie stared at Jason as if searching his face for some clue as to what to do. He appeared to be doing the same. After a moment, he reached across and took her hand in his and nodded. She nodded back. Decision made.

"We will help. Though, to be honest, apart from the abilities which come with shifting, we are not fighters," she told them.

"You could have fooled me," Sylvanis corrected. "You saved my parents and fought off two strong Trues long enough for reinforcements to arrive. Believe me, Stephanie. If it hadn't been for the two of you, I would have been killed, same with my parents."

Kat took a step forward. "I can teach you how to fight. I have been training for this my whole life it would seem."

Stephanie and Jason nodded to Kat.

Sylvanis regarded each of them again. Her smile was wide, and her heart was light.

"Okay, so I guess that is it. Thank you, all of you. You may not realize it yet, but you are not only helping me, but all of mankind by doing this."

Smiling at the group, they smiled back at her, feeling her optimism.

It was Clint who broke the moment with a valid question.

"So, what now?"

Sylvanis pondered this. She had many ideas as to what Kestrel would do next, but one thing was more likely.

"I believe we need to try to accomplish two goals. First, we need to start gathering others who wish to join our cause. Those who wish to become lycanthropes and those who don't. Second, we need to try and stop Kestrel from getting the rest of her minions together."

Hank considered something.

"How did she find you? And can you not find her the same way?"

"Kestrel found me because I opened myself up to the Earth to call all of you. Normally I would hide my presence within the biosphere, but I needed to get you here and it was the only way," she told him. "She hides herself and will continue to hide herself. We will not find her the same way. But, I do believe I know how we can find her."

"How," Sim questioned.

Sylvanis turned to Clint. "You said you had a confrontation with the Boar?"

Clint nodded.

"Was it visible to the public? Did others see you?"

Again, Clint nodded.

"It is a decent chance the last remaining True out there, the Rat, has heard of it and will most likely try and find either of you. The trick is to have them find you first, not the Boar."

"Right," Clint agreed. "We must go back to Chicago. Which is fine with me, and it will give me another chance to kill the son of a bitch!" His anger was evident.

"There is one thing I think we should mention." Kat chimed in.

"What is it?"

"There are three of them."

Sylvanis was confused. "Three of whom?"

Wincing a little, Kat explained. "Three boars. One True? And two Pures?"

Sylvanis let out a breath. Bad news.

"Well," Hank interjected, "if what Sylvanis says is true, all we have to do is take out the one and the others will lose their power. And besides, three of them can't be all bad."

"Four," Clint was staring at his feet.

"Aw, shit, you're right, Clint." Kat granted. "There's also Sarah."

Clint glanced back up, tears welling in his eyes. "She wouldn't do anything towards us, though."

Sylvanis took a step towards him and put her hand on his arm.

"I don't know how to tell you this, Clint, but she will not have a choice in the matter."

Clint wiped a tear away and stared at her, hard.

"What do you mean, she won't have a choice?"

Sylvanis searched Clint's eyes. She didn't want to have to tell him this, because she was all too knowledgeable of what horrible things could occur.

"A Pure is under the control of a True. They must do as the other commands. If the Boar commands her to attack us, she will be forced to do so, though she will do so halfheartedly. Another reason Kestrel's army failed. You can command people to fight, but if it isn't in their heart, or the cause isn't just, they may fight, but they won't do it well."

Clint was staring at her, as if he hadn't heard what she had said. She could see it in his eyes, though. He was beginning to understand all too plainly what it might mean for the Boar to have control over Sarah. What he might, no, *would* do to her, and make her do as well.

The anger swiftly grew in Clint, and she stepped back as he threw his head up and arched his back, letting out a monstrous roar.

"NOOOOOOOOO!!!" He shifted instantly and stood before them in his wolf form, panting hard, his lips curled back to reveal sharp, slavering fangs.

"Clint, you must hear me," Sylvanis called to him. "You can do nothing for her alone. Get a hold of yourself."

Clint wheeled on her, letting out a low growl and stepped forward.

Hank was between them in a second. Clint turned away, but spun and back-handed him, sending him flying.

Simon turned into a Bear and made to intervene as his father did but was brought up short by Sylvanis' outstretched arm.

"Stop," she told him, not taking her eyes off Clint.

"Fine, go to her," she told him. Clint stood before her, chest heaving from full, deep breaths, his golden wolf eyes boring into her. She stood her ground. Spinning around, he ran out of the house.

"Why did you let him go?" Kat demanded of her. "We need him."

Sylvanis turned to study her.

"I know we do. There was no stopping him. Not without bloodshed, and I will not have that amongst friends." Turning to the side of the room, Hank was dusting himself off, trying to remove the drywall dust from the wall he partially went through when he hit.

"Are you okay?"

"More or less," he told her. "More surprised than hurt. The kid packs quite a punch. Though, if he hits me again, I am going to hit back, and he will find I hit a whole lot harder."

Sylvanis smiled at him. She thought he was jesting. Well, perhaps not. The truth was, she didn't know these people. She knew their ancestors, but not them. They must be noble people to offer their help, knowing they might not survive. She didn't know them, but she could get a sense of each of them, and she felt confident they would be enough to stop Kestrel.

"Well, I would suggest we rest for the night. There is plenty of room here for all of you to sleep. Tomorrow, if Clint hasn't gained control of himself and comes back, we will go to Chicago, and hope to intercept him there."

She noticed Stephanie and Jason were not paying attention but were arguing about something.

She watched them for a moment. Realizing the room had gone silent and they were now the focus of the attention, they each stood and stepped closer to the rest.

"I don't think we should go to Chicago," Stephanie told her.

"Really? Where do you think we should go?" Sylvanis asked.

"Oh, no," Stephanie laughed, blushing. "I don't mean you shouldn't go to Chicago, only Jason and I shouldn't go."

Sylvanis raised her eyebrows inquisitively.

"It's just one of the goals you listed was recruitment. We believe we know a couple of people who we might be able to convince to help us. So, we have to go back to our college." Sylvanis thought this over. It was likely Kestrel would figure out the same thing about where her last minion would end up. So, it was likely if they ran into each other, it would be her, Kat, Sim, Hank, and hopefully Clint, against Kestrel, Syndor, the Croc and four Boars, assuming Kestrel didn't get to the Rat first.

She did not like those odds. But, Stephanie did have a point, and one thing she learned from Stephanie's predecessor, Adonia, was the Fox always planned ahead. Now, whether Stephanie was anything like Adonia, she couldn't be sure, but it would have been like her to split up and try to accomplish two things desperately needing to be done. Would it be harder without them? Most likely, but it did seem necessary.

"Very well, you and Jason return to your college and see who you can get to help. Try and meet us in Chicago as soon as possible. For we will be sorely pressed without the numbers your presence would bring us."

"Thanks, Sylvanis." Jason told her. "We will meet up with you as soon as we can." He glanced to Stephanie, then back to her. "If it's all the same to you, we will leave tonight. The sooner we get there; the sooner we can make it back to you."

Smiling at them both, she considered herself lucky to have these two on her side. They turned and left, leaving Sylvanis there with the others.

"Kat," Sylvanis turned towards the young woman. "How do you think the Boar found Clint?"

Kat shrugged her shoulders. "Not sure. It is possible he found him the same way as me." Kat sat down on one of the couches.

"I watched the news, read the papers, trying to find anything which would lead me to someone like me. You see, my parents *knew* about the lycanthropy. My mom was entrusted with the secret. One day, she knew, we might be called upon to serve again. She knew there would be others as well, most likely. So, when I transformed the first time, we knew it was time. It was before I found Clint when I started to feel your… summons?"

Sylvanis nodded, admitting it was an accurate description of what had happened.

"Well, I decided to leave and come here when I hadn't yet tracked down any other sign of what I had read in the news, about a large animal, possibly a bear seen in Chicago. It was luck which made me decide to wait one more day. So, I walked the beat, so to speak and sniffed him out."

"Sniffed him out?" Hank asked.

"Yeah. Can't you smell it?"

He shook his head.

"Well, possibly because there are too many of us in this room, and there is no way to tell the difference. The point is, if you are in a room full of non-Weres, you can *smell* the Were in the room. I'm not sure how else to explain it, but the moment I smelled it on him, I knew he was one of us." She peered off in the distance, as if remembering the moment.

"I lost him the first day. But, I had got a decent view of him. It was plain luck he decided to come out for a walk in the same area again. Though it might have been bad luck, because it might have been how the Boar found him as well." She turned back to Sylvanis.

"I guess you are right. Seems odd you both could follow a vague lead like a news story and end up finding him." Sylvanis mused.

"There was one thing about him, the Boar I mean, struck me odd."

"What was it?"

"He had a British accent. I mean, it was hard to tell, you know, because we all sound a little different when we shift, but I thought I detected it in his voice and the words he used."

It wasn't what Sylvanis wished to hear. It confirmed the worst of what she had thought. If the Boar was British, likely he was sent there by Kestrel to try and take out Clint.

This meant Kestrel had located everybody except the Rat. Sylvanis knew it would be harder to defeat her this time. Sure, there were outside forces which would make Kestrel's attempts harder to accomplish, but Sylvanis watched the news, she saw the people protesting in the streets. There was a horde of people out there who felt the same way as Kestrel — humans were destroying this world and they must be stopped, at any cost. These people had been dangerous, in their own way, before. Now, with a leader like Kestrel, they could be deadly.

Kestrel wouldn't make the same mistakes as last time. She would target those who would agree with her cause and would fight harder because of it. Syndor had been around all this time, and she doubted he had been inactive. They would have the money and the resources to accomplish what they wanted. The Croc and Boar were not Por and Answi this time. She would make sure they would not try anything stupid and get themselves killed. Of course, Clint wasn't Calin, either. Renwick had been a coward, and there was no telling if the Rat would be so, again.

Sylvanis sighed.

"What's wrong?" Sim asked her.

Smiling at him, pleased by his concern, it was important they liked her and cared for her, though she would not try and force it.

"Just thinking about how daunting our task is. This is a different time from the last time Kestrel and I clashed. There are a lot of uncertainties, and I am not the leader of some vast army as I once was. All I have is the six of you, but I am sure it will be enough. It just won't be easy.

"Well, I think we should go to sleep. We have a long and difficult day ahead of us tomorrow and we will need our rest. I believe I am going to check on my parents to see what I can do to speed along their recovery. I bid you all goodnight."

Climbing the stairs, she left the others below to work out sleeping arrangements.

Lying in their bed where Stephanie and Jason had left them, she found her parents. They were still unconscious, and she took a moment to examine them. She had been afraid from the beginning they might have been wounded beyond the superficial and may have gotten lycanthropy from the Croc. But a quick examination showed they only had taken a blow to their heads, and there were places where the fire had burned them enough to cause some blisters.

215

They would live, and more importantly, they would not become Weres under the control of the Croc. Placing her hands upon each of them in turn, she took some of their pain away, and they went from unconsciousness, to sleep by the rhythm of their breathing. Crawling up in bed between them, she snuggled as she used to when she was a little girl. She laughed quietly to herself. Yeah, a little girl. Like what, a couple of months ago? She genuinely loved her parents, yet in a way, they were strangers to Sylvanis.

Snuggling closer to them, to feel their warmth, she hoped they could forgive her for taking away her childhood from them. When she left tomorrow, she didn't believe she would be back, and she hoped they would have another child, and live happily with one they could watch grow at a normal pace. She had not intended her spell to do what it did. Not seen the consequences of her actions. But, what choice had she had? She couldn't let Kestrel come here, now, and do what she tried to do back then.

It wasn't fair. She gave up her life then to stop Kestrel and had to do so once again. She was not able to grow up at a regular pace because of Kestrel, and she had been robbed, once again, of a chance to grow up and live out her life in peace.

She cried for the loss of her parent's daughter, and the loss of herself. She cried till she fell asleep, cradled in the arms of her parents, in the arms of strangers.

Chapter 8

Shae stood on the sidewalk of Chicago's magnificent mile and watched as repairs were underway on several buildings around her. There were fewer people on the streets today than yesterday as the novelty began to wear off. Of course, it was still busier than any town she ever been in. She could sense Daniel back at the hotel. They had fought again about coming here, but in the end, she told him to shut up and he had little choice but to do so. It was a strange relationship they shared. He disgusted her and many times she wished him dead, yet she couldn't be without him. Occasionally, she would use him, but it was mainly to humiliate him, for she found little pleasure in their sex. It was a part she believed her past had killed within her– the pleasure of intimacy, and she didn't think it would ever return.

Brushing her ruddy brown hair out of her eyes, the wind which gave Chicago its nickname blew hard cutting her skin like a knife, leaving no wounds only reddened chapped skin. Pulling her overcoat tighter around her, she checked her Sais, as she learned the knives were called, to see if they were secure at her waist. She practiced daily handling the twin daggers. Whether she could fight well with them, she couldn't tell, but she could handle them with familiarity, which would help with any casual encounter where she might need them. If she dealt with someone who knew how to defend against them, or had a similar weapon, she would have to rely on her shifting ability.

Daniel and she had been here for two days.

They had been living off the grid in extended stay hotels for around seven months. Daniel was independently wealthy and took most of his money out of his accounts before they left New York to have cash so they couldn't be traced using credit cards. Seven months they had traveled and lived aimlessly. Not sure where to go and what to do. Until they saw the news of what happened in Chicago. There was no mistaking the descriptions of other Weres.

She woke Daniel in the hotel room they were staying at and told him they were leaving. After driving all night, they arrived in Chicago in the afternoon. Shae dragged Daniel downtown that night and they both examined the damage and listened to the talk about what happened there a couple of days ago.

Of course, the stories varied, since most heard it from a friend, who heard it from a friend. The following morning, Shae returned, without Daniel, and questioned more people. In the end, she located a woman from one of the damaged stores who had witnessed almost everything. She had been reluctant to talk about it at first since many people didn't believe her or called her nuts, regardless of all the video of it on the internet. Shae assured her she would not think her crazy and would believe her. Something about Shae convinced her to talk.

The woman missed the beginning of the fight, but others had told her a huge man, with a face like a boar with tusks and everything, emerged from somewhere and attacked a man and a woman. That is when she exited her shop to see what was happening.

"It was the most frightening thing I'd ever seen. This *boarman* lifted this woman into the air, right in front of the man who may have been her boyfriend, or perhaps husband it was believed, because of the way the *boarman* was taunting him with the woman. Just when it appeared the monster was going to eat this woman, he was attacked, not by the man, but by some *tigerwoman*."

Pausing to peer at Shae, she undoubtedly wanted to check to see if she was going to laugh, but Shae was transfixed to the story, and only nodded for the woman to continue, which she did.

"At this point, the woman the boarman had been holding was dropped and the tigerwoman and the boarman fought. The boarman was downright beating the hell out of the tigerwoman, and I was sure this fight was going to end soon with the boarman winning.

"In fact, the boarman had everything going his way. He had beaten the tigerwoman to unconsciousness and was, once again, about to grab the other girl when the man who had been with the woman transformed into a *wolfman*. I wouldn't have believed it, if I hadn't seen it with my own eyes," the woman told Shae. "Anyhow, the man transformed, like a...a...werewolf. He transformed and attacked the *boarman*. They fought, and the tigerwoman, who I'd thought was a goner, helped, and together they saved the other woman and escaped. The cops arrived and the boarman attacked them. The cops must have shot the thing dozens of times, but it didn't stop, it tore through them and was gone.

"At any rate, no one knew what happened to the *boarman, tigerwoman* or *wolfman.* Rumor had it, the cops knew the identification of the *wolfman*, but not of the others. The woman was in the hospital, but from what I heard, three *boarmen* came in and took her. I'm not sure I believe it. It sounds more like others trying to join in on the hubbub around the attack."

It was all she knew, she assured Shae. Her eyes sparkled with finally being able to tell someone who took her seriously, and didn't think she was either crazy, or lying. Thanking her for the information,

Shae returned to the hotel to find Daniel and tell him what had happened. He was torn between his desire to help her and to study these others. She reminded him that part of his life was over; he would never experiment on another person ever again. He sulked, but knew she was right.

The next day she spent at the stores, searching for any sign any of those people who might still be around. She knew it was silly, and Daniel told her as much. Why would those responsible for this destruction return to the same spot, but it was all she had. This was her only link to others like her. She returned the following day as well. Daniel stayed at the hotel; he lived in a perpetual state of self-loathing which didn't allow him to spend much time out. Or, it might be he was afraid he would change, though they had learned to control the change in the seven months they had been traveling around together, he was still uneasy about it.

The sudden appearance of others like her got her wondering. It seemed an impossibility. Suddenly, three Weres, like her, appear out of nothing? She wondered if they changed for the first time at the same time she did? It was unlikely, but she couldn't fathom another reason around the same time she had this thing awaken within her; others would show up as well. She needed to find the others, she needed answers.

Her acute nose picked up a new scent in the air. It was not something she had ever smelled before and couldn't quite place it. It smelled…bestial, was the only word she could find to describe it. As she was trying to place the smell, a dark shadow stole the sunlight from her.

"Hello, lass, it seems the Lady guessed right when she said you might come here," a man said from behind her with a rough British accent.

Turning around, she saw a man looming over her. Easily over six feet tall, with black greasy hair, slicked back, which only accentuated his oversized forehead. He was a somewhat fat man, with a portly gut. He smiled down at her with a gapped-tooth smile and beady eyes.

Her hands stole within her overcoat to grab her Sais.

"There is no need for those, lass," the man told her. "You are among friends and others like you."

"What do you mean? Like me?" Despite his assurance of friendship; she didn't like him or trust him in the least.

He smiled wider at her. Yeah, she didn't like him at all.

"I think you know what I mean, lass, but it's best to not discuss this here. Come with me and I will answer your questions. And, when the Lady gets here, she will answer the rest of them."

"Which one were you?" Shae asked, suddenly curious.

"Which one?" He raised an eyebrow.

She nodded in the direction of the damaged buildings.

He smiled at her again. "Which one do you think?"

Shae scrutinized him before answering. "The pig."

The smile was gone in an instant and a low growl emitted from him. Shae thought she might have gone a little too far.

"Leave her be, Blain, you know the Lady would not be happy if anything happens to her."

Turning, Shae noticed a couple of men she hadn't seen before. The one who talked was tall with a narrow face. A stick of a man, made to appear more so by the overweight man next to him. This one was short and ugly with thinning hair and pale skin. He was sweating, though it was a cold day. The tall man approached her.

"My name is Taylor. What's yours?"

Shae felt a little more comfortable dealing with this one than she did with the other one.

"Shae."

"Well, Shae, I am Taylor. You've met Blain. This other one next to me is Joseph. We were asked to find you by someone who

221

would like to meet you. You see, you are a special person, and like us, she has need of you."

"I won't be used," Shae told him.

He chuckled disarmingly.

"Of course not, Shae. No one is going to use you. In fact, she wants to make sure no one will ever harm you again."

Considering what he said, she decided she would go with them. She had little to lose. Not caring much for her life, and if they could give her some answers, it would satisfy her for now. If not, she would leave them, if she could, or die, if she couldn't. It was better than it was now, either way.

Suddenly, she thought about Daniel and worried for him. Why she should feel this way, she didn't understand. She hated him, but she also cared for him. she wondered what would happen to him if she died.

He would be better off, she decided.

"Alright," she turned back to Blain. "Let's go."

Without a glance back at the damaged buildings, or the hotel housing Daniel, she left with them.

Officer Ben Charles hadn't come to Chicago for this, but this is what he now found himself involved in. He watched as the three men led the small girl away. Yesterday, she had caught his attention as she watched the repairs of the buildings. It appeared to him the girl was there for similar reasons.

It had been a long road bringing him to Chicago from Sacramento. It was a hunch, one which got him put on leave from the force. His gut told him the person, or thing, he had to admit the possibility now it wasn't human, which killed the man back in Sacramento, was here in Chicago, or at least, had been.

The case had grown cold in Sacramento when there was no physical evidence to provide any definitive leads. The only physical evidence didn't make any sense, or at least, didn't at the time. It did now. It did to him. His captain wasn't too keen on his theory and accused him of going all *National Enquirer* on him. The problem was, the only piece of evidence forensics claimed to have found was tiger hair, which was next to impossible in Sacramento. All the tigers were accounted for. Ben had made sure of it, going so far as to track down private owners who had exotic animal registrations. All tigers in the area zoos were locked up and hadn't escaped. The backgrounds and alibis of all handlers and private owners verified and vetted accordingly. It was, like he said, a dead end.

Then, there was the news out of Chicago, and the accompanying internet footage of a humanoid tiger. It was the break in the case Ben was waiting for. The problem? No one else thought it had anything to do with his case. In fact, most of the other officers thought it was some joke, or fraud. For Ben, it was too obvious a link, one he couldn't pass up. When he pushed his Captain to let him pursue it, he was denied. It went badly after that. Things were said which shouldn't have been said. The next thing Ben knew, he was on 'personal leave.' He flew out to Chicago the next day.

That was two days ago. The first day he came down to this corner, the one where he was standing right now, he noticed the girl.

It was difficult to put an age to her, but he marked her no more than fifteen. She was wearing a gray overcoat and a pair of black sandals, which was peculiar footwear, considering the temperature. Pale skin, she was marked by freckles he could see from across the street. Ruddy brown hair which had been cut short at one point, given the growth she sported now. Something about her caught his eye, and it wasn't until he noticed she kept touching the sides of her coat, at her hip, he realized she was packing.

At first, he thought he might have been mistaken, but after a few minutes of quiet observation there was no mistaking the nervous touching someone does when they keep checking to make sure their weapons are still there. It was a common trait of someone who had little use of guns and was nervous about using and carrying them.

He continued to watch her for a few more minutes. Curiously, he wondered as to why he hadn't crossed the street and confronted the girl. It was clear her intentions were not wholesome. Quite possibly, she was going to try and kill someone, but the way she kept surveying the damage, it left him with the idea she was there waiting for the beasts. It intrigued him. Either she had an idea of who they were, or she would somehow recognize them when she saw them.

What was more worrisome was, for some reason she believed, with the weapons she was carrying, she could deal with them. Given the footage he saw on the internet, this surprised him. After all, he wasn't sure he would know how or be able to deal with any of them, let alone three of them.

It was that belief which kept him from approaching the girl. He continued to watch her and others in the crowd for the rest of the day. Many people came to those buildings to inspect the damage made by the monsters which caused more excitement in this town than fear. Many came, but all left, all but the girl – the girl and him.

A few times, she entered Starbucks, presumably to pee. For the same reason, he entered a restaurant once or twice, but always returning to the same area, as did she. It was surprising she didn't seem to notice him. It was if she knew, somehow, he wasn't one of the ones she was searching for, and so her eyes flowed over him.

It was midnight when she left. He followed her to a local hotel but decided against following her to her room.

Instead, he stopped at the desk and flashed his badge to the clerk. "That girl who just went through the lobby?"

"I'm sorry. I didn't notice a girl, officer. What's this about?"

"Police business. The girl, about fifteen, short reddish-brown hair, pale skin and freckles?"

The clerk thought it over for a minute and shook his head.

"Doesn't ring a bell, officer. But, if she checked in during the morning shift, I wouldn't have seen her come in. You don't have a room number perhaps?"

Damn his decision to not follow her up.

"No. I don't. Who was on staff this morning?"

"Kelly. But she's gone for the day and won't be back until tomorrow morning."

Ben gave it some thought.

"What time?"

"Her shift starts at six am," the clerk informed him.

"Alright, I'll be back."

Ben left, determined to go back to his hotel and get some sleep. He considered checking out and staying at the same hotel as the girl, but he was worried if she saw him too much, she might get suspicious.

It was fifteen minutes to six when Ben arrived at the hotel. The girl had been out at the street, same outfit, same spot. Knowing she was there made Ben hurry back to the hotel, hoping nothing happened while he was gone. It was a chance he was going to have to take.

The same clerk was working the desk when he entered the lobby. A little bleary-eyed when he saw Ben, but he recognized him right away. As Ben approached the desk, the clerk raised a finger to indicate he should wait there a moment before disappearing into a side room next to clerk's posts. Ben overheard some muffled conversation.

The clerk returned with a thirty-something woman with black hair and a cute face. Somewhat plumper than he liked them, but her face and eyes would have made up the difference for him, if he was here for that sort of thing.

"Kelly?" He prompted.

"Yeah, Shawn here says you have a question about someone who is staying with us?"

"Sure do. I am searching for a girl, early teens, who might have come in the past few days. Reddish brown hair, though more red than brown, short, like it is growing back from being shaved off, pale skin and freckles. Ah, I see by your expression you know whom I'm talking about?"

The woman hesitated, trying to figure out if she should confide in him.

"Go ahead," he encouraged her.

"Yes. I saw her. She came in, maybe two days ago, with an older gentleman. They paid for a week, in cash."

Pausing, she let it sink in for a moment. It only took him a moment to realize the significance. They were in downtown Chicago; a week's stay would almost be around two-thousand after taxes. Not a small amount to lay down in cash, but it wasn't exactly damning.

"This gentleman, can you describe him?"

She described him as best as she could. It was clear something about the gentleman bothered her. He pressed her on it.

"Well, it's just he was easily in his forties, and as you know, the girl is in her teens. You might think father/daughter, but they shared no similar features. Her red hair for instance was natural and he had dark hair." She paused, again unsure of stating the next part. Nodding for her to continue, he was trying to be patient.

"The other strange thing was their relationship. It was definitely not father/daughter, but what it was, I don't know, either. He deferred to her, as if asking permission for his actions. There was also a weird type of attraction between the two. I don't know. It was weird, okay? It made me feel uncomfortable. I almost called the police because I thought there might be something illegal happening between the two, but I couldn't be sure, you know? It would be my job if the police showed up, accused someone, and nothing was happening."

She glanced at him apprehensively. "Now you are here, I am starting to think perhaps I should have."

Smiling at her reassuringly. "I don't know anything about what you are referring to. In fact, I didn't know there was someone else staying here with her, so you probably did the right thing. If there is anything illegal going on, you can be sure, I will deal with it." Turning to go, he suddenly turned back.

"Do you have their room number?"

"Of course, it is room 112, through there," she pointed to a short hallway which teed at the end. "Turn left at the end, go to the end of the hall and turn right. The room is almost all the way at the back of the building."

Smiling again, he thanked her, turned to leave, and once more, turned back.

"Curious. Did they request the room?"

Her eyes grew big and her mouth made a small 'o'. "Now that you mention it, yes, they did. They wanted a room on the first floor, near the back of the building. How did you know?"

Smiling again for the last time, he left, not answering her. It was best not to explain how most people who do things illegally frequently want a room on the ground floor and as far away from the front as they can, so getting away was easier. No need to alarm the poor girl, as he planned to take care of all this today.

As he hurried back to where the girl was hopefully still standing, he wondered why he had yet to see the man who arrived with the girl. Plainly, he wasn't going to the corner with her. But why? Did he even leave the room? Could he? There were all sorts of nightmare scenarios running through his mind as to what could be, but he let it drop. He didn't have enough information to come close to drawing a theory.

Half jogging, half walking back to his scouting spot, he was in time to see the large man approach the girl. At once, he didn't like the appearance of this guy at all, but he didn't match the description the clerk gave him of the guy who came with her, so this was someone new. Perhaps, this is who the girl had been waiting for. Perhaps, this was who he had been waiting for.

The first thing he realized was he had been right about her packing. When the guy approached, she immediately reached into her coat for whatever was hiding there, but something the man said made her relax... to some extent.

Ben pondered whether he should go over and somehow break up whatever this was, but something about the appearance of the guy made him rethink his idea. It was then he noticed the other two. They were off to the side, close enough to do something, but not close enough for the girl to have figured out they were together.

This was going from bad to worse in Ben's eyes, and he felt helpless to stop it. For the first time in his career, a feeling of cold dread stole over him. His gut was screaming at him to walk away, perhaps run. Continuing this plan of action was going to get him killed, but he couldn't let anything happen to this girl. Despite all the evidence pointing to this girl being as bad news as these guys were, she was still just a teen. Maybe she had a chance to change. Even after all he had seen in his career as a cop, he was still a little naïve. He couldn't help it.

The conversation unfolded as he watched. Words were exchanged, and at one point the girl must have stood up for herself because the big man almost made to lunge for her but was pulled up short by a word from the taller of the two guys who were off to the side. For the first time, the girl realized the guy was not alone and her posture changed to someone who appeared ready to flee.

The taller guy approached her, and whatever he said calmed her. He talked to her some more, and to Ben's surprise, they left together.

It took Ben a moment to realize they were, indeed, leaving. Ben crossed the street while they were only a block away. Trailing them for several blocks, he watched them enter a luxury apartment high rise. Entering shortly after they did, he was in time to see them enter an elevator.

He had two choices; follow them once he knew what floor they got off on, which didn't seem likely he would find them after he got to that floor. Or, he could hope for the best, and the doorman would know what room they were headed to. The big guy was discernible and disconcerting enough, the doorman might know which room they leased.

It seemed like this was Ben's best option and he jogged over to the man, trying to gain back some time. Luckily for Ben, the doorman did indeed remember the big guy and told Ben what room he was staying in. Ben dashed for the elevators. He knew he would get there after they did, but perhaps he could hear what was happening and be able to act if something did occur. They were on the tenth floor, and Ben considered what he had discerned about criminals typically taking ground floor rooms. The only ones who didn't bother to do this, he realized, were the extremely dangerous ones — the ones who weren't afraid of the police, or anyone.

When the elevator opened on the tenth floor, Ben hesitated a moment to glance out, making sure he didn't run into them outside the room. The longer they had no idea who he was, or what he was doing, the better it was for him. There was no one in the hall. Ben made his way to room 1008 and crouched in front of the door, listening. Voices

229

reached him through the door but couldn't make out what was being said. There wasn't any yelling or screaming, which was good.

Considering his options, Ben realized they were few, but he needed to hear what was happening inside. Glancing around, he headed for the door next to this room, and knocked lightly upon it. After a moment, the door opened a crack, a middle-aged, finely combed sandy brown hair of a man in dark glasses peeked out. Blue eyes peered at him through the crack and gave him the once over.

"Can I help you?"

Ben flashed him his badge and the man straightened somewhat.

"I need to use your apartment for a while."

"Excuse me?"

"I need to make use of your apartment, for a short time, I am hoping. If you could let me in and make yourself scarce for the rest of the day I would appreciate it."

The man was irritated by the idea and continued to press the issue.

"Why do you need to use my apartment?"

"Official police business, now, if you will please allow me the use of your apartment, it is somewhat a matter of urgency."

"Don't you need a warrant?"

Ben had had about enough.

"Sir, you watch too many police shows. I do not need a warrant because I am not searching or entering for the purposes related to this particular apartment. Furthermore, I could have done this the rude way and talked to the apartment manager and had him toss you out for the day. I decided to be polite and ask you, instead. Now, will you please step aside and allow me to enter?"

The man seemed to think mayhap he should press his luck. Perhaps, what Ben had told him was the truth? Most of it wasn't. In the end, he decided being an asshole for no reason was silly and stepped aside, allowing the door to open enough for Ben to enter.

"Thank you," Ben told him as he moved past him. "Now, I hate to ask this of you, but for your own safety you might want to go find something to do somewhere else for a while." Ben smiled at him in what he hoped was apologetic.

The man stared at him for a moment, grabbed his wallet and keys off the small hall table, and left.

Ben hoped too much time had not been wasted on gaining entry and rapidly made his way to the wall adjoining the two apartments. Removing his pocket knife, he always carried from his pocket, he pulled out the small saw blade to start working on the drywall.

Cutting a square, larger than his head, between the two studs slowly and carefully finally cut two small holes to see into the room. As soon as he cut one hole, he could make out a conversation occurring on the other side.

"…told you, the Lady will be here in a day or so, and she will answer all of your questions." It sounded like someone with a British accent.

"Yeah, but what does she want with me?" A girl's voice, forceful, but with a slight quiver to it. Acting braver than she was.

"I told ya. I don't know what the hell she wants with ya, only she does. And if you keep asking me these stupid questions over and over again, you won't get any answers because I will toss ya out the window."

"Lay off the girl, Blain. You know you won't do anything of the sort. The Lady is already pissed off at you for allowing the wolf to get away, along with the tiger." Another voice, also British, interjected, one of the other guys.

Ben put his head into the wall and his eyes up to the holes to see what he could. What he saw was the side of a bed lengthwise. Sitting on the bed, back to him, was the girl. Opposite of her was the brutish man he had seen initially talking to her in the street. Now he could see him up close, Ben was warier of him.

The man wheeled towards where Ben assumed the other man was.

"The wolf was mine, if only that bitch of a tiger hadn't interfered. If it is anyone's fault, it is the Lady. She told me only the wolf would be here; she never mentioned anything about no tiger."

"Don't get riled up, Blain. Taylor is telling you how it is, no reason to get pissed at him. If you remember, we said you should have taken us with you, and the wolf and the tiger would've been dealt with." This must have been the voice of the third guy Ben had seen.

"Shut up, Joseph. I don't need you spoutin' off, too." The man named Blain turned back to the girl.

"Now, in the meantime, you are going to stay here and be quiet. I may not be able to toss you out the window, but you ain't so young I wouldn't hesitate to rape your scrawny little ass." Blain loomed over her. She leaned back a bit, so his face wasn't so close to hers.

As soon as he turned, she was up and was headed for the door. Blain was expecting the move and his meaty hand flashed out, grabbing her by the elbow and tossed her back. She landed on the bed and something happened Ben couldn't believe.

The girl bounced when she hit the bed, and before she landed again, her body went through an amazing transformation. Her face elongated to take on a kind of rat-like features. She was covered almost entirely with hair, except

232

near her ankles and wrists, which were hairless. Elongated fingers, ending in sharp looking claws, sprouted from her hands. Ben ducked as a hairless tail ripped out of the back of the girl's clothes and slammed against the wall, right above where his eyes were, knocking drywall dust and insulation down on his head.

The thing which was once the girl was standing on the bed, somehow wielding two wicked looking daggers with wavy blades. He hadn't seen her pull them, but he now knew what she carried under her coat. They appeared too small for her form now. In fact, at second glance, Ben realized the girl must have grown at least a foot or two in height. Visibly, she was bulkier in shape than before, as well.

Standing upon the bed, daggers pointed at the man named Blain, she threatened him.

"Oh, come now, lass, you can't be serious?" The man took a step forward and the rat girl took a swipe at him with one of the daggers. It was so quick, Ben wasn't sure it happened until he saw a line of blood appear from a cut in the man's arm.

It was there only a second, and for the second time that day, Ben saw something which would live with him forever. The man shook himself and transformed right in front of him. It only took a second and the monstrous form the man took shook Ben to his core. He was undoubtedly the boar creature he had seen in the video but seeing it in person was a whole other story. It was huge, and it towered over the girl, more so, because it was forced to duck, otherwise it would be too tall for the room.

Ben saw the girl creature hesitate, then leap at the boar. She was nothing if not fierce, Ben thought. The boar grabbed her as if she was nothing and pinned her arms to her sides. She fought hard against him, but it was in vain. He was too strong for her. What Ben saw in the beast's eyes as he glared at the girl made him want to leap through the wall to rescue her, even knowing it would see him dead. He was about to, when he heard another's voice, a woman's voice, quiet and frightened.

"Leave her alone, Blain."

The boar glanced to the side of the room where the voice came from, then back at the girl. Ben saw the moment of fury was gone, and he relaxed. The boar released the girl who slumped to the floor, daggers dropped. She rubbed the spots on her arms where Blain had squeezed.

"What's your name, girl?" the woman asked.

Trying to twist in the wall to get a peek at the woman, Ben couldn't see much past his limited view of the side of the bed. As he glanced back, the girl returned to her human form, huddled in the shelter of her overcoat.

"It's Shae."

"Well, Shae, I'm Sarah." Ben wondered if it was the same Sarah who had been involved in the fight on the street, the one later taken from the hospital.

"I'm afraid it is best if you do what Blain says. I know you heal swiftly, like the rest of us, but it won't stop him from causing you a lot of pain, which he won't hesitate to do. It will be easier on you to stay here with me, and we will wait for this Lady to show up. Hopefully, we will get better treatment. Okay?"

The girl peered in the direction of the voice; a tear trailing down her cheek.

"Why don't you come over here by me, I'll keep you safe."

The girl scrambled up and moved out of Ben's vision. The boar returned to his human form and gave a laugh.

"Don't listen to her, lass, she can't even protect herself. Of course, she can't do much of anything without me telling her. But, she is right about one thing, as long as you shut up and behave, you should have little problems from me. You step out of line though... well, ask Sarah there to find out what happens."

234

Blain walked out of his vision, and Ben had to strain to hear the rest of the conversation.

"How long till the Lady gets here, Blain?" one of the other guys inquired.

"Dunno, she said she was going to take care of something tonight and hopefully be here in a couple of days. I suppose she will call us tonight to let us know."

"What happens if the wolf or the tiger show up in the meantime?" It was the voice of the other guy, most likely the fat one.

"Well, first of all, they don't have any way to find us. But if they did, we would tear them to pieces. Right, Sarah?" he asked with a particularly mocking tone in his voice.

"Clint will kill you, Blain."

The sound of the slap was almost deafening to Ben, which was followed by a heavy thud as a body hit the wall further down in the room. The entire wall shook, and the drywall bulged on his side from the impact.

Ben heard the girl scream, and Ben braced for the sound of the next slap. It never came. A groan came from the other room and dry wall dust fell again as the woman pulled herself from the wall.

"That's where you got it wrong, lass. I made the mistake last time by not finishing the job, but I won't make that mistake, again. Your boyfriend shows up, me and my mates here are going to destroy him. And if the pussy shows up, we'll kill her, too, but like I said, it doesn't matter, because they won't find us. They don't have an idea we are still here."

Pulling himself out from the wall, Ben stared off in the distance. These were bad men, worse than men, they were monsters. Literally. If this wolf and tiger were against these men, they couldn't be all bad. In fact, from what he heard on the street, a vast many thought of them as heroes.

To Ben, the girl didn't belong with these men, the woman, Sarah, plainly didn't. But, what could he do about it? This was beyond anything he was prepared to handle.

He gave it some more thought. It was more than he could handle, but perhaps the wolf and tiger could handle it? The problem was, he had no idea where they were, or if they were in Chicago anymore. However, if they were in Chicago, or if they came back, chances are they would start their search where he had found the girl. He decided it would be best to go back to the corner and wait. It was all he could think to do.

It never occurred to him to find out about the guy who arrived with Shae in Chicago.

Epilogue

The wolf tore through the woods and had done so for several days. Aware of little else but the anger in its heart. It had traveled through the woods, or at night when it must travel the more populated areas. It ran on four legs, though it was partially aware it could have run on two, its mind was little more than animal, vaguely aware it was more. Something caused this change, but it didn't matter anymore. It had a destination, and a target for its anger. When it reached its target, it would rip its throat out with its teeth and taste its flesh and blood.

It smelled a deer and shifted direction a little to intercept it. It had feasted upon a couple deer over the past few days, along with two hunters with their orange vests and slow reactions. It was the first time it had tasted human flesh. The flavor lingered on its tongue, even now. It would not go out of its way to hunt humans, but if the opportunity presented itself again, it would not hesitate.

Part of it screamed against this, a part stronger than the animal, but weakened more and more. Soon, it believed, the voice would disappear altogether, and it would be free of its human protests, free to hunt, and free to kill.

The Saga will continue in
"The Gathering"

If you have enjoyed this novel, please take a moment and post a review on Amazon and or Goodreads. Thank you.

You can find more information on my website, https://www.michaeltimmins42.com
Facebook page,
https://www.facebook.com/LycanWarSaga/
Or you can follow me on twitter or Instagram.
https://twitter.com/mtimmins_author
https://www.instagram.com/mtimmins42/

This is a work of fiction. All of the characters, and events portrayed in this novel are products of the author's imagination.

THE AWAKENING: PART TWO

Michael Timmins lives in Toledo, Ohio with his wife and two sons. His inspiration for writing came from his many years making modules to run for his D&D group. It has been a dream of his to one day get his work published, and now with ease of self-publishing he has made his dream come true.

Made in the USA
Lexington, KY
23 October 2019